Suspended

By
Rob Ashman

www.bloodhoundbooks.com

Print ISBN 978-1-912604-72-2

Praise For Rob Ashman

"Five stars from me, would have been six if Amazon and Goodreads went up that high!!" **Donna Maguire - Donnas Book Blog**

"Faceless is fast paced, it's twisted and it packs one hell of a punch into every page!" **Sharon Bairden - Chapter In My Life**

"I'll definitely be reading more from this author in the future. Loved it." **Philomena Callan - Cheekypee Reads And Reviews**

"The story is very fast paced with lots happening and lots of twists and turns that kept me on the edge of my seat, sometimes quite literally!" **Joanna Park - Over The Rainbow Book Blog**

"Faceless is a fantastic, jaw-dropping journey as I was introduced to DI Roz Kray." **Yvonne Bastian - Me And My Books**

"It is jam packed with tension and OMG moments in fact there is nothing not to like and is the best book I have read this year so far...." **Shell Baker - Chelle's Book Reviews**

"This is a seriously addictive read. There were so many shocking twists and revelations..." **Lorna Cassidy - On The Shelf Reviews**

"Dark, nauseating, intense, destructive, yet incredibly written..." **Kaisha Holloway - The Writing Garnet**

"If you want a seriously twisted and deranged serial killer thriller, then look not further!" **Jessica Robins - Jessicamap Reviews**

"His writing is so slick that you cannot help but be drawn into this fascinating novel." **Kate Eveleigh - Portable Magic**

"...it's a read that will keep you guessing from page to page..." **Jo Turner - Life Of Cri.me**

"A brilliant start to a brand new upcoming series that is bound to blow us all away!" **Gemma Myers - Between The Pages Book Club**

"My jaw is on the floor, but I loved every single second of this fabulously sadistic read." **Katie Jones - Katie's Book Cave**

"Faceless is a gritty, compelling and thrilling serial killer thriller that kept me utterly engrossed..." **Eva Merckx - Novel Deelights**

"The story itself is exciting and addictive in the way a good thriller should be." **Susan Corcoran - Booksaremycwtches**

"A super unique and thrilling story line that had me feel uncomfortable even in a room full of people." **Susan Hampson - Books From Dusk Till Dawn**

"Faceless is a rollercoaster of a ride with twists and turns at every corner." **Caroline Vincent - Bits About Books**

"I love Ashman's books and recommend anyone that loves a good, bloody, and gory thriller to check them out." **Jessica Bronder - JBronder Book Reviews**

"One thing I will say for Rob Ashman OMG he certainly knows how to catch the reader's attention, with a opening chapter that's guaranteed to make you squirm you find yourself eagerly devouring chapter after thrilling chapter." **Lorraine Rugman - The Book Review Cafe**

"A strong foundation of engaging characters and compelling plotlines with superbly executed twists means that I always know I'm in for a cracking read when I pick up one of his books." **Sharon Bairden - Chapter In My Life**

"His style of writing is easy to follow and I could see this as a gripping T.V drama." **Nicki Murphy - Nicki's Book Blog**

"I can honestly say that Rob has fast become one of my favourite authors and I'm waiting with bated breath for the next installation in this new series." **Debbie Binnersley - My Eclectic Reads**

"The storyline was well thought out, in fact it was an epic storyline that sucked me right in from start to finish." **Philomena Callan - Cheekypee Reads And Reviews**

"This was one dark and twisted book!" **Berit Lohn - Audio Killed The Bookmark**

"Definitely five stars from me – this is another book that will definitely be in my top reads of the year..." **Donna Maguire - Donnas Book Blog**

"This Little Piggy has quadrupled my intense satisfaction for a high octane story which delves deep inside my very imagination..." **Diane Hogg - Sweet Little Book Blog**

"Always gritty, graphic, and guaranteed to make some readers squirm, but that never stops a thriller fan!" **Jessica Robins - Jessicamap Reviews**

For Jeff, who is a never-ending source of ideas and plotlines, none of which would ever make it into print.

Preface

'We donned our battle gear to protect our citizens, and our way of life, from those who sought to destroy it. When all along the powers that be couldn't give a toss about either.

'When the final reckoning comes I will be able to say I stood up for what was right; when you chose to remain seated, content to let it happen.

'If you had done your job, there would be no need for me.

'You failed … there is every need for me.'

Chapter 1

'I fought for my country but I never fought for this,' I mutter the words through clenched teeth. My fury growing with every step. I tug my hood forward and dig my hands deep into my pockets, trying to clear my mind and focus on the task in hand. It's cold and the stars are on parade. I like the cold, I can't ever see myself returning to a hot country. Not after Afghanistan.

I cross the road and turn down Bloomfield Crescent, flanked either side by semi-detached properties in a suburb of Blackpool, pretending to be more affluent than it is. The car comes into view, parked at the side of the road, and I run through the procedure in my head; rubber, window, hook, lock, twist and away. I've practiced as many times as I could, or to be more precise, as many times as I could find cars that fitted the bill. I enjoyed spending my Saturday afternoons trawling the breakers yards. It was the same story every time.

'Excuse me, mate, I'm looking for an old banger for my son to learn to drive. You know the sort, something that runs okay but won't break my wallet when he wrecks it.' I would say to the man in the filthy overalls.

'Try at the back, over by the fence, mate, there's a few you might be interested in.'

They always seemed to be stored 'over by the fence'. I honed my skills on as many as I could find, putting into practice what I had learned from the Internet. When I had exhausted the scrap yards the next step was to find one that was kept outside somebody's house and not behind high fencing topped with barbed wire. Bloomfield Crescent provided just the ticket.

It was the right age, the right size and most importantly it was parked on a street with no CCTV. Perfect.

I quicken my stride closing in on the vehicle, trying to keep my anger in check, I need to stay calm and controlled. My eyes scan the road ahead for movement. Nothing. I draw level with the driver's door and crouch down, a final look around before I go to work.

I force the flat end of the chisel between the window and the rubber trim running around the outside. It slides into position and I lever the tool against the door sill, prising the glass towards me. With my other hand, I feed the wire loop through the gap and hook it onto the door knob. One subtle flick of my wrist and the door clicks open.

I jump in and hit the switch to kill the interior light, my senses are assaulted by a gagging mixture of cigarette smoke and lavender air freshener. The driver's seat slides back as far as it will go to accommodate my long legs. I take a Pozidrive screwdriver and a hammer from inside my coat. The tip of the screwdriver fits into the ignition lock and I deliver two heavy blows to the handle. The screwdriver smashes through the tumblers in the lock. *One more should do it.* I thump it home.

I twist the screwdriver and the dashboard lights up, another turn and the engine tells me it's ready to go. I pull away from the kerb and drive off.

My knuckles taut and white under the orange glow from the streetlights. I realise that I'm grinding my teeth. All I can see is that little girl with her mum. My blood begins to boil.

I look down and see I'm doing well over the speed limit, I ease my foot off the accelerator and suck in a few deep breaths. Getting pulled over for speeding is definitely not part of the plan. For the rest of the journey I rehearse the next steps, over and over in my head. In no time I find myself outside the Hawk's Head pub, pull the car over to the side and step out. I remove my jacket and drape it over the steering wheel to hide the offending screwdriver. The cold bites at my skin through my clothes.

I put my shoulder against the door and shove it open, the bar is hot and smells of old socks. The low ceiling and flaking walls does nothing to welcome me in and the guy behind the bar looks like he's straight out of an episode of *Shameless*. I order a beer and sit in the corner away from the gaggle of men gathered around the massive TV on the wall. There is a football game playing but no one is the least bit interested. A speaker the size of an armchair bangs out a song that I don't recognise above my head. I scan the crowd and realise that dressed in jeans and a shirt I stand out like a spare prick at a wedding - there are more tracksuits on display than at an Olympic track day.

Then I see him, dressed in a grey hoodie with a heavy gold chain hanging around his neck. Dangling from the end is an oversized crucifix, an ironic symbol given the man wearing it. He's holding court amongst his brain-dead cronies; telling his jokes and recounting his tales to the delight of his adoring followers. I want to sip my beer but I can't unclench my fist. I put my hands in my lap and try to relax, this is proving harder than I thought.

He elbows his way to the bar and I hear him shout his order.

'Oi, Jim! Ten pints of Stella mate, and don't spare the horses my man.'

The crowd behind him whoop and holler their approval. He turns with his hands raised in triumph. He has a lot to celebrate.

He takes a roll of bank notes fat enough to choke a horse from his pocket and peels off a couple of twenties.

'Make it eleven, I'm fucking thirsty,' he calls out.

The guys behind him go berserk, shouting and punching the air. I finally manage to pick up my pint and take a sip. The sudden change in temperature irritates my cheek. My eye twitches as I pull out a handkerchief and dab it against my face. Even now, after all this time, I still struggle to resist the temptation to rake my fingernails across the offending skin to alleviate the irritation – which of course it never does. I take the medicated cloth away and look at the surface in the dim light – it is clear. That's five weeks now.

I've seen enough, sink the rest of my beer in two large gulps and head for the door, the cold of the night tugs at my cheek again and it itches like a bastard. I hold the hanky to my face and walk across the road to the car.

All I have to do now is wait. The time ticks by and my breath begins to condense in the air, the windows glaze over with frost. I switch on the heater to keep them clear. When it's time to go I have to be ready. I watch the door to the pub and wait. The digits on the clock click over to 11.30pm.

The door flies open and five men spill out onto the pavement. He's in the middle of them doling out gangster rapper style handshakes and man-hugs. My adrenaline spikes.

They spend the next five minutes saying their exaggerated goodbyes and eventually he peels off and staggers down the road on his own. He is well oiled and needs the full width of the pavement to avoid stepping into the road. I start the engine and pull away slowly with my lights off.

I cruise behind him, keeping a safe distance, and watch as he weaves his way down the street, bouncing off the occasional car or hedge. He hangs a right into Clinton Avenue. This is where things get serious. I have to be flexible, adapt to the situation, no amount of planning can predict the next three minutes.

He leans into the corner and hugs the wall. He's taking two steps forward and one to the side trying to negotiate the bend. Then he stops, unzips his jeans and takes a piss against the brickwork. He disappears in a cloud of steam. Then, with a quick shake, he's off again zig-zagging his way up the pavement.

I close the gap between us, edging the car forward. Any minute now.

He reels to his left and stumbles into the road.

Shit! He normally crosses to the other side much further on, it catches me by surprise. I gun the engine and, despite the age of the car, it lurches forward, gathering speed. He hears the roar and stops in the middle of the road, his body twisted at the waist, staring in my direction.

The car accelerates hard. I hit the switch and the headlights come on full beam. He puts his hand to his forehead to shield his eyes. The engine screams in protest as I max out the low gear.

I can see his face, parchment white in the glare of the lights.

I want him to see me coming.

Chapter 2

Acting Detective Chief Inspector Rosalind Kray cruised to a stop at the side of the road. Up ahead she could see the flapping yellow tape strung across the mouth of the junction and behind it the blue lights of a squad car danced off the windows of the surrounding houses.

Stepping from the car, she pulled her coat around her to ward off the cold. She signed her name on the clipboard and the uniformed officer nodded as she ducked under the tape.

The other end of the street was blocked in the same way, the flashing blue lights gave the place an eighties disco vibe. Up ahead, Kray could see a knot of white suited people standing in the middle of the road, the glare from the array of lights on either side making them fluoresce against the dark. Despite it being almost one o'clock in the morning every house had someone silhouetted in the front door or at a window, craning their necks for a better view.

A police sergeant approached Kray.

'Ma'am.'

'What do we have?'

'A hit and run.'

'Any witnesses?'

'The guy at number forty-six said he saw something and called 999 when he discovered the man lying in the street.'

'Where is the victim now?'

'Left in an ambulance about fifteen minutes ago. He was in a bad way but still alive.'

'Have we identified him?'

The officer consulted his notebook. 'Jimmy Cadwell. He had a credit card in his wallet.'

'I know that name.'

'Yeah, we all do, ma'am. Fancies himself as a local hotshot. He's into all sorts.'

'Number forty-six you say?'

'Yes, ma'am, one of your guys is already there.'

Kray dug her hands into her pockets and marched off to find the house.

She pushed open the front door and was greeted by the warmth from the hallway. In the lounge she found a middle-aged man sitting on the edge of his armchair in his pyjamas, sporting matted bed hair. He was talking like his life depended on it. Opposite him on the sofa was DC Duncan Tavener; a Scotsman in his mid-twenties with boy band looks and the stature of an international lock forward. Kray didn't have favourites, but if she did, it would be him.

'Good evening, I'm Acting DCI Roz Kray.' She introduced herself not waiting for the man to acknowledge her presence. He stopped mid-sentence, six empty lager cans lay around the base of his chair.

'Oh hi, are you here because of …' he said.

'I am, yes.' Roz replied, wondering if there could be any other reason why two coppers were in his living room.

'Hey, Roz.' Tavener went to stand and Kray waved her hand for him to remain seated.

'It's as I was saying to your mate here …' The man saw a gap in the conversation and went for it. 'I was watching TV when I heard a thud outside, you know, the same type of noise when a rubbish bin falls over. So, I didn't think much of it. Then I heard a screech of tyres. Or it might have been a screech of tyres then a thud, I'm not sure. Anyway, I thought hang on a minute what's going on? I looked out the window to see a dark coloured car speeding away up the street. I thought *that's weird*. That's when I saw something in the middle of the road … at first I thought it was a bag of clothes. So I went outside and it was that guy. He was all twisted and bashed up and bleeding so I called an ambulance.'

Tavener glanced at Kray as if to say, 'That's as far as I got'.

'When was this?' asked Kray.

'It was about midnight I would say.' The man reached for his phone and hit a couple of buttons. 'Eleven forty-five to be precise.' He handed Kray the phone to confirm the time of his call.

'Did you get a look at the vehicle involved?'

'Not great. It was driving away from me, up the road that way.' The man pointed his finger to the right of the lounge window. 'But I do remember it was a dark colour.'

'A saloon car?' asked Tavener.

'Yeah I suppose so.'

'Did the victim say anything?' asked Kray.

'No, he was out cold.'

'When you looked out of the window and first saw the car, was it moving or stationary?'

The man struck a theatrical pose to accentuate the fact he was thinking. 'It was moving, definitely moving.'

'Are you sure?' said Kray.

'Yeah, pretty sure.'

'Okay, we'll need a formal statement from you, Mr …'

'Lewis, my name is Reg Lewis.' He could barely contain his excitement.

Tavener opened up his pocket book. 'Can you start from the beginning, Mr Lewis …'

Kray nodded to Tavener and walked back down the hallway into the night air. By now, the outside was awash with piercing white light from four banks of LED lamps. Kray could see the bloodied stains on the tarmac where Cadwell had come to rest. White suited people were peppering the road surface with yellow markers to indicate anything of interest, while others were snapping away with high-resolution cameras.

She surveyed the scene. The scars across her back began to tingle and she spun her wedding ring round and round. Something wasn't right. She donned a pair of overshoes and meandered her way between the yellow markers. The tingle escalated into an uncomfortable burn.

This is bollocks.

Kray ran through the chain of events in her head. She could see the vehicle hurtling around the corner, the driver slamming on the breaks and Cadwell being thrown into the air as he bounced off the bonnet. Then she saw the car screech to a halt as the tyres fought with the tarmac for traction. She walked to the first set of skid marks, shimmered black in the sanitised light. Then paced out thirty strides to the other set, scorched onto the tarmac further up the road.

'This isn't right.' She muttered under her breath.

'What isn't?' Tavener was stood beside her breaking her train of thought.

'Shit! For a big guy you don't make a lot of noise do you?' Kray said jolting herself back to reality.

'Sorry, I didn't mean to …'

'Never mind.' Kray looked her colleague up and down. 'You do know it's January, right?' A reference to him wearing a white cotton shirt that looked as if he'd borrowed it from a much smaller friend.

'Yeah, I know, I left my jacket in the car.'

'Jacket? You need an arctic explorer coat in this weather never mind a bloody jacket.'

'Thanks for the advice, ma'am, I'll make sure it's on my shopping list for the weekend,' he replied, knowing full well Kray hated being called ma'am.

Kray gave him a withering look, like she was scolding a wayward teenager. 'Did you get a statement?'

'Got it. I couldn't shut him up and every time he repeated his story it was slightly different. Keeping track of it was a nightmare. Not sure the beer helped matters.'

'Go back and have another go if you're not happy.'

Tavener paused, it was his turn to look his boss up and down. 'It appears you're the one who's not happy. What is it, Roz? I've seen that look enough times to know all is not well.'

'Maybe.' Kray continued to examine the scene.

'Well, what is it?'

'What do you think happened?'

'The driver came around the corner and saw Cadwell in the road. He or she slammed on the anchors but failed to stop and ran him over. They came to a halt further on.' Tavener pointed to the two sets of skid marks. 'When he or she realised what had happened they drove off. That fits with the witness statement.'

'Yeah it does. But it doesn't fit with this.' She waved her hand around the blood spatters in the road. Tavener rotated on the spot taking in the extent of the markers.

'The car must have been going a fair speed,' he offered.

Kray removed her phone from her inside pocket. 'Hi, this is Acting DCI Kray can you get a Forensic Collision Investigator over to Clinton Avenue. Tell them to ask for me when they arrive.' She hung up.

'Collision investigation? Why do we need that?'

'This wasn't a hit and run, this was attempted murder.'

Chapter 3

*I*t *was the day I came back from the dead.*

The first rays of the sun skirted over the mountains, sharpening the lengthy shadows on the ground. It was going to be another blistering spring day. My boots hit the shale as I jumped from the Snatch Land Rover, sending a cloud of dust into the air. My wrap-around ballistic glasses protected my eyes but my mouth soon clogged with the perpetual taste of sand being carried on the wind. I rubbed a cherry chapstick around my cracked lips. The dry climate and high altitude played havoc with my skin.

Up ahead I could see the burley figure of Donk perched on top of the Jackal, panning the barrel of his heavy machine gun across the outcrop of buildings in front of us. He had been given that name after one of the guys noticed his uncanny resemblance to the character in the Crocodile Dundee film. Donk was a giant of a man, the kind who couldn't spell tank but could pick one up. The rest of the team piled out of the vehicles to greet the day.

This was my second tour. Like many before me, I would describe it as ninety-eight per cent boredom interrupted by two per cent of sheer terror. To my shame I had to admit that I craved the two per cent. And being stationed in Helmand Province, a land mass half the size of England, and expecting it to be effectively patrolled by a little over one thousand troops, ensured we were never too far away from our share. Looking back now, it was the only time I felt normal.

Patrolling the Northern Valley was a no-win situation. 'Protect and reconstruct' was the mission statement but that was tough to do when nobody wanted us there. Not the Taliban, not the drug barons and not the tribesmen. It reminded me of the time I visited my girlfriend's family over Christmas the previous year – only with less agro.

We had received an intelligence report that a lethal arms cache had been hidden by insurgents in a village thirty miles to the west of Sangin - though experience had taught us to take the word *intelligence* with a huge pinch of salt.

All the fighting was focused around the district centres of Sangin, Now Zad and Musa Qala and the drone footage of the area had shown it to be deserted. We weren't expecting any unwanted company.

To call it a village was a little overstating it. A ramshackle collection of four dwellings, set in a square with a dust bowl of a courtyard in the middle, could hardly be considered a village. We scanned the surrounding hillsides. Nothing moved.

We scurried to the nearest house leaving Donk on his perch, raking the terrain through a set of field glasses. I pressed my back hard against the wall as Jono ran inside, followed by Pat, Ryan and Bootleg. I filed in behind.

The building was derelict, with half a roof and debris strewn across the floor. The sun had baked the brittle orange walls to dust. The occupants had long since gone, taking everything with them except for a paprika-red headscarf which was draped over a makeshift washing line. I reached over and snatched it free, folded it into a neat square and stuffed it inside my combat jacket. To this day I have no idea why I did that.

The others were chatting in a close huddle. We looked out at the three other buildings about thirty yards away, each one in a similar state of disrepair. All was still. To the right of the house was the wall. A curious twenty-feet long by four-feet high stone and mud structure in the middle of nowhere. What the hell purpose it served was beyond me. It wasn't connected to anything, it just stood there. It was like some guy had built it, got bored, thought 'that will do' and left. That was our target.

I took out my map and spread it onto the dirt.

'Yup, that's the place. The cache is hidden beneath the base of that wall, on the south side.' I nodded to the others.

'Time to deliver justice, boys.' That was the phrase Jono uttered on every operation. None of us knew exactly what it meant, but it suited the occasion every time. It had become our team mantra.

We crouched down, keeping tight to the outside and entered the nearest home to the left. It, too, was stripped bare. Then we made our way onto the next, then the next. They were deserted.

Jono marched out to the middle and signalled to Donk, who raised his hand. I unpacked my detector and snapped the handle in place.

Ryan followed me over to where X marked the spot.

'What the hell was this used for?' he said pointing at the wall.

'Buggered if I know. Maybe it was the start of a fifth house and they thought better of it.'

'I got neighbours like that. I wish they hadn't bothered.'

I flicked the switch on the detector and slowly tracked along the base of the stonework. The machine started to do its stuff and the needle bounced around as it picked up fragments of metal on the ground.

Jono and Bootleg showed up.

'Anything?' Jono asked.

I shook my head, continuing to fan the detector head in arcs across the sand. Five strides further on, the needle went off the scale and the shrill beep told me there was something heavy hidden below. I took out my knife and began delving the tip into the gravel. It was not unusual for arms dumps to be booby-trapped, so it paid to be cautious.

After several minutes I had dislodged the top layer of shale. It was safe.

I unfolded my shovel and began to dig at the sandy soil. After ten minutes I struck something solid. Bootleg lent a hand and we quickly uncovered a thick plastic sack. I ran my hands across the surface and could feel the curved outlines of AK-47 magazines. We heaved it from the ground.

'That's gonna hurt Terry Taliban,' Jono said as he grabbed hold of one end and Bootleg took the other. 'Let's get it to the Snatch.' They waddled off with the bag hanging between them.

I picked up the detector and continued to search, inching my way along the wall. Three feet further along the needle did its electronic happy dance again. I went through the same routine as before with the tip of my knife, this time grinning like a Cheshire Cat. It was all clear.

My shovel broke the ground and I piled mounds of sand and rocks to the side. I could feel the warmth on my back disappear as the rest of the team appeared behind me, putting me in the shade.

'Makes a change for the scribblies to get it right,' said Pat.

'Looks like they hit the jackpot this time,' replied Jono.

'We got this,' said Pat nudging me out of the way. He and Jake dropped down and started to claw at the ground with their shovels.

I resumed my snail's pace walk along the wall. The needle went berserk again.

'Got another one,' I said and allowed Jono to do the honours with his knife. A little further along and it happened again. 'And another. This is a good day, my friends.'

Pat and Jake tugged at the handles of a green metal box, freeing it from its shallow grave.

'Fucking RPGs,' Pat said wiping away the layers of dirt from the top with his gloved hand and flipping open the catches.

'Nice one,' Jono said.

I took out my knife and knelt down at the latest site. To the side of my face, a black scorpion emerged from a gap in the stonework to soak itself in the first heat of the day. I watched it find a suitable spot, stretching out its tail and front pincers. I put the point of my knife in the centre of its body, there was a crack like the splintering of eggshell.

I lifted the scorpion from the wall and gazed at it, it's legs pumped the air as it fought against being impaled upside down on the blade. The sting in its tail stabbed repeatedly at the metal. The creature contorted its body trying to free itself.

A puff of dust erupted from the wall to the left of my head. I caught it in my peripheral vision, snapping my eyes away from the scorpion. A second fragment of wall disintegrated into the air. Then we heard the pop-pop-pop of rapid fire.

Jono leapt to his feet yelling 'Incoming!' just as a shell tore into the calf muscle of his left leg. I launched myself to the side to avoid the exploding debris from the wall. I hit the ground hard and took a mouthful of dirt for my troubles.

Pat and Jake swung around to engage the enemy but there was no one there.

Where the hell is it coming from?

Jono went down clutching his leg. 'Shit!' he cried out.

Another line of bullets exploded against the mud surface of the wall, everyone hit the ground. The bang-bang-bang of Donk returning fire with his 50-calibre echoed off the buildings.

I looked up. *Where the hell are they?*

I shuffled to a crouch position and grabbed hold of Jono by his arm. 'Get over the wall!'

Pat and I bundled him over the top and he landed in a heap the other side screaming in pain. Jake dropped to the floor as a black hole appeared in his upper chest. A starburst of red exploded across the stonework behind him.

Donk was spraying bullets about the hillside as if he was doling out sweets on Halloween, sending plumes of dust and rock into the air. Then all of a sudden everything stopped. Silence. Pat scrambled over the wall followed by Bootleg.

Then another round thudded into Jake but he didn't flinch. I felt a sharp pain in my right shoulder and a bullet tore through my fatigues, grazing my flesh. I grabbed my weapon and hurled myself into the air but my feet slipped from under me on the loose gravel. I arched my back like a high jumper and came crashing down on top of the wall, knocking the wind out of me. In my dazed state I writhed around trying to right myself and tip my body over the top. I heard a fat metallic clunk against my helmet and the force catapulted me over to the other side. I landed flat on my back staring up at the blue sky with a loud ringing in my head. Then the craggy features of Bootleg filled my field of vision. He had one hand on my chest and the other on my neck.

'He's gone,' he yelled. 'Jarrod's gone.'

I stared up at him through my unblinking eyes and thought, *is this what it's like to be dead? I imagined something different.*

He disappeared and I was once again drowning in a sea of deep blue. I could hear the retorts of assault rifles as Pat and Bootleg blasted away, and was aware of being showered in debris from the top of the wall. Jono was barking orders.

I lay there unable to move, imprisoned inside my inert body. As the mayhem swirled around me I could feel sand in my eyes but could not close them. The tiny particles felt like boulders. Jono was shouting something about a tourniquet while Bootleg was yelling about the radio. My arms and legs refused to move. I couldn't call out, the sound of a thousand air raid sirens screamed in my ears.

Boots pounded around me as the guys changed position trying to lay eyes on where the enemy was hiding.

Then with a massive intake of breath I sat bolt upright, frightening Bootleg to death. He leaned over and pulled me against the wall.

'I thought you were fucking dead,' he said.

I rubbed the grit from my eyes and tried to speak. Nothing came out. I stared down at my hands turning them over and over as if I was seeing them for the first time.

I'm not dead ... The words churned over and over in my head.

The far end of the wall exploded. The blast blew us sideways and sent the whole world spinning in a shower of rock.

Chapter 4

'Today's the day,' Kray sang the words over and over as she drove to Victoria Hospital. This was despite having given herself a stiff talking to while waiting at a set of traffic lights and telling herself to calm down and get a grip. Even so, the knot of expectation in her stomach would not go away.

She checked the clock on the dashboard, 9am exactly. At this precise time, three days ago, she had been sitting in front of an interview panel being put through her paces for the role of Detective Chief Inspector. ACC Mary Quade was chairing the panel which was a mixed blessing because Quade flipped between being Kray's number one fan one day - thinking she was the best thing to happen to Lancashire force since Curry Fridays - to hating her guts the next, and wanting to destroy her career. The problem was, it was never clear to Kray which ACC Quade would show up for work.

All the candidates had been through the selection board on the same day. It was a prestigious position and the candidate list was long. DI Dan Bagley was one of them. The Mancunian tosser from Greater Manchester Police who Quade had drafted in to 'support' the Palmer case. Though in Kray's mind she substituted the word 'support' for the more appropriate phrase of 'almost fucked up'.

Kray had performed well during the hour-long grilling and had flown through the In-Tray exercise and the presentation. At one point she had to steel herself away from the mess of pens and pencils laying on the desk. Her OCD went into orbit … everyone knows pens go on one side and pencils on the other. She resisted the temptation to arrange them in their rightful place, blanked out her anxiety and ploughed on. After all, she was the star of the show, having cracked two serial killer cases in a year, she was the woman in form. Though she had to admit it was a challenge to speak for twenty minutes on the topic 'Delivering effective policing in an environment of austerity.' Despite her reservations they had appeared impressed with what she had to say. She was quietly confident the appointment would go her way but the nerves would not let her anxieties rest.

Kray parked up and entered the sprawling building. She didn't bother with the lift, choosing instead to bound up the stairs to the landing with the sign hanging above the corridor that read: Mortuary, Bereavement Office and Pathology.

On reading the sign another image burst into her head. A dishy, blond haired, Home Office pathologist with a liking for wearing waistcoats and trousers that fitted where they touched. The prospect of seeing Dr Christopher Millican was definitely an added bonus when having to view a dead body at this time of the morning.

Kray reached the mortuary and pulled on her protective gear, growling under her breath at the white coverall that swamped her small frame.

She rolled her eyes to the ceiling as she grabbed hold of a yard of material and pulled it away from her body. *I'm meeting Doctor Ding-dong and I look like a child wearing her father's overalls.*

She berated herself. *What the hell difference does it make what I look like? It's not as if I'm interested in him.*

It was a lie Kray had told herself every day since she had joined him for a coffee, closely followed by an after-work glass of wine at his favourite bar. It had happened the day after she solved the Palmer case and she put it down to an 'emotional blip'. She had taken the initiative and called him suggesting they met up. He had been the perfect gentleman, listening politely as she unburdened herself while ensuring her glass was never empty. He was a good listener and an even better barman.

But the thing she remembered most was giggling. She could not recall when she had laughed so much in the company of another person. That is since Joe died, of course. She had laughed so much her jaw ached and went home, on her own, feeling warm and fuzzy.

The next morning she'd been racked with guilt, a feeling that had stayed with her ever since. She had never been unfaithful to Joe but reckoned if she had, this is what it would feel like. A weird position to take as his ashes were buried in a cemetery.

Millican had called several times following their night out but she had put him off with lame excuses. He stopped calling after a while. This was the first time they had met since that fateful evening. For a woman who was convinced she didn't care, she had butterflies in her stomach the size of condors.

Kray pushed open the door and inhaled the sickly smell of rotting chicken and formaldehyde. The mortuary was shiny and new, courtesy of an injection of funds into the Victoria Teaching Hospital. The place was bright and clinical with three stainless steel tables lined down the centre of the room. Each table had a drain at one end and metal scales hung from the ceiling. Hoses and nozzles were connected to the frames and a set of gleaming steel work surfaces and sinks ran around the walls.

Doctor Ding-dong was huddled over a dish containing what looked like chopped liver. He looked up, his eyes flashed a warm 'Hello' long before his mouth uttered a word.

'Hey, Roz, how are you doing?'

'I'm fine thanks,' she replied, trying hard not to respond too eagerly. 'How about you?'

'Good.' He gave her his winning smile again, she chose instead to look at the liver in the silver container. The air between them crackled with unsaid conversation.

'What have we got?' She broke the silence, conscious that her cheeks were beginning to flush pink.

Millican snapped into work mode. 'James Arthur Cadwell, twenty-eight years of age, was admitted around half past midnight.' He tugged at the blue sheet covering the corpse and rolled it down to waist level. The signature Y-shaped scar stood proud on his chest.

'Shit,' Kray blurted out.

'Yeah, shit, exactly. Multiple blunt force trauma to the head, crushed rib cage, fractured pelvis, a collapsed lung, ruptured spleen, broken radius and ulnar, broken scapular … the list goes on. He died in ICU from massive internal haemorrhaging. His chances of survival when he was admitted were slim. The file says suspected hit and run?'

'Yes, that's the original line of inquiry, but I think this is a murder investigation.' Kray cast her eyes over the broken body lying on the slab.

'His injuries are more consistent with being run over by a fleet of lorries rather than a single vehicle.'

'That's what I thought. The blood spatter at the scene was extensive, much more than you would expect from a car and pedestrian collision. My view is the driver hit the victim, then reversed over him and finished off by running him over a third time.'

'That would do it. Under normal circumstances the victim would have primary impact wounds where the vehicle strikes them, usually the lower body and head. In the case of James Cadwell there are so many impact areas it's impossible to give you a sequence of his injuries.'

'Anything else that I should know about?'

'He had a high level of alcohol in his blood. It will all be in the report.'

'How much alcohol?'

'His blood alcohol concentration was point one-five percent.'

'What's that in old money?'

'He was well tanked up. Given his age and weight I would say he'd had seven or eight pints?'

'Thank you for rushing this through, I needed to get an early confirmation on our thoughts.'

'That's what we're here for.'

Krays phone buzzed in her pocket. It was Tavener.

'Yes I can be there in twenty minutes.' She hung up. 'Sorry, I have to run.'

'Okay, let me know if you need anything else.'

'Thanks.'

'Roz, before you go—'

'Sorry I have to dash.' She cut him off knowing full well what was coming next.

Chapter 5

I'm standing by the coffee machine when I overhear the news about Jimmy Cadwell.

'Hit and run, they reckon. He died in hospital from his injuries.'

I try to keep my emotions in check and not allow my elation to shine through.

'CID are carrying out an investigation.'

I keep my eyes glued to the floor.

In the absence of being able to race around the office with my arms stretched out and my jumper pulled over my head, I decide to celebrate with a Mochaccino instead of my usual Americano with milk.

I sip the coffee as I walk back to my desk. It tastes extra good.

I have been in work since seven-thirty this morning. We have a regular start time of eight-thirty but the first hour of my day is the most productive. Not because the phone is silent, or that we don't have meetings, not even because I'm the only one in the office at that time; it is the most productive hour of the day because at seven-thirty the case files get delivered.

You would think in this day and age the documentation would be processed electronically, but not when you're dealing with the courts system. It's paper, paper, paper all the way. Some old habits take generations to die off.

An early morning start provides the opportunity to sift through the incoming cases and pull out the ones that interest me the most.

I've been working here now for little over a year and it suits me down to the ground. It gives structure to my life and keeps me out of the pubs during the day. It also pays me a salary, that I can live on, which means I don't have to draw on my army pension. But the most important facet of the job is it makes me feel alive. I return to my desk with my coffee.

It's almost lunchtime and I can feel the adrenaline coursing through my body. At twelve-noon exactly the office empties and I am left alone. To everyone else working here I am the guy who keeps himself to himself, the one who chooses not to go to lunch with his co-workers and the man who comes in early when he knows he doesn't get paid for it. Oh, and he fought in Afghanistan or somewhere. The man who's a little odd.

I pull the buff coloured file from the pile and open it up. My heart is thumping with giddy expectation. I flick through the paperwork.

Boom! I knew it. I fucking knew it.

This case had all the hallmarks of the perfect storm. My pulse rate spikes as I consume the transcripts and file documents. The more I read the more a knot of anger builds in my stomach. I feel beads of cold sweat on the back of my neck.

I fought for my country but I never fought for this. The thought ricochets around my head.

I put my life on the line to protect the people of our country from the tyranny of rogue states that wanted to harm our way of life. I was injured in the pursuit of delivering that aim. I lost brothers in the pursuit of delivering that aim. And while I was being shot at, blown up and having my head screwed, the powers that be in this country were putting those very same people at risk by their own dereliction of duty. Through their own liberal incompetence, they were putting those very same people who I swore to protect in harm's way.

I read on.

'The victim has an above average interest in sex for a child of his age.' What the fuck! The key word of that sentence is *child*.

My pulse hits the roof when I read: 'So it has to be said that in this case the child contributed to his own abuse.' My fists are balled tight under the desk.

I close the file and cast my eyes to the ceiling. *What was the point?*

The words jump off the page. My breathing becomes erratic.

'The defendant is of below average intelligence for someone of her age.'

What was the point of all that suffering if those in power don't play their part to protect people? We were over there busting a gut and having bits blown off us when all the while the bad guys in our towns and cities are being allowed to run riot.

I bang my fists into the underside of the desk and stand up.

This one is perfect.

She's on the list!

Chapter 6

It was the day I looked a man in the eye, smiled, then blew his brains out.

The mortar shell left a three-feet wide crater where the end of the wall used to be. The explosion spewed stone and dirt in all directions, throwing us sideways in the blast.

'Get the fuck out of here!' Jono levered himself up on his good leg and began firing over the top. 'Go! Go!' he screamed. 'I'll lay down cover while you get the truck.'

I flashed a look at Pat.

'I'm staying with you,' Bootleg said checking his weapon.

'No, we all have to get out of here,' I yelled. 'They have the range with that mortar and the next one will be right on top of us. We all go, now!'

Jono thought for a second. 'You go. I'll slow you down.'

I hooked his arm across my shoulder and heaved him to a crouching position.

'Yeah right.' I plunged a vial of morphine into his leg. 'On three.'

Pat counted down with his fingers and sprinted from behind the wall, crabbing across the dustbowl to the nearest house, firing as he went. A torrent of rounds slammed into the dirt around him. Me and Bootleg bolted into the open with Jono slung between us.

It was the longest fifty feet of my life.

Jono tried to hop but we were moving too fast. He put his weight onto his shattered leg and yelped in pain. By the half-way point we were half dragging, half carrying him. The sand around us seemed to come alive with shells bursting against the ground.

Pat reached the corner of the first house just as there was an almighty bang behind us. The wall disintegrated, sending rubble spewing into the air. A heavy stone caught Bootleg in the middle of his back and all three of us crashed to the floor. We scrabbled around trying to right ourselves.

Out of nowhere Pat appeared, gripped Jono by the back of his collar and hauled him along the floor. I struggled to my feet, picked up the guns and threw myself behind the cover of the house, Bootleg landing on top of me. How the hell they missed us I will never know.

'We gotta get one of those vehicles,' Pat said adjusting the tourniquet around Jono's leg.

I could see the pearl white, jagged edge of his shin bone protruding through his trousers. He was bleeding out. His blood soaking into the earth.

'They'll hit these buildings next, we need to move fast.'

We took a moment to catch our breath. The vehicles were parked about thirty yards away.

'Let's go.'

Bootleg and Pat heaved Jono to his feet and manhandled him to the far corner. I held up my hand for them to stop.

'It's too far. They will pick us off, we won't make it. I'll go get the vehicle and bring it here. It's the best way.'

Before they had a chance to protest I darted from behind the house, keeping low, zig-zagging my way over the open space. My heart was in my mouth. I was blowing hard and could feel dust choking my throat. There was a second of glorious silence which seemed to last forever, I was covering the ground fast, closing the distance to the trucks. Then there was a terrifying cacophony of gunfire. The ground around me erupted, rounds kicking up the sand. My legs pumped as I hurtled towards the Jackal. I glanced up to see Donk slumped over the big gun.

I skidded feet first under the vehicle like a baseball player sliding to first base. My breath was ragged and I was hyperventilating, my blood thumped a deafening rhythm in my temples. I tried to calm down and take stock.

Then I heard a different noise, it was the sound of people shouting. I swivelled around on my belly trying to locate the voices. I peered out from under the truck to see five insurgents racing down the hillside toward the village.

'Shit!'

I turned and clawed myself out, climbing up the side of the Jackal. I grabbed Donk with both hands and heaved his bloodied body to one side. The Taliban fighters were two hundred yards away and closing fast. I crouched behind the gun, took hold of the grips and swung the long barrel towards them. The rapid bang-bang-bang of the M2 ensured they got no further. The belt fed smoothly through the chamber and with a few short bursts they were cut down. I checked the mountainous terrain for others – all clear. But I knew more would be coming soon.

I heard the ping of a mortar shell being launched and saw two men silhouetted on a ridge. A schoolboy error.

I held my breath. *Where the fuck was it going to land?*

I crouched down expecting the worse.

The shell overshot the houses and exploded ten yards away from where the other three were hunkered down. A near miss. They wouldn't make that mistake a second time. I took aim and began emptying the magazine box. At six hundred rounds a minute, the ridge exploded as the bullets tore up the ground, shredding everything in its path. I paused to get my bearings and squeezed again. Another ten second salvo and I stopped. The top of the ridge was empty.

I dropped down into the driver's seat and cranked over the engine. It wouldn't start. I tried again. The big diesel chugged but refused to fire. I slammed my hands into the wheel and leapt from the cab.

I'm not sure who was more surprised – me or the middle-aged man who was crouched at the side of the Jackal. He jumped to his feet as my boots hit the dirt, he was so close I could smell the stink of his body odour. He was dressed in dark coloured robes and his heavily weathered face stared at me, wide eyed, from beneath his

Peshawari cap. But more importantly he was carrying a battered AK-47.

I reckon I was still suffering from the bang to the head because he reacted first, lifting his weapon and yanking the trigger.

Click

That's twice today.

The gun jammed. He looked down at his rifle and then at me.

In that split second our eyes locked. He wasn't scared, his face told a story of being angry and confused. *Why the hell doesn't this thing work?* I half expected him to hand me the gun to see if I could fix it.

I smiled back at him, with a sympathetic grin that said *that's gotta be tough.*

The muzzle of my rifle kicked up as I fired from the hip. The bullet entered under his jaw bone and blew out the back of his head.

Chapter 7

'This is good work, Duncan,' Kray said negotiating a sharp bend that took them into a new housing estate.

'It wasn't difficult, I followed the motive. Cadwell has a list of associates as long as my arm who would gladly run him over in a car.'

'And back again.'

'Yeah, but this one stuck out from the pack.'

They drove past a large sign that read 'Woodland View, an up-and-coming estate for the upwardly mobile.' *Nice,* Kray thought as she looked at the show homes at the entrance to the development.

'How do you want to play this?' Tavener asked looking at the well-kept front lawns of the houses as they passed.

'I don't want to bring anyone into the station if we can help it. Let's try to keep this low key, you know, sound them out first.'

'Got it.'

Kray pulled up in a cul-de-sac and pointed to the three-bed detached property straight ahead of them.

'It's the one with the red door.'

They both got out of the car and made their way up the driveway. A Ford Kuga sat on the drive, Kray pressed the doorbell.

Moments later a thirty-something-year-old man stood before them dressed in his pyjamas and carpet slippers. He seemed to stare right through them and had the complexion of someone who had spent ten years in a darkened room. He said nothing.

'Mr Jack Stapleton?' Kray asked.

'Yeah.'

'I'm acting DCI Kray and this is DC Tavener. I wonder if you would help us by answering a few questions.' She held her badge up for him to read. He ignored it.

'Fuck off, I'm not interested.'

'Mr Stapleton, we believe you may have information relevant to an on-going investigation—'

'Are you deaf?' He went to close the door, Kray put her hand up to stop him.

'Mr Stapleton, we would like to conduct this with as little fuss as possible but if you refuse to cooperate I will be forced to arrest you and we can do this down the station.'

Stapleton looked over Kray's shoulder at the towering figure of Tavener and back to her.

'If this is about fucking Cadwell, I don't want to know.'

'Mr Stapleton can we come in please?'

Stapleton walked into his lounge leaving the door open. Kray nodded to Tavener and they followed him inside.

The house smelled of fresh flowers. In the lounge two huge bouquets flanked the fireplace and cards cluttered the mantelpiece and window sill.

'Someone's birthday?' asked Tavener.

'Fuck me, you're sharp.' Stapleton slumped down into an armchair and switched off the TV.

Kray picked up one of the cards. *To Liz, happy birthday, thinking of you always. All our love Kirsty and Pete x*

'Is your wife at home?' asked Kray, replacing the card and taking a seat on the sofa.

'No, she went back to work a few weeks ago. She reckoned the routine would do her good.'

'And what about you?'

'I went back for a while but had a big bust up with a kid, and was signed off with stress.'

Kray nodded her head and looked at the carpet.

'When was the last time you saw Jimmy Cadwell?' asked Tavener.

'So, this *is* about him! I knew it. When will you people leave us alone?' Stapleton was on his feet, glowering down at the two of them.

'Jack, can I call you Jack? Where were you last night at around half eleven?'

'I've said all I have to say about that bastard.' Stapleton sat down hard in the chair.

'Please answer the question, Jack,' Kray said. 'Where were you at around half past eleven last night?'

'In bed.'

'And your wife would be able to verify that?'

Stapleton stared out of the bay window.

'Jack, would your wife be able to verify that you were home in bed at that time?' Tavener asked the question again.

'No,' he replied.

'You were here alone?'

'Yeah, I was.'

'Your wife is a teacher as well isn't she? Is she away on a course or something?'

'No, Liz was at her sister's place!' He got up and began stomping about the room. 'She's staying there for a few nights while we ...' He failed to complete the sentence.

'Has your wife moved out, Jack?'

'Yeah you could say that. We are having a few ... well you know.' He tailed off again. 'Look what the fuck is this about? Haven't you people done enough damage?'

'What car does your wife drive?'

'A Corsa. What the hell has that got to do with anything?'

'What colour is it, Jack?'

'Dark blue.'

Tavener flashed a sideways glance at Kray.

'Is there anyone else who could confirm you were at home at that time?'

'Yeah, there's loads of people in my house at that time of night when I'm tucked up in bed. What do you think? You people crease me up with your bullshit lines of questioning. Why don't you leave me and my family alone?' He stopped and put his head in his hands. His shoulders began to shake and tears ran through his fingers. 'Oh, silly me I forgot for a minute. I got that wrong didn't I?' he yelled, jumping to his feet. 'I got that wrong because I haven't got a fucking family, have I?' He yanked a picture off a side table showing him, a woman and a small smiling child on a trike. He shoved it into Kray's face. 'I don't have a family because she's dead, killed by that bloody Cadwell. And where is he now? In prison where you would expect? No, he's roaming around free as a bird because between you lot, the CPS and the judge you fucked it up.'

'We are deeply sorry about what happened to your daughter and deeply sorry that the judge chose the sentence he did, but you have to understand that is out of our hands,' Kray said with all the compassion she could muster. Her brow creased in sympathy.

'You're all the same, each one shoving the blame onto the others. My daughter is dead and he gets off with it.'

'Jack you need to calm down,' said Kray.

'Oh yeah, calm down. Calm down. Because that's what a father does when his four-year-old kid gets knocked down by a car and killed, and the driver is handed a suspended sentence. That's precisely what you do - calm fuckin' down! We got a bedroom full of toys and unopened Christmas presents on her bed and neither of us can bear to go in there.'

'Jack we know how hard this must be—'

'No you don't, you don't have a clue. If you did, he would be behind bars getting his arse ripped open every night by a big bloke with tattoos who wants to be called Brenda. If you cared one jot, that's where he'd be right now, not walking about laughing his fucking head off.' Stapleton spat the words at Kray.

He backed away, slumping back down in the chair and gazed teary eyed at the photograph. His face flushed red.

Kray looked at Tavener and shook her head. There was nothing else for it.

'Jack, put some clothes on we need to do this down at the station.'

Stapleton launched himself at Kray.

Tavener took him off his feet with a shoulder charge that saw the pair of them land in a heap on the lounge floor.

Not exactly what Kray had in mind when she had said 'low key'.

Chapter 8

Kray sat opposite Stapleton in the interview room. She was flying solo this time having dispatched Tavener to pick up Liz Stapleton and bring her in for questioning.

'You are not under arrest, Jack but you are under caution, and this interview is being recorded. You have been advised of your rights and have a solicitor present.' Kray paused for the middle-aged woman sat to Stapleton's left to state her name.

'Audrey Piper, duty solicitor.'

'We need to ask you a few questions and I understand that talking to the police is difficult for you, but I want you to remain calm. Is that clear?'

'Yes it's clear. I'm sorry about earlier, some days are worse than others and this morning wasn't good. Will you be charging me with assaulting a police officer?'

'I'm not sure what you're referring to, Jack, I would much prefer that we move on. But I do need you to cooperate.'

Kray's eyes locked with Stapleton's and that was all she had to say.

'I understand,' he said, casting his gaze to the ceiling.

'For the purpose of the tape I will summarise what was said at the house.' Kray continued, content that the message had been received loud and clear. 'You told us you were home alone, in bed at around eleven-thirty last night. There is no one who can vouch for your whereabouts. You and your wife are going through a bad patch and she is currently staying at her sister's house. You also told us your wife drives a dark blue car. Is all that correct, Jack?'

'Yes, it is.'

'When was the last time you saw James Cadwell?'

34

Despite his assurances, Stapleton flashed with anger at the mention of the man's name but managed to hold it together this time. 'It would have been the final day in court when the sentence was handed down. If you can call it a sentence.'

'You haven't seen him or been in contact with him since?'

'No I've steered well clear of the little shit. If I did manage to bump into him, I'd kill the fucker!'

Piper nearly had a seizure and grabbed his arm, pulling him in close and whispering frantically into his ear. Stapleton pulled away and looked at her.

'Well what else am I supposed to say? Oh, if I met him again I'd take him to McDonalds and buy him a Happy Meal? The man killed my daughter, he mowed her down in his car in broad daylight. She died at the scene. She was walking hand in hand with Liz, when he mounted the kerb and knocked her fifteen feet along the road. The impact took her clean out of Liz's grasp. All because he was texting on his bloody phone. What else do you expect me to say?'

'So you admit to wanting to see James Cadwell dead?'

Piper lurched for his arm again but it was too late. 'Of course I do, wouldn't you? Cadwell beguiles the court with some cock and bull story about having to look after his mum who has dementia and the family relies on his money to scrape by. Judge Fuckwit swallows the lot and gives him a suspended sentence. When the truth is he hardly ever sees his bloody mother and his money comes from his criminal activities. It was a circus, and we are the ones living the sentence, not him.' Stapleton had his fists clenched on the desktop trying to keep himself in check. 'Look I'm sorry about earlier but it doesn't change anything. Cadwell killed my daughter and walked away, any father would want him dead.'

'Which is why we need to ask about your whereabouts,' Kray said, 'and there is no one who can confirm where you were last night?'

'Has something happened to him? Is Jimmy Cadwell dead?'

'I am not at liberty to—'

'Fucking hell, he is, isn't he? It was on the news this morning, a report about some bloke being killed in a hit and run. They didn't give the victim's name but it was Cadwell, wasn't it? That's why you wanted to know the type of car Liz drove.'

'We cannot confirm or deny—'

'Oh my God.' Stapleton flung himself back into his chair almost toppling over. He tilted his head back and buried his face in his hands. 'He's dead, someone killed him.' Stapleton jumped up from his seat giving Piper the fright of her life.

'Jack, you need take it easy,' Kray said. 'We don't want a repeat—'

'Don't worry I'm not about to kick off, I could not be happier.' Stapleton bent over at the waist putting his hands on his knees like he was out of breath. 'I can't believe it. This is the best news ever!'

'Jack can you sit down. You need to answer our questions.'

Stapleton returned to his seat, tears in his eyes. 'I will do whatever you want, I'll answer any question you want. You have just made my day, no my year! That is brilliant.' He slumped forwards and began sobbing. There was a loud knock at the door.

Kray terminated the interview and found Tavener standing in the corridor. She stepped out, closing the door behind her.

'Sorry, Roz, can I have a word?'

'Yeah, you can have several.'

'How's it going in there?'

'He saw a news item this morning saying a man was killed in a hit and run, put two and two together and come up with four. I've not confirmed or denied it but he's like a dog with two dicks in there. He couldn't be happier.'

'Can't say I blame him.'

'Yeah, I know what you mean. Anyway I don't think he had anything to do with Cadwell's death. He strikes me as a man who struggles to get himself dressed during the day let alone someone with the capability to plan a murder. What do you have?'

'I have good news and some bad news.'

'Good news first.'

'I think we've got the vehicle used to kill Cadwell. It's a dark blue Vauxhall Vectra, a couple of uniformed officers found it burned out on a patch of waste ground about five miles from Clinton Avenue. The inside is gutted, so fingerprints are unlikely, but forensics have found fragments of grey material snagged on the broken headlights and the bumper which match the clothing Cadwell was wearing on the night he was killed. There are also several blood traces on the back and front of the Vectra which have been sent off to the lab. We are also comparing the skid marks found at the scene with the tyre treads. They will take a while to come back but I'm pretty confident it's the right car.'

'That's a result.' Kray paused. 'Doesn't that strike you as odd?'

'What?'

'That you would go to the trouble of torching the inside of the car to cover your tracks and not burn the outside as well.' The scar on her cheek began to itch and tingle.

'I'm not with you?'

'Whoever mowed down Cadwell didn't pour the accelerant over the bodywork when he set it on fire. If he had, we wouldn't have fragments of his clothing and blood stains.'

'I see what you mean. Maybe whoever did it just got careless.'

'No, it's more like they only did half a job.' Kray drifted off, fidgeting with her wedding ring.

Tavener was growing impatient. 'Do you want the bad news?'

'Oh, erm, yes. What is it?' Kray snapped back to the present.

'Liz Stapleton has done a runner. She was at school this morning and left, suddenly. We checked her sister's place … she's not there.'

'Shit!'

'What?'

'Stapleton must have made a phone call when he was getting dressed before we dragged him here.'

'I don't get you?'

'Take over for me with Jack Stapleton.'

'Why where are you going?'

'Liz Stapleton hasn't done a runner, I know exactly where she is.'

Chapter 9

*I*t was the day I found my friend's severed leg.

I had abandoned any further attempts at starting the Jackal and tore over to the Snatch Land Rover, throwing myself into the front seat. It roared into life first time. Ever since I had shredded the hillside with the M2 it had all gone quiet. There had been no sign of the mortar boys and the insurgents were either dead or dying.

The wheels spun on the shale as I powered the short distance to the house. Pat had heard me coming and had Jono up and waiting. I swung the front end around and backed up. I could hear the doors being flung open and Jono cried out as he was bundled on top of the sack containing the AK-47 magazines. Bootleg jumped into the front passenger seat.

'Go, go!' Pat yelled.

'No, no wait,' Jono said, trying to get up. 'We need to get Ryan and Donk.'

'They're gone, Jono, we gotta get you to a hospital.'

'I'm not fucking leaving them.'

'Jono, there's bound to be more Taliban around. We need to get going.'

'I'm not leaving without them. They hung American contractors from a bridge in Falluja after mutilating their bodies. They are not doing that to any of us.'

'But that wall took two direct hits, not sure there's anything left of Ryan … and Donk took one while he was blasting away on his perch,' said Pat.

'Then let's go and see.' Jono slumped back as the pain washed through him.

Bootleg shot me a glance.

I shoved my right foot into the floor and slewed the truck around. As we bumped and jerked across the dust bowl we could hear the distant pop-pop-pop of assault rifles.

'Shit, there's more of them,' Bootleg shouted over the growl of the engine.

I looked to my left and could see a group of men working their way down the hillside. I stamped on the break skidding to a stop close to the wall. Pat threw open the back doors.

There on the ground, laying in a crumpled heap, was Ryan's body. He had been thrown clear in the blast.

'He's here!' Pat called out and we both jumped from the cab to help. Plumes of dust kicked up around our feet as the shells missed their mark. Pop-pop-pop, the frequency was intensifying. We each grabbed a part of Ryan and heaved his body into the back of the Land Rover.

I eventually slammed my foot on the accelerator and we skidded away. The staccato sound of metal on metal filled the confines of the cabin as the rounds cracked against the side. The back window blew out showering Bootleg with glass.

'I'm okay, I'm okay,' he yelled.

I drew level with the Jackal, trying to give us as much cover as possible, and shuddered to a stop. All three of us piled out. I scrambled up on top of the turret swinging the machine gun into position. I could see the bobbing heads of a dozen insurgents running towards the village, firing as they went.

The gun jolted in my hands as I strafed the hillside. One by one I watched them fall as the trail of bullets overran them. A few of them turned in my direction to return fire but they were no match. I kept them in my sights and mowed them down.

I released my finger and could feel the heat from the barrel waft towards me. Job done.

Bootleg was beside me while Pat waited, crouched. We pushed and shoved Donk's body off the top and lowered him to the ground. Then with one last effort he was laying on the floor in the Land Rover.

'Feeling better now?' Bootleg asked.

'Much,' I said as we powered up the dirt track away from the village.

'Lima 1 this is Foxtrot 4, over,' Pat shouted into the radio, while trying to pour water into Jono's mouth.

'Foxtrot 4, what is your status?' The detached voice cracked through the speaker. Pat had already called into base and a Medical Emergency Response Team were on their way.

'Lima 1, we are evac and enroute, repeat, evac and enroute. Request immediate medical support. Two down and one injured. Repeat, two down and one injured. Over.'

'Roger that, Foxtrot 4. Support is in the air. Over.'

'Roger that, Lema1. Out.'

'The MERT are on their way.'

The village was fast disappearing into the side mirror. I was driving like a maniac and could hear the munitions banging against the floor of the truck as we lurched around.

'Where are they taking him?' I asked.

'Role 3 hospital, Camp Bastion, it's about sixty-five miles from here.'

'Nice one. We could—'

There was a massive explosion and the Land Rover was lifted into the air on a ball of fire, spinning along its axis. The road seemed to be rising up to meet us. The whole world went into slow motion. The windshield folded in on me and I could feel a searing heat against my legs. The vehicle became a giant tumble dryer. Rifles, people and the bag of amo twisted and turned in mid-air. The structure of the Land Rover flexed under the force of the blast. We landed on our side and skidded off the road into a ditch. My driver's side window shattered, showering my face with glass. We came to a juddering stop.

I looked across at Bootleg, he was staring directly ahead, held in place by his seat belt. I reached for my weapon and shook him by his left shoulder.

'Get out!' I shouted at him. 'Open your door and get out.' I hit his belt release and he toppled onto me. The left side of his head was missing. I screamed and tried to shove him away.

'Pat, Pat, Bootleg is dead.' I turned in my seat. The back of the land Rover was gone. I could see body parts, bits of metal and AK-47 magazines strewn across the road marking our direction of travel. The dirt track looked like a butcher's block on a busy Saturday.

I fought my way around Bootleg and clambered over the back of my seat. My head felt like I had spent a week riding on a fairground waltzer. I sat down with a bump and keeled over onto my side. The debris on the road oozed in and out of focus. I felt a warm trickle of blood run across my face and the sharp sting of embedded glass. The taste of bile welled at the back of my throat. I blinked rapidly trying to clear my vision.

Then I saw movement.

I sat up and tried to get to my feet, but my legs buckled and I toppled over. I tried again and managed to plant my feet on the floor and stand in a half-crouch. I could see someone moving. It was Jono.

I hobbled over to where he was lying face down on the ground. His right leg was gone. Arteries and veins protruded from the ragged stump, pumping blood onto the road.

'Aghhh,' he croaked.

I pulled a tourniquet from the pocket in my sleeve and secured it in place, next I plunged another vial of morphine into what was left of his upper thigh.

'It's okay, Jono, the chopper is on its way.' It was the only thing I could think to say. I staggered to my feet and wandered about looking for Pat. I only found enough of him to fit into a Tesco shopping bag. I located the remnants of the radio and what was left of Ryan. Then it struck me, the Taliban would have heard the bang. If there were any left, they would be heading my way.

I found a rifle and a hand gun and dragged a groaning Jono into a ditch as far from the road as I could. I returned and sliced open the sack of AK-47 magazines with my knife, scattering more of them over the road. I figured Terry Taliban might be more interested in them than us. I pulled the sacking free and returned to Jono, wrapping him in the material. All we had to do now was wait.

In the distance, I could hear two things. The whoop, whoop of two sets of massive rotor blades cutting through the air and the fierce revving of engines. I saw the dust trail from the trucks first. They were racing across the valley floor, heading our way. Two pickup trucks with men sat in the back.

I pulled Jono further down into the ditch and checked my weaponry. I had enough to hold them off but not enough to go to war. The whoop, whoop got louder. My face burned with a hundred hot needles. I ran my fingers over my cheek and felt the shards of glass embedded in my skin, I could taste blood in my mouth.

The flat-beds were speeding towards us, I counted about ten or twelve insurgents. Then I heard the sound of 50-cal bullets tearing into what was left of the Land Rover, followed a split second later by the staccato bang as they left the muzzle. I had missed the heavy-duty machine gun attached to the roof of one of the trucks.

The place erupted in flying metal and rock. I held onto Jono and did what I could to protect him, a large patch of blood was growing in the sand.

The air was filled with a loud fizzing noise, followed by two thunderous explosions. I ducked my head down, convinced that this was the end. But as the sound echoed away, I looked up to see two scorched craters where the pickup trucks had been. The Apache Attack helicopter came into view, banking around the head of the valley. It remained in the air as the Chinook touched down. The Force Protection Unit spilled out of the gaping tail like the huge machine was vomiting them up. They fanned out securing the area.

I stood up and the MERT team reached us in seconds.

I did what I could to tell them what had happened but I was all over the place and kept falling over. The next ten minutes were foggy, it was as though my brain had shut down. The last thing I can remember was finding Jono's leg and bringing it with me when I boarded the chopper. I knew it was his because the tourniquet was still in place, wound tight below his knee. At the time, it seemed that finding it was the most important thing in the world.

I laid it next to him as the medics pulled me away for treatment, then I passed out.

Chapter 10

Kray cruised around the sharp bend leading into Woodland View and took the third cul-de-sac on the left. At the far end she could see a dark blue Corsa sitting on the driveway of the house with the red door. She parked up and walked across the grass verge. The front door was ajar. She pushed a finger against it, lightly, and it cracked open.

'Hello, anybody home? I'm Acting DCI Roz Kray, I want to ask you a few questions. Liz are you here?' There was no response. Kray bobbed her head into the lounge but it was empty. She made her way up the stairs to the landing and found what she was looking for. On the door to the right was a sign, it read: Eve's Room.

Kray softly knocked and eased the door open. The room was pink and bright, with unicorn and rainbow wallpaper. Toys and clothes were strewn over the floor. Against the wall, under the window, was a single bed with a quilt cover sporting even more unicorns. But Kray couldn't see much of the quilt design because it was obscured by a mound of presents wrapped in Christmas paper piled up against the head board and the vacant figure of Liz Stapleton, sitting with her knees tucked up under her chin. Her glassy eyes stared right through Kray as she entered the room.

'Liz, my name is Acting DCI Roz Kray.'

'I heard you.' Liz Stapleton pressed a child's pyjama top to her face. She was around the same age as her husband, with dark brown hair that was cut into a bob and framed what was once a pretty face, but now one ravaged by sadness. 'I can still smell her you know. After all this time, when I come in this room she's still here. I can hear her playing and singing along to her

Disney songs. I can see her dolls lined up as she plays school and pours water into plastic tea cups because it's break time. It never goes away you know?'

'How long has it been?'

'Two months and two weeks, tomorrow. Hence all this ...' She nodded her head towards the pile of presents. 'We couldn't bring ourselves to do Christmas this year.'

'It was your birthday,' Kray said changing the subject.

'Yes, a couple of days ago.' She straightened out her legs, took a tissue from her sleeve and wiped her nose. She turned the pink pyjama top over and over in her hands. 'Let's just say, it wasn't much fun.'

'Did Jack call you, this morning?'

'He went completely overboard with the flowers; one bunch delivered to work and another waiting for me when I got home. It was like he was trying to make up for me not having a gift from Eve. Like he was overcompensating. Fucking idiot.'

'Liz, did Jack contact you?'

'Why are men so shit at this stuff? I'm hurting just as much as him, yet he's the one who collapses in a heap and can't even make a cup of tea, then he flips into being Mr Angry and it's like sharing a house with bloody Rambo. And the flowers are supposed to make all that okay? I don't think so.'

Kray lightly tiptoed her way around the toys and sat on the floor with her back against the wardrobe. She might get her turn to talk, but not yet.

'I persuaded him that going back to work would be good, you know to get a bit of routine back into his life. Then that judge has a total brain-fart and allows Cadwell to walk free, and it all kicks off again. Jack has a stand-up row with a pupil in the classroom and storms out. I don't know what to do with him. I can't take any more. I'm hanging on by a thread myself, taking one day at a time, and he thinks two bunches of flowers is going to make everything okay? Fucking idiot.'

'Mrs Stapleton—'

'I don't feel *anything* anymore. I don't get angry, don't get sad. It's as though someone hollowed out my insides. Jack hates you lot, and what he wouldn't do to that judge is nobody's business. Me? I just feel numb.'

'Did your husband contact you this morning?'

'Oh, erm, yes he did. He said you had come around asking questions about Cadwell. Where is Jack now?'

'He's down at the station helping us with our enquiries.'

'What the hell has he done?'

'He's been answering questions, that's all.'

'What about?'

'Where were you last night, Liz, around eleven-thirty?'

'I was at Anabel's house, she's my sister. I'm staying there for a while until we get back on an even keel.'

'Was there anyone else at the property who can vouch for you?'

'Yes, I was with Anabel. We were watching some rubbish on TV. I'm not sleeping well so there's no point going to bed. She stayed up to keep me company and we turned in about half past midnight.'

'We will have to confirm that with your sister.'

Liz Stapleton simply shrugged her shoulders.

'So what is this about? Why are you asking us questions about Cadwell?'

Kray paused, weighing up her options before answering. She allowed compassion to get the better of her. 'James Cadwell was hit by a car last night and died of his injuries.'

Liz Stapleton bounded from the bed, her bottom lip trembling. She towered over Kray, her fists balled at her sides. 'Jesus Christ, is there no fucking end to this?'

Kray stared up at her. 'I need to—'

'And you think we might have had something to do with it?'

'We are following a number of lines of inquiry.'

Stapleton spun on her heels and returned to her place on the bed, picking up the pyjama top and tucking her knees under her chin. 'I'm sorry, I don't know where that came from.'

'It's okay, I appreciate this is a shock.'

'Well I can't say I'm not pleased to hear that, but it doesn't change things, it won't bring Eve back. He took her from us and we have to live with that for the rest of our lives. What should have happened is that he went to prison for life – that's what *should* have happened. Him being dead doesn't give me closure. It will make me smile from time to time I'm sure, but I would rather think about him being in jail for what he did. When that judge allowed Cadwell to walk free from court he condemned us to an existence where we had no closure.'

'He didn't walk free, he got a ten-month sentence which was suspended for two years. He was out on strict license.' Kray looked up and into the face of Liz Stapleton. She regretted her comments immediately.

'Oh please, save me the sob story about poor Jimmy Cadwell and how shit his life is under the threat of his suspended sentence. He ran down the steps of the court punching the air for all he was worth. He's a career criminal who doesn't give a flying fuck about your licensing conditions. You know he had a curfew right? So how come he fell out of the pubs at all hours of the day and night?' Kray wanted the doors of the wardrobe behind her to open and swallow her up. 'That judge destroyed our lives for a second time when he believed the bullshit that was being spouted off in court. Cadwell pleaded guilty to the lesser charge of causing death by dangerous driving, along with the fantasy-land tale of having to provide for his sick mother and he has the whole courtroom in tears. He was fucking texting when he mowed down our little girl. And her life is worth a twenty-eight month driving ban and he got to walk about … free as a bird. So please don't give me the 'suspended for two years' speech. I'd swap places with him tomorrow, well maybe not now he's dead.'

'I'm sorry, Liz.'

'It's not your fault. It's the judicial system we have in this country. We wanted to see justice done for little Eve - Cadwell being dead is not justice.'

'Your husband has a different view.'

'Yeah, he will have. When you've finished with him he'll be straight to the pub to celebrate.' She eased herself forward and got off the bed. 'You got time for a cup of tea?'

She walked out leaving Kray sat on the floor.

Kray's phone buzzed, it was Margaret Gill, ACC Quade's PA. There was only one reason why she would call her today – they had made their decision.

Back in the car, Kray's heart began to race. She had spent the last ten minutes making her apologies to Liz Stapleton and telling her she would have to take a rain check on the cup of tea.

Kray drove the short journey to the office, her mind running amok with ambition, the details of the Cadwell case could not compete. She parked up and forced herself to take the lift to the ACPO suite on the top floor. She didn't want to be out of breath when she got there however much she wanted to sprint up the stairs. The lift seemed to take forever, Kray jigged on the spot like a child needing the toilet. Eventually the doors dinged open and she rushed out into the rarefied atmosphere of the top floor, filled with the smell of furniture polish and gilded seniority.

She made a beeline for Quade's office. Margaret rose from her desk and stopped her.

'Mary has someone in with her at the moment, Roz. I'm sure she won't be long.'

Kray noticed the office door was shut and could hear the soft murmurings of voices coming from the other side. She glanced at the outlook diary on Margaret's computer screen but it was too far away to read the name on the appointment.

Margaret closed down the window and began typing an email. Kray was trying to control her excitement.

The sound of laughter echoed from the other side of the door just as the handle was punched down and the door flew open. Bagley stood before her, looking like he'd just found a fifty-pound note in the pocket of an old suit.

'Thank you, Mary, I will give you a call,' he said over his shoulder.

'Keep me posted,' Quade replied, out of sight.

'Hey, Roz,' Bagley said blocking her path. 'Good to see you.' He held out his hand which she took in a limp apology for a handshake.

'Hi, Dan.'

'Look, I have to get back to Manchester otherwise I would suggest we catch up over a coffee.'

'That's a shame, maybe next time,' Kray replied; her second lie of the day.

'Roz, please come in and take a seat,' Quade announced from inside the office.

'Good to see you.' Bagley slipped past and she could hear his heels clicking their way across the hardwood floor to the stairwell.

Kray stepped into the enormous office. Two drained coffee cups sat on coasters on the low table surrounded by comfortable chairs. Quade flopped her considerable bulk down behind her desk. She motioned for Kray to take the seat opposite.

'Come in, Roz and close the door.'

Chapter 11

I drag the tin sheeting to one side and squeeze myself through the gap, tugging it back in place. The cold wraps around me and the sound of my footsteps echo against the blank walls. I flick on my head torch and a white cone of light cuts through the darkness. The chill seeps through my clothes, pricking at my skin. It's an exhilarating feeling.

I scan the ground floor taking in the familiar surroundings, an obstacle course of broken pallets and makeshift work benches litter the floor along with rubble and breeze blocks. I move through the remnants of the bar to the reception area, a grand space with a vaulted ceiling. Or it would be if it weren't for the long reception desk being reduced to matchwood and bare plaster walls. I skirt around the debris to the back and climb the service stairs. The noise of my boots hitting the concrete steps fills the stairwell.

At the top I push open the only door left in the place and enter onto a landing. Shards of light dance off the metal lift doors as I pass through into the main corridor. Up ahead it is pitch black, the smell of plaster board and dust hangs in the air. I walk through a large archway into a huge room – the penthouse suite.

I found this place nine months ago when I was roaming the streets trying to rid myself of the sound of small arms fire and chopper blades raging in my head.

The Lakeland Hotel, an imposing four-storey building on the promenade, still boldly advertises 'Lifts To All Floors' on a plaque on the front. It is in a prime location with parking for twenty cars, but the developer either ran out of money or lost interest because it hasn't been touched for over a year. It is a perfect retreat; isolated, derelict and cold.

In the summer months I can watch the sun retreat behind the horizon through the broken metal shutters fitted to the panoramic windows - the Ferris wheel standing proud on the central pier silhouetted against the pink and orange glow. But the best part of all, when I was running down the street trying to find the helicopter for my extraction point, I noticed is was sand coloured. The same sun-baked orange as those houses in the village in Afghan. It drew me like a moth to a flame.

The penthouse suite is on two floors with a spiral staircase running down to what should have been the living space beneath. I sit with my back to the wall and watch the lights outside swing back and forth as the wind whips in off the Irish Sea. No wonder it is so cold, even in summertime.

I love this place, I feel safe here. There is no one for me to harm and no one to tell me everything will be all right when the dogs of war kick off in my head. I used to come here when life got tough with Julie.

Now I use it to reflect on life and to plan.

I joined the army when I was twenty-one years of age and by the time I was twenty-three my parents were dead, cancer took them both in the same year. I used to think they caught it off one another. But Mum died from having smoked since the age of ten and having lungs the consistency of barbecue coals. Dad developed bowel cancer, diagnosed just as Mum was breathing her last breaths.

'Trust me to get it up the arse,' he would say. My dad could never be accused of being liberal minded when it came to homosexuality.

When I came back from Afghan the second time, I was only back in body, not in mind. I was still eating hot sand in the northern valley of Helmand Province. For the first month I enjoyed the novelty of being home, pretending to Julie that I was okay and that things would work out. She even started talking about moving into a bigger place. You know the way women plan and us blokes simply nod, hoping it goes away. I suppose she thought looking to the future would take my mind off the present.

But I knew something was wrong. Julie knew something was wrong.

One morning, I remember shaving in the bathroom sink and noticing a crack running down the reflection of my face. Not as a result of the healing scar on my cheek, this was a jagged fracture which started on the right of my forehead and finished to the left of my mouth. I wiped my hand across the glass – it was smooth.

I stared at my misting-reflection as my hand slid back and forth across the surface of the mirror and I realised, the crack was inside me.

My very being had a fracture running through it. To the left of the line was the man I once was, leading the life I once had; to the right was the man I am now with no life at all.

I fake it, every day I fake it.

I now live on the dead side of the fracture and pretend to the outside world that I still exist on the other.

My side of the line is hollow, devoid of meaning, devoid of feeling, devoid of content. Yet in my previous life I had been a good boyfriend, heading towards being a terrific husband with the potential to be an amazing dad. All of that was gone. Lost in a fog of flashbacks, night sweats and panic attacks. Even now, when I look at my cracked reflection, I cannot understand how others cannot see it. When I look in the mirror it is obvious, plain as day. The only one to see it was Julie - and she suffered the most.

Sometimes, when I'm at work, I can't breathe. If one of my colleagues slams the filing cabinet too hard, I'm back there in an instant. Fighting for my life, fighting for survival, fighting for breath. And in that moment, sat in my air-conditioned office – I can't breathe. I have to hurry from behind my desk and head for the gent's toilet. I try to suck air in but my throat is closed, like it was when the truck turned over and sand ploughed into my mouth through the shattered window.

I lock myself in a cubicle with both hands on my knees. My chest burns, my head spins. I know if I stay like this for long enough my throat loosens up and oxygen penetrates deep into my lungs. Then with a massive gasp I will straighten up, trying to regain my composure.

As time went on the night terrors got worse. Vivid dreams of picking up dismembered limbs, watching Jono's face mouth the words 'save me', my own face dissolving into a soup of melting flesh.

Julie was amazing, taking it all in her stride. When I woke in a bath of my own sweat, she would change the sheets while I took a shower, and we were back in the land of nod in no time. What was not so easy for her to overcome was the bruises.

What started out as a kick here, or an elbow there, soon gave way to all out fist fights with faceless assailants, each one intent on cutting me up while I slept. Julie took the brunt.

At first she would try to calm me down, talking to me with soft tones, engulfing me in gentle hugs, but as time went on that became too dangerous. My flailing arms and legs striking out at my attackers, dealt her some heavy blows. Eventually, when I was gripped in my private war, she would leap out of bed and stand against the far wall. My arms and hands were a mess of cuts and abrasions as they slammed into the headboard and side tables, but at least she was out of harm's way.

Then, following a 3am admittance to A&E and a terrifying interview with a police inspector who took ages to be convinced this was not a case of domestic violence, Julie could take no more. I moved into the spare room and we removed all the furniture, save for the bed. When I look back I think that signalled the end. She forced me into counselling but I pissed around, unable to take it seriously, because taking it seriously meant admitting I had a problem. Separate rooms quickly led to separate lives.

The therapy was run by people who had no fucking idea what I was going through. They thought they did, which made it worse. Their scripted declarations and progression plans drove me crazy. The final straw came when Julie took a call from the lead counsellor asking why I had not showed up to the session that day. Which was unfortunate, because earlier I had spent twenty minutes telling her how enlightening the session had been.

She didn't shout, she didn't lose her temper, she just packed a bag and left.

'I will be at my mum's. Call if it's urgent, if it's not urgent don't call,' she had said, lifting her car keys off the hook in the hallway. 'I will be back in a few days for the rest of my stuff.' And with that she was gone and a piece of me was kind of relieved. I no longer had to feel guilty for dragging her through my living hell. Now I only had myself to damage.

One by one my friends went the same way. I didn't cover them in bruises but I hurt them enough that they didn't want to stick around. Eventually only two people remained, which was tragically reduced to one. I regret that every day, but it's easier that way.

I get to my feet, retrieve a folder that is tucked into the waistband of my khaki trousers and walk over to the opposite wall. I run the torchlight over the collage of pictures and documents pinned to the plasterwork. I pick up a marker pen and draw a big fat X across the face of Jimmy Cadwell, he looks much better that way.

I will deliver justice, Jono.

From the file I take three more and pin them in their place. The face of a young boy stares back at me – a young boy with an above average interest in sex for a child of his age. The boy that contributed to his own abuse. Next to it is a mug shot of a person who is described as being below average intelligence.

The details are straightforward: A twenty-three-year-old adult had sex with a twelve-year-old child. On four separate occasions. Bang to rights child abuse, you might think. A mandatory term of fifteen years with no chance of parole until after ten.

But this open and shut case had three fatal flaws running through it. Three factors which I spotted right from the start as I trawled through the case files early one morning. The presiding judge was Bernard Preston who has an admirable track record of being an incompetent liberal dick - more interested in courting favour amongst the great and the good rather than dispensing justice.

The Defence Lawyer was Christine Chance who is either incredibly lucky, incredibly good or is blackmailing every court judge on our circuit – or a mixture of all three. And thirdly the defendant was a woman.

Fuckwit Preston handed down a six-month jail sentence, suspended for two years. If it had been a man they would have thrown away the key.

I clench my fists and imagine what her face will look like when we meet. But she will have to wait, a pair of beady eyes are competing for my attention; his narrow face and sunken features compelling me to look.

I switch off my head torch, walk over to the front wall and look through the gaps in the shutters. I can see the vast wood and metal structure stretching out into the sea, with the massive circle perched on top. Even out of season, when the party lights are switched off, the dark silhouette cast against the horizon is the best view in the world.

I turn my head to where a spiral staircase is cut into the floor. Above the gap hangs a heavy rope secured to a ceiling joist with an eye bolt, it has a noose dangling at the end. The slip knot has thirteen turns of the rope. It hangs as a constant reminder that I can end things at any point.

But not today. I check my watch ... time to go fishing.

Chapter 12

*I*t was the day I was attacked by a killer and never felt a thing.

My consciousness bobbed just below the surface. I knew I was somewhere special because for the first time in months I couldn't taste sand in my mouth. I opened my eyes to see a solid white roof above and felt cool air wafting across my face. The fluorescent fittings set into the ceiling blurred in and out of focus. It felt like I was floating.

Where the hell am I?

I looked down at the blue and white sheets covering my body, the bedding was crisp and smelled of washing powder. Two IV lines hung from empty bags, each one suspended from a metal stand. It was difficult to tell if the needle stuck in the back of my hand had punctured a vein as my skin was a patchwork of bruises and abrasions. A wave of nausea washed over me. I ached like a bastard.

A woman with dark hair pulled back into a ponytail appeared next to me, wearing a blue plastic apron and combats. She had a nice smile and the tag on her sleeve read Cpl Jane Rogers.

'How do you feel?' Her Yorkshire accent made me feel at home.

'I'm not sure. I think everything hurts.'

'Do you know where you are?'

I shook my head.

'You're in Role 3 hospital, you came in with lacerations to your face, a bullet wound to your shoulder and minor burns to the backs of your legs. Oh, and concussion caused by being shot in the head. Your helmet saved you, we kept your stuff, you might want that as a souvenir.' She continued to check her clipboard.

Her words seemed to bounce off several satellites before they landed in my brain. Then, piece by piece, it all came flooding back.

'Shit!' I said and tried to get up.

'Wow there, you need to take your time.'

'How is? When did we? What about ...' The words spilled from my mouth.

'The MERT team brought you in four hours ago. You've been out since you arrived.'

My mind raced. 'What about the others?' I blurted out, a split second before my brain processed the memory that they were all gone.

No wait, what about Jono?

'Captain Ellis Johnston, I came in with him. How is he?'

'He's still in theatre.'

'But is he ... will he be okay?' I tried to lever myself up on my elbow.

'Until he comes out we won't know. Do you have any acute pain?'

I ran my hand over the padded gauze dressing covering the left-hand side of my face and the turban-like bandage wrapped around my head. 'No, I'm not in pain, I just feel like I've been run over by a truck.'

She busied herself, replacing the pouches. I sat up, taking in my surroundings. I could have been in a hospital anywhere in the UK but with better facilities. Rows of beds lined the walls, two of them were occupied. Staff wandered about administering to the patients and filling in medical details onto large white boards.

'Have you been here long?' I asked.

'Three months, I'm just coming to the end of my deployment.'

'This is my second tour.'

'I've lost count. I'm a senior trauma nurse in a Manchester Hospital, joined the Reserves nine years ago and here I am. I hate it when I go back.' She finished changing over the bags and adjusted the flow, the drips started to dispense their industrial strength medication. 'In a few hours, if you continue to improve, we will transfer you to the recuperation area.'

'Can you let me know when Captain Johnston gets out of theatre?'

'Sure. Now get some rest.'

I didn't need to be told twice and slid myself down in the bed. I drifted off into a dreamless sleep.

I woke with a jolt. My brain was on some kind of time delay and I went through the *where the fuck am I?* routine again. I sat up, the bags connected to my arm were empty. Corporal Rogers came over.

'Had a good sleep?'

My brain clicked back into my surroundings.

'Yeah I went out like a light.' I shook my head to clear the cobwebs and felt much better. 'Any news on Jono?'

'He's out of surgery and recovering in ICU.' She paused. 'He's still in poor shape.'

'But he's alive?'

'Yes he is.' She scribbled onto a clipboard as I looked around. The two original guys I had seen previously had been replaced by four new soldiers, each one hooked up to a variety of machines. She followed my gaze. 'They go out on patrol in the morning so we tend to get busy later in the day.'

Despite my wounds, I was the fittest bloke in the place.

'Do you feel well enough to be moved?' she asked.

'Yup,' I said pulling the sheets to the side. Rogers held onto me and I swung my feet over the side and onto the floor.

'How does that feel?' she asked removing the cannula from my arm and pushing the drips to one side.

'Pretty good. But my head still feels like its stuffed with cotton wool.'

'It's the pain killers. You will have to be careful when they start to wear off.'

I took a few tentative steps. 'I feel okay.'

A man came in, barking instructions that I didn't understand, it was full of numbers and abbreviations. The look on Rogers' face told me life was about to get a whole lot busier. She ushered me through a set of doors and down a corridor to another part of the building. I was in a smaller room containing four empty beds. I rolled into the one nearest the door.

'I gotta go,' Rogers said making sure I was comfortable. 'I will look in on you later. Your stuff is in the bag.' She hurried out and the door swung shut behind her.

I glanced over the side of the bed to see a plastic bag containing my combats, boots and helmet. I opened it up and fished out my helmet, a black dent on the right-hand side stood out against the camouflage cover and the interior padding was deformed.

'Saved my life,' I muttered under my breath. Out of the corner of my eye I caught a glimpse of the paprika-red scarf poking from beneath the folds of my jacket. I rummaged in the bag and pulled it free. It shimmered against the fluorescent light. I remembered picking it up in the first house and stuffing it into my tunic.

Why the hell did I pick this up?

I stuffed it into the helmet and tossed it on top of the bag. My eyes were heavy and I felt dog-tired all of a sudden. I pulled the sheets up to my chest and drifted away again in a drug-induced slumber.

The tiny killer freed herself from the confines of the scarf. The past six hours had been a traumatic ride but somehow she had survived. She flicked her wings and launched herself into the unusually cool air. The trials of the journey had made her hungry and she didn't have to travel far to find a feast.

Exposed flesh and warm blood.

Chapter 13

Kray banged the door shut with such force the panes of glass rattled in their frames. She kicked her shoes off against the wall and tossed her bag into the corner of the hallway, then threw her coat at the hooks on the wall, it landed in a crumpled heap on the floor.

She stepped over the coat and headed straight for the kitchen, yanking a half full bottle of wine out of the fridge and picking a glass off the draining board. The wine chugged into the glass while she was pacing around the lounge. The first glass didn't touch the sides. Kray filled it again.

'Fuck!' she yelled at the top of her voice. 'Fuck!' The second glass of wine went the way of the first and she stomped back to the fridge, pulling a full bottle from the rack. The top twisted off and a third of the bottle made it into the glass.

'I don't believe it.'

The chat with Quade had not gone well. To be precise, it had been a disaster. Kray had sat there speechless while ACC Quade had explained how well Kray had done in the assessment centre and how she had done herself and the force proud. But there was a sting in the tail, 'on this occasion you have been unsuccessful' Quade had chirped. After that Kray hadn't paid much attention to the rest.

She did, however, tune in when Quade had said, 'I think given the circumstances it is only fair to let you know we will be appointing DI Dan Bagley to the role. I'm sure you will treat this with the utmost confidentiality until we make a formal announcement. You and he will make a formidable team'.

Kray couldn't get out of there fast enough.

She continued to march in circles in the lounge, bottle in one hand, rapidly emptying glass in the other. 'Dan fucking Bagley!' she shouted, slopping wine onto the carpet. 'That snivelling little shit.' She poured wine down her throat like she was putting out a fire in her belly – which in essence she was.

She crumpled down onto the sofa and stared into space.

That bastard Quade sold me out, that job was mine. Dark thoughts crashed around in her head. She drifted back to the assessment centre – what could she have done differently?

There's no point going over what I did. The job was his as soon as he put his name on the application form.

Her anger began to subside as the wine took effect. The worst part was she was annoyed with herself. She had allowed her ambition to run away with her and for that she was kicking herself. It was a schoolgirl error, made by those who were less experienced – not her. And yet she had fallen into the trap of believing she would get the job on merit but life doesn't work that way, and she knew it.

Kray took a deep breath and was just about to get another top-up when there was a knock at the door.

Standing on her top step holding a bottle of Champagne was Chris Millican.

'Hi,' he said, his smile lighting up his face. 'I brought you this.' He held out the fizz for her to take.

'Hi, Chris, thanks for coming.' Kray gave him half a smile and walked back into the lounge, slumping down onto the sofa again.

'I presume it's okay for me to come inside,' Millican said appearing at the living room door.

'Oh yes, I'm sorry. Please come in and have a drink. You'll have to excuse me I'm not at my best this evening.'

'That's okay, you said on the phone that there had been a problem at work and you would like someone to talk to.'

'Shout at, more like.'

'Oh, that bad, eh?'

'Worse, and I couldn't face drowning my sorrows while watching cooking programs and quiz shows.'

'Well I'm delighted, even if it did take a disaster for you to call. Do you want more? I seem to recall the wine disappeared quickly the last time we met.' Millican found his way into the kitchen and opened the fridge.

'Yeah, that would be nice.' She followed him and propped herself against one of the units, nursing her glass. 'I'm sorry, I'm not being a very good host. It's been a crap day.'

'That's why I'm here.'

'Actually, I lied. When things like this happen I normally go to the graveyard and talk to my dead husband like a crazy person, and then come home to get pissed in the bath. I thought this time it might be better if I spoke to someone who was, you know … alive.'

'You going to tell me what happened?' He splashed wine into her glass and topped up his own.

'It's silly really,' Kray said and then took a giant swig. 'I went for a job and didn't get it and now I feel like shit.'

'Sorry to hear that. It has obviously hit you hard.'

'Yeah it has. It was the DCI role and I thought I had it in the bag.'

'It's tough when that happens. Do you know who got it?'

'Unfortunately, yes. I worked with him before on a case.'

'And you were less than impressed?'

'Let's just say the guy is …' Kray paused trying to find the right words.

'Is what?'

'A complete wanker.'

Millican cracked a smile at the blunt analysis, then his smile turned into a stifled giggle.

'I'm sorry,' he said. 'It's just that …' He could hold back no longer and burst out laughing. Kray looked down into her glass and began to laugh along with him. 'Remind me never to go for the same job as you.'

'Shut up. I was upset, I'm still upset.' She sniggered into her wine.

'Then why are you laughing?'

'Because of you.'

'Well that's good, isn't it?'

'Look I haven't finished being angry so it's no good you turning up here and making me laugh.' She now had a full-blown bout of the giggles. 'And besides, you've brought a bottle of fizz and you know I drink dry white wine.'

'I do. I'm celebrating but given the circumstances it now appears to be the most inappropriate celebration of all time.'

'Why?'

'You are looking at the new resident Home Office Pathologist for your patch.'

It took a while for the news to sink in. 'You got the job!'

'Yup, I was told today.'

'That's fabulous news, Chris, congratulations.' She chinked her glass against his.

'So when we've drunk this, if you would like some fizz?' he said.

'Fuck that.' Kray picked up the Champagne and started to remove the foil from the cork. 'Let's have it now.' She twisted off the metal cage and popped the cork free from the neck.

Millican looked at the pile of dirty glasses in the sink. 'Did the cleaning maid not call today?' He walked around the kitchen, opening and closing cupboard doors, then triumphantly pulled out two mugs. 'These will do.'

He held them while she poured the fizz into the cups and they chinked them together.

'Congratulations!' she said. 'Thank you for coming over so I could shout at you.'

'Thanks for allowing me to celebrate inappropriately.'

Millican leaned in for a kiss. Kray flinched. Her instinct was to pull away, but she stopped herself.

Their lips met.

It was the softest touch.

She tilted her head and pressed her mouth against his. Her mind was spinning, she had not kissed a man in so long.

His hand moved to her neck and pulled her into him. She felt his tongue slip into her mouth. He tasted of wine.

They floundered around putting their cups onto the worktop. Kray placed her hand on his chest. She could feel the contours of his muscles beneath his shirt.

He wound his arm around her waist, drawing her against him. His hand slipped beneath her shirt, his fingers running over the rippled scars across her back.

She jumped at his touch, and he removed his hand.

'I'm sorry, I didn't mean—' he said, his breath short.

'It's okay.' She kissed him hard, guiding his hand back under her top. His body pressed her against the worktop. Kray pushed him away.

'No,' she gasped.

'I just—'

She placed her finger on his lips.

'No, not here.' Kray picked up the bottle with one hand and took his hand with the other. 'Get those,' she said nodding to the cups on the worktop.

She led him through the lounge and up the stairs.

Chapter 14

This is my third fishing trip in as many weeks. The others came up blank but this time my hopes are high. I sit and wait in the armchair facing the TV. I've done all that I can, the rest is up to him.

It has been four months in the planning and getting to grips with the methodical way in which he goes about his business has been a challenge. The strict patterns and schedules have often made me wonder if he had a military background. But that's a stupid idea – when it is patently obvious this is all he has ever known. After weeks of tracking him I was able to gauge his next move. His predictability was his Achilles heel.

The whole place is in darkness apart from the light of the street lamps washing the room with a pale orange glow. I can feel a cold draft around my feet as the night air blows through the open window in the bedroom.

This is a nice flat, it has two bedrooms, a kitchen, a good-sized bathroom and comfortable lounge-diner. I asked the agent how long it had been on the market and he was suitably evasive. I suspect it has been vacant for a while due to it being located above an Indian restaurant. Even for a curry addict like myself I think I would have to think twice before leasing it; though, as I sit here and the minute hand on my watch sweeps past 3am, the residual smell is making me feel hungry.

This was the fifth property I viewed. The others all had issues of one sort or another – some had alarms fitted while others were too well lit or didn't have suitable access. This one was just right. I had spent ages casing the outside of the building working out the best method of entry. The bedroom window seemed ideal and my plan was to leave it cracked open, allowing me to gain entry whenever I wanted. However, when I visited the place to have a look around, and the agent dropped the keys onto the sideboard, it was a simple case of creating a diversion and slipping one off the ring. He had previously been banging on about how they have to cut so many copies of the keys to manage multiple viewings. So it seemed rude not to take one. If I had known that was going to happen I could have saved myself a ton of effort. The agent seemed genuinely disappointed when I told him I would not be taking the flat, my acting skills must be improving.

My senses are tuned to high alert and my head is playing havoc with the sounds of the neighbourhood asleep. Every noise has me ready to go, only to come to nothing. Then I hear a cat howl like a baby in the alleyway at the back, I strain my ears and can hear a shuffling coming from outside the back of the property. There is a 'clunk' from the bedroom as the window is pushed up, the wooden frame clattering in the runners.

Fuck me, game on.

I ease myself out of the chair and hide behind the door to the living room. The sound of feet landing on the floor wafts towards me on the cold air.

I hold my breath.

It all goes quiet.

The only thing I can hear is my blood thumping through my temples. I catch the sound of carpet fibres, brushing under a door as it opens. Then silence again.

A thin cone of light flashes into the lounge from the hallway beyond, it criss-crosses the floor and walls. The tall, lean silhouette of a man moves into the room scanning the contents with the tiny beam. It's him.

The beam lands on the Sky box sitting under the TV and he hurries towards it. He pops the end of the pen light into his mouth and sets to work disconnecting cables.

The figure is kneeling down, reaching around the back to the sockets on the wall. I see him tug at the wires to free the devise. He slides it towards himself and tucks it under his arm.

I swing the sock packed with sand, bringing it down hard. He catches sight of me in his peripheral vision and dodges to his right, it thuds into the top of his shoulder and he yelps in pain. I take a backhand swing, but he ducks away and it glances the top of his head. The force of the blow sends him spinning sideways and he lands on his side with his back to me. He turns and throws the Sky box, it smacks me full in the face.

You little shit!

My calm resolve evaporates and now I want to kill him with my bare hands.

He scrabbles to his feet and bolts for the door. I launch myself at him and grab his ankle, forcing him to topple over, landing heavily against the doorframe. He yelps again.

I claw myself over him and straddle his back, he is bucking and lurching trying to throw me off. I grasp his head with both hands and slam it into the doorframe. His hands claw at mine trying to prise them loose, I crack his head against the wood once more and he collapses beneath me.

I roll off to the side and suck air into my lungs. *Fuck I made hard work of that.*

I grab the back of his coat collar and drag him across the floor, down the hallway to the bathroom. I need to work fast, he is out cold but it won't last long. My bag is already tucked under the sink. I unzip it and remove a tea towel, ramming it past his teeth to fill his mouth. Then I take a roll of duct tape and wind it across his mouth and behind his head to keep the towel in place. I tip him over onto his front and bind his wrists tight with the tape as well as securing it above his elbows. I repeat the process with his knees and ankles. Before long he's trussed up like a chicken. I shove him across the floor and heave him over the rim of the bath. He slides in like a wet fish.

I take a few minutes to collect myself and he starts groaning. A few minutes more and he is screaming through the gag while writhing around fighting against his bonds. I stand up and look down at him lying face up in the bath, his eyes are bursting from their sockets the size of pool balls.

'Hello, Billy.'

Chapter 15

Kray pressed the flashing blue button and took the ticket as it protruded from the slot, the barrier went up allowing her to drive in. This was going to cost her an arm and a leg but it was worth it to get out of the bumper-to-bumper traffic and, besides, by this time the station car park would be full. She was late and couldn't care less.

Waking up with a man in your bed, after such a long time without one, had been a shock. Especially when Dr Ding-dong had made it very clear that he wasn't keen on having breakfast, but rather that he had his mind set on something else to start the day.

Kray had stood in her kitchen, waiting for the kettle to boil, and was amazed that with everything that had happened in the past twelve hours, the oddest feeling was making coffee for two. The other thing that felt odd was the fact that she didn't feel guilty. Not one bit.

She had surprised herself how comfortable she had been baring her scars to him. He was more interested in her to notice, while she was more interested in him to care.

She got out of her car at the fifth floor and made her way down in the lift. As she stepped out into the thin winter sunshine she wanted to bask in the afterglow of last night, but instead she could feel the fury of bitter resentment growing in her stomach. Every step she took the rage grew and grew.

DCI Dan Bagley?

By the time she had reached the main thoroughfare any thoughts of Dr Ding-dong were long gone, replaced instead by a toxic mix of self-loathing and raw anger towards Quade and Bagley. She puffed away on a cigarette oblivious to those around her, storming along the pavement like a one-woman protest march. She bumped shoulders with a man coming in the opposite direction.

'I'm sorry, I wasn't looking where I was going,' she said holding her hand up to cement the apology. He scowled at her and carried on. Kray was so engrossed in her black mood she almost missed it. She backtracked and read the poster in the window.

'Fuck 'em,' she said causing the woman walking her dog to glance over, probably expecting to see a rowdy teenager not a woman in her late-thirties dressed in a smart coat and suit. Kray pushed her shoulder to the door and went inside.

Ten minutes later she emerged with two sheets of paper which she stuffed into her bag. She looked at her watch, 9.20am. She was late and she couldn't care less.

Kray reached her office to find ACC Quade lurking in the corridor.

'Morning, Roz, I've been looking for you.'

'Sorry, ma'am, I had car trouble this morning. How can I help?'

At that moment Bagley came around the corner. 'Hey, Roz, how are you doing?' He offered his hand, which she took.

'I'm fine, Dan, I wasn't expecting you to—'

'We thought a prompt start was in order and Dan got himself released early from GMP, so we thought why not start now,' Quade interrupted.

I bet they couldn't wait to get shot of him. The bunting must stretch all the way down Deansgate.

'We want to make the announcement at nine thirty, will you be able to do the honours and show me around, introduce me to the team?' Bagley said with child-like enthusiasm.

'Yes I can, but can we do the tour about ten to allow me time to follow up on a few items from yesterday and make sure the guys are on track? And I have to pop out at two thirty to pick up my car from the garage,' Kray lied.

'I could give you a lift if you want,' Bagley said trying to make friends.

'It's okay, I already have a lift thank you.'

'Sure, me and Mary could grab a coffee and I'll see you back here at ten.' He was grinning like a maniac. Quade nodded and they both scuttled off.

Me and Mary can grab a coffee. Kray sang the words as a schoolyard chant over and over in her head. She busied herself completing paperwork and called Tavener. Her one productive thought on her way into work was to check if they had CCTV installed on the show houses on the Woodland View estate. If they did, maybe they could corroborate Jack Stapleton's alibi that he was at home all night. Tavener was still chasing up Liz Stapleton's sister.

'Oh shit,' Tavener said mid-sentence.

'What's wrong.'

'I've just seen the announcement from ACC Quade.'

'Yeah, it didn't go my way.'

'Roz, I'm so sorry.'

'Forget about it we got work to do.' She hung up not wanting to prolong the conversation.

'Forget about what?' Bagley appeared in the doorway.

Shit, was it that time already?

'Oh nothing. Now how about if we start by me giving you the low-down on our live cases?'

'Sounds good to me.'

The next four hours flew by. Kray had impressed herself with her comprehensive grasp of the department's workload and issues. Shame ACC Quade hadn't been there to hear it. She had introduced Bagley to those members of the team who were working in the office and took him around some of the other departments. For many of those they met it was like an old school reunion. Congratulatory back slapping, excited exchanges and the re-telling of old anecdotes. All of which served to piss Kray off.

'I have to go pick up my car and then I have to chase down some leads in the Cadwell case,' Kray said, looking at her watch.

'Yeah, I think you are really onto something with the husband and wife of the little girl he killed. You need to keep me in the loop.'

'As I said, I'm not so sure it has anything to do with the Singletons. They don't strike me as—'

'No, you need to pursue it, they have every reason to do Cadwell harm,' Bagley interrupted.

Kray went to stand her ground but found herself smiling at him instead. She picked up her coat from the stand and collected her bag.

'I really appreciate this, Roz and I'm sure you and I will make a great team. No hard feelings eh?' he said.

'None on my part. See you tomorrow.'

Kray walked out of CID and down the stairs, two words screaming in her head.

Fuck 'em.

Chapter 16

It was the day my face exploded.

Jono was flown to Queen Elizabeth Hospital in Birmingham, thirty-six hours after being admitted to Camp Bastion. I never did get to speak with him. Corporal Rogers told me that they had to amputate his other leg above the knee because it was full of ball bearings from the blast.

I stayed at Camp Bastion until my wounds had healed sufficiently for me to be posted back to my unit. Five guys that I had never met before welcomed me into their ranks like an old friend. They took the piss out of my face with its criss-cross of scars and said I made Freddy Krueger look like someone from the Nivea advert. It felt good to be back amongst the Brotherhood.

The months passed and I relaxed back into my role with my new team, trying to blank out the terror that had gone before. The faces of Pat, Bootleg, Donk and Ryan haunted my dreams. Their disembodied heads came and went, emerging from a haze of memories only to sink back into the blackness. They never said a word, they would float around and stare at me, cracking the occasional smile and then be gone.

Then life began to change. It started out as an irritant, a tiny blemish on my right cheek that constantly itched. It felt like a gnat bite that you might get while sitting in the garden on a warm summer's evening. But is wasn't.

I tried every off-the-shelf remedy the supermarket at Camp Bastion had to offer but it seemed the more creams and potions I applied the worse it got. One morning I got up and it had developed into an angry red swelling beneath my skin. It was our rest day, so I made my way over the Med tent.

'How long have you had this?' said the male medic, pushing and prodding it with his gloved fingers.

'A few months. I reckon I got bitten and it will won't heal. It itches like a bastard and I can feel it throbbing when I lie down.'

'It's infected. I will give you a course of antibiotics and an antihistamine cream. If it doesn't clear up in a week come back.'

It didn't take a week. Oh boy, the little fucker loved that antihistamine cream. I applied it in line with the instructions and popped my tabs like a good boy. The swelling got bigger and bigger, and angrier and angrier. The endless itching drove me to distraction and it reached the stage where I struggled to focus when we were out on parole.

'Maybe it gets worse with the dust.' One of my new team mates had chirped up following an explosive bout of swearing on my part. That seemed like a cracking diagnosis at the time – you have to love getting medical advice from non-medical people. So, one day I took the added precaution of covering it with a medical gauze while we were out searching for munitions. The bloody thing went into overdrive. By the time I got back the swelling was so bad I looked like one half of a fucking chip monk. It was hot to the touch and throbbed in time with my heartbeat.

I went back to the Med tent and saw a different medic. We went through the same courteous discussion and I left with a stronger course of antibiotics and a stack of dressings to stick on the side of my face.

Three days later I woke in the middle of the night to find my pillow covered in blood. I rushed to the bathroom and to my horror my cheek had split open like a water melon and was oozing both blood and puss. I rushed to the medics who admitted me into a room and set to work.

The next day my cheek ruptured into a volcanic glob of exposed flesh. I freaked out. I saw a specialist who examined me for about fifteen minutes then declared, 'You have leishmaniasis, a disease carried by sand flies that is sometimes called Baghdad Boil.'

'Bagdad what?' I answered not really taking in what he had said.

'It's commonly called Bagdad Boil.'

'What the hell is that?'

'You've been bitten by a female sand fly that has injected a parasite under your skin. The parasite evades the body's natural defence mechanism by hiding away in white blood cells. There they multiply and eventually the cell wall ruptures, allowing more of the parasites to hide in more white blood cells, and so the cycle repeats itself. It is a progressive infection that results in the skin bursting, as it has done in your case.'

'Christ! So can you give me some shit to clear it up?'

'I'm afraid it's not that easy.'

'How come?'

'I will need to run tests to determine which strain of leishmania you have and depending on that we will prescribe a course of treatment. How long do you have left on this tour?'

'About two months.'

'The treatment can be traumatic, so I think it's fair to say your tour is over.'

And that was that. I had the first course of my treatment at Camp Bastion and was flown home to finish it off. That doctor wasn't kidding – they gave me a cocktail of drugs that screwed up my liver, aggravated my pancreas and gave me so much joint pain I was literally immobile at times. Six months later I was medically discharged. Sent back into civvy street with a rancid hole in my face and a head full of nightmares.

My cheek healed slowly. Julie was a rock, looking after my every need and caring for me while I got better. But as my physical health improved, my mental state declined. I gradually spiralled into a pit of depression. The nightmares returned with a vengeance, while panic attacks regularly punctuated my day. I began to drink heavily and the night terrors turned into day terrors.

I was living on the edge. I felt dead inside, a hollowed-out husk of the man I used to be. Julie left and I was on my own.

Then one day I did something that made me feel alive again.

Chapter 17

'Fuck 'em,' Kray said a little too loudly.

'Come on, Roz you don't mean that,' replied Tavener.

'Don't I?' He watched as she upended the wine bottle and drained the last of it into her glass. 'I solved two of the highest profile murder cases the force has had to deal with in years, got bloody injured on both occasions and made a damned good job at the Acting DCI role. And they go and give the job to that Mancunian prick Bagley.'

Tavener wasn't listening, he didn't have to, he'd heard the same speech five times already.

She glugged at her drink and stared into space. Tavener motioned to the barman who began preparing another bottle. The place was starting to fill up with early evening revellers which was not good considering Kray's lack of volume control. He glanced at his watch, it was just gone 7pm.

'Roz, you need to take a step back, that's all I'm saying. Don't do anything rash.'

'Like what?'

'Like apply for a job as an office manager in a solicitors?'

Kray flashed him a look. 'How the hell—'

'It boosts my confidence no end when you forget I'm a detective.'

'Have you been following me?'

'Didn't have to. You left the job advert and the print off of the email confirming your interview on your desk. You had other things on your mind today so I put it into your top drawer to avoid prying eyes.'

Kray paused. 'I wondered how the damned thing had got there.'

'How the hell did you end up applying for that?'

'I saw it advertised in the window of a recruitment agency when I was walking to work this morning. I went in and applied. They invited me to come in for a chat this afternoon.'

'You walked to work?'

'Don't ask.'

'Christ, Roz you only found out about not getting the DCI role this morning.'

'No I found out about it yesterday. And let's just say I was feeling impulsive.'

'Impulsive? More like reckless.'

'It made me feel better.'

Tavener paused then said, 'how did it go?'

'Oh, erm, it went fine.' Which, given the conversation she had with the fourteen-year-old girl from HR – Amanda - was not her biggest lie of the day.

Kray zoned out and replayed the interview in her head.

'Where do you see yourself in three years time?' Amanda had asked.

Fucking dead the way my luck is going. Kray thought.

'Well, Amanda, I have a five-year plan,' she had replied in her best office manager voice. 'I need a change in career direction ... blah ... blah ... blah.' The lies tripped off her tongue like a cabinet minister voicing support for a colleague.

'Tell me, how do you manage conflict?' Amanda had been pulling out all the stops.

I flash my warrant card and try not to punch them in the face.

'I find it essential to understand the other person's point of view. Only then can you ... blah ... blah ... blah.' Kray was on fire, spouting fluent management bollocks, Amanda was lapping it up.

'What particular qualities will you bring to Willis and Broughton to compensate for your lack of experience?'

Bloody hell, Amanda, that was below the belt. Well let me see, I have galloping OCD, an eating disorder and can drink enough wine to kill a medium sized horse.

'I see my lack of experience as an advantage. In my current role … blah … blah … blah.' This was proving way too easy.

'And finally, Roz, do you have any hobbies?' Amanda had finished strongly.

I get shit-faced in the bath, if that counts.

After forty-five minutes, Kray had walked out of there feeling like she had nailed it.

She snapped her head back to reality and sipped at her wine, giving herself a well-deserved pat on the back. After all, she hadn't put her foot in it once by being either genuine or truthful. She had to think positive, it had been a confidence boost if nothing else and it stuck two fingers up to Bagley and Mrs Blobby.

'Is that why you suggested we meet up for a drink?' she asked.

'Yeah, I thought I might be able to talk some sense into you.'

'Do I have to remind you how far I outrank you?'

'No, Roz, that's plain for everyone to see. You do know this is not the answer, right?'

Kray didn't reply and once more lapsed into a one-thousand-yard stare. Eventually she said, 'it was a weird experience.'

'What was?'

'Being interviewed by someone who's life experiences consisted of cramming for exams, getting trolleyed in Ibiza and occasionally visiting the STI clinic.'

'I'm curious, what reason did you give for wanting to leave the force?'

'To get a better work life balance.'

Tavener spat the last of his wine onto the table. 'You only have work. There's nothing to balance it with.'

'Yeah, alright. But she doesn't know that.'

'That job isn't for you, Roz. And it's not like you to throw in the towel,' he said mopping up the drops with a beer mat.

'Yeah, well I can't stay where I am, I know that.'

'Bagley might not last.'

'Oh come on, Duncan.' Kray downed her wine as the new bottle arrived. 'He's so far up Mrs Blobby's arse he's had to move in his office furniture.'

They both laughed out loud.

'It sounds like you're dead set on doing this,' Tavener said cracking the top off the latest bottle.

'Yes I am. My heart isn't in it any more, it's time to give someone else a chance.'

'That's what I thought you'd say, so … I got something for you. I figured you hadn't seen it as you've been busy.' He slid a piece of paper towards her and poured them both a drink.

'What is it?' She read the article. It was a job advert to head up the Criminal Justice Unit for Lancashire Police, a central department where they managed the criminal intelligence databases and file preparation teams.

'There's no drop in rank, so I presume your pay and rations would stay the same, it's on your doorstep, and there's no need to leave the force. The closing date for applications is the day after tomorrow.'

Kray re-read the ad, churning the options over in her mind.

'You trying to get rid of me?' she asked.

'You're going to go anyway. At least this way I might get to see you from time to time in the canteen. I'm not sure how it stacks up against a job in the solicitors?'

'It's a tough call. The office job paid less than a third of what I'm on now, had less holiday entitlement, no health care provision and a minimal pension. So, I'm not sure …'

Tavener held up his glass. 'Here's to getting rid of you.'

She raised her glass and chinked it against his.

'Thank you.' She leaned over and planted a kiss on his cheek and immediately regretted it.

Chapter 18

Kray was perched on the edge of Tavener's desk sipping at the coffee that she hoped would blow away the cobwebs from the previous night. She had consumed far more wine than was wise to on a school night and had gone home in a taxi to conduct a one-woman assault on the bottles in her fridge.

She had been on tenterhooks while getting ready for work, conscious that if she was to blow into a bag, she'd be catching buses for the foreseeable future - completely forgetting her car was still at the station. She left her house with the job advert for the role in CJU tucked away safely in her bag, ensuring there was no chance of leaving it on the desk this time.

When she arrived at work the station was in full swing.

'How are you feeling?' Tavener asked.

'Oh, you know.' She tilted her hand from side to side.

'You must have drowned your problems last night?'

'I gave it a good go but I'm afraid to say they are still there.'

'You did that all right.' Tavener leaned in close. 'I think we had a lovely evening and if I'm not mistaken you thanked me with peck on the cheek.'

'That's quite enough of that, Detective Constable Tavener, I put it down to being tired and emotional at the time. Now did you get anywhere with the CCTV at the show homes?' Kray asked trying to ignore the banging in her head and the fact that her underling was gently taking the piss out of her.

'Not just the ones at the entrance. The developer had cameras everywhere to cover the site while the build was going on, they are still there. The footage is with the imaging team but from what I saw on the night Cadwell was killed, Jack Stapleton never left his house.'

'What about the alibi for the wife?'

'We got hold of the sister and she confirmed they were at home watching TV at the time. I reckon we can strike them off the list. Unless ...'

'Unless what?'

'Unless they paid someone to kill Cadwell?'

'They could have but they don't look the types to do that.'

'I agree. I'm compiling a list of Cadwell's business associates who we will want to speak to.'

'By business associates do you mean Blackpool's best and brightest in the criminal underworld.'

'Yeah, something like that.' Tavener sniggered.

Bagley stuck his head around the door.

'Roz can I have a word?'

Kray pushed herself away from the desk and found Bagley in her office. He was sat in her chair, rearranging the pens and pencils on the desk. Her OCD spiked into the red zone.

'Come in and shut the door.'

'What is it?'

And will you stop fucking about with my things?

'I don't want you to back-pedal on the Stapletons. If I was in their position I would want Cadwell dead, they have a copper-bottomed motive.'

Kray jolted herself to focus on what he was saying.

'They do, but as I told you yesterday—' Her hackles were on the rise.

'Yes you did, but I'm not so sure. It would be great to kick off with a big win.'

'Kick off with a big win? What does that mean?'

'Well you know, with me being new in the post, it would be good for all of us if we could put this one to bed, pronto.'

'Put it to bed pronto? We will conduct this investigation in line with our processes and procedures. I do know how to do this, you know?'

'I know you do, Roz, but I want to be sure we keep focused. I don't want us to squander what is right in front of us just because we have fallen at the first hurdle. I don't want us to drop the ball on this one.'

Kray balled her fists at her sides and wondered if this was the right time. She decided it was.

'Dan we may as well get our new working relationship off on the right foot. Number one: I have no intention of dropping the ball. Number two: I always work for the good of the department as a whole, not for any one individual, and number three: either I am going to run this case, or you are going to run the case, but we sure as hell aren't *both* going to run it.'

Bagley clucked his tongue against the roof of his mouth, shaking his head.

'You're right, Roz.' He scattered the pens and rose from the chair. 'We should get our relationship off on the right footing. I was hoping you would be open to working together but it doesn't sound like you are. Now I'm a straight up and down kind of guy, what you see is what you get, so I want to make myself clear. If you can't move on then it's probably best if you move out. Think about it, Roz.'

Bagley crossed the office, punched down the handle of the door and marched out.

Kray was about to call after him, she hadn't finished with her 'getting their relationship off on the right foot' speech, when her phone rang. Anything more she wanted to say to Bagley would have to wait and besides there was a desk in desperate need of tidying.

I slept like a baby last night. I am used to functioning on little sleep when the helicopters, small arms fire and explosions keep me awake, but when I sank into my pillow and closed my eyes

I enjoyed the sleep of the dead. I'm feeling remarkably calm and level-headed this morning, very different to when I took care of Cadwell. Then I was wired, like I had drunk ten espressos laced with speed.

I have the day off today, which is why last night fitted so well. It is time I am owed from working late and coming in on a couple of Saturday mornings to reduce the backlog in files. No one else fancied it, so I put my hand up. Having the time off is worth more to me than the overtime payment.

I'm sat in a Greggs bakery, looking out of the window nursing a coffee, the clock on the wall tells me it's ten to eleven. Today is Wednesday, the only day of the week she gets out of bed before noon. I look up the street to see her ambling in my direction, cigarette in one hand and an energy drink in the other. She passes in front of the shop and crosses the road, flicking the butt end towards the gutter as she goes. She is early for once.

She disappears inside and I watch her take a seat at the window. After a while she is called forward and I lose her from view. I wonder how long it will take this time. Her record is five minutes. The hand sweeps the dial of my watch and at the nine-minute mark she re-emerges still clutching the can. They must dread it when she shows up, no wonder the meetings are short. She is an old hand at this and I can imagine how the conversation goes with her Work Coach.

'Have you been actively looking for work for your agreed number of hours?'

'Yes.'

'Do you have evidence of that?'

'Yes.'

'Have you attended any interviews?'

'No.'

'Are you still registered with the same recruitment agencies?'

'Yes.'

'Is your CV up to date?'

'Yes.'

Blah, blah, blah, and so it must go on, they reel through their stock questions and receive one-word answers in return. So, with all the boxes ticked on her Claimant Commitment agreement she leaves happy in the knowledge that her allowances will drop into her bank account and that's it for another two weeks. A job well done.

I watch her hang a left down Brigg Street, I don't need to follow her because I know exactly where she is heading. I finish my drink and saunter after her, making my way to the Cat and Mouse pub.

I reach there in fifteen minutes, just in time to see her first pint disappear down her throat. This place has the dubious honour of being known as the worst pub in Blackpool, though by what yardstick they measure that is beyond me. I take a seat in the corner at the far end of the bar. Then I remember, the last time I was here a woman emptied her bladder while perched on a bar stool near to where I'm sitting. I swear I can still smell piss and disinfectant. The woman apologised, which apparently made it okay.

My target belches loudly.

'Oh, excuse me,' she calls out. 'Another one in there, Chief.'

The pub is empty apart from a few stragglers, her posse has yet to arrive. I watch her flip a tenner from a bulging wad of notes. She tosses it onto the bar.

This is going to be a long day.

Chapter 19

It was the day I tried a different pub and finally felt alive.

I tended to drink in the downbeat pubs around town, you know the sort, where they pull a decent pint but can't find a decent cleaner. They were the pubs that suited me. Just me, my beer, a bar to lean on and zero conversation – no matter how many people were standing next to me.

By this time, I had worked out that the beer helped right up until the point that it didn't. Then it had the effect of magnifying every horror I was trying to forget. The trouble was I had no idea where to draw the line, and when in full flow I could be three pints the wrong side of the line before I realised. My life was unravelling fast.

A new bar had opened near to the tower, it was a chrome and mirrored gin palace with a decorative vaulted ceiling. The owners must have spent a ton of money doing it up in time for a Christmas opening and the place was doing a roaring trade. And for some inexplicable reason, which I still can't fathom, I thought it would be good to give it a try.

I was propping up the end of the long oak bar drinking my past away, oblivious to the raucous celebrations kicking off around me. It was half five in the afternoon, I was already six pints down and the atmosphere was thick with Christmas cheer. The office party brigades were making their presence felt, staging a full-scale assault on the two hundred and twenty different varieties of gin on offer.

The whole pub felt like Christmas, not that I felt anything much in those days, just a dull nothingness, like I'd been hollowed out in the middle.

I cocked my head towards the door as a group of people tumbled past the doorman. I spotted Julie. She was corralled in amongst the knot of revellers wearing a pink party hat and a necklace of tinsel. Leading the charge was Kail, a bull of a man who headed up their department. Julie disliked him with a passion and had always described him as a walking gob on a stick. He shoved his way to the bar and she appeared at his side. It seemed Julie had changed her mind.

He barked out a long drinks order in a deep baritone voice that suited his Pavarotti physique. A hassled barmaid ignored him and continued serving the guy next in line. Julie began to dance on the spot waving her arms above her head and throwing her head from side to side. Her hat fell off revealing her long blonde locks as they tumbled around her shoulders. A few of the others joined in, Kail wobbled and bobbed his broad shoulders to the thumping beat beside her. Julie always had the ability to start a disco in the vegetables aisle in Tesco.

Kail turned his attentions back to the poor barmaid, who was trying to look at anyone but him.

'Over here, sweet cheeks, over here,' he yelled out.

She finally gave in and Kail bawled his order at her. Pints of beer, glasses of wine and gin cocktails were shuttled back to the waiting party-goers. He handed Julie a fish bowl full of gin and something-or-other. I can remember thinking, *she doesn't even like the stuff.*

I watched from the other side of the room, keeping myself obscured by the punters at the bar. The place pulsated to festive songs, everyone singing along.

How am I going to get out of here without being seen?

The thought rattled around in my head as I stared into the full pint in front of me. The bubbles rose through the glass saying, 'Drink me.'

But I need to go now before she spots me. An awkward meeting with Julie was not what I wanted right now.

Hmmm … maybe I could keep myself hidden in the crowd for another few minutes. Just enough time to make this pint disappear. A big mistake.

Try as I might, I couldn't help but glance across at Julie and her workmates. She was hands down the most beautiful woman in the room but she looked different to how I remembered. Her hair was the same and I had seen that dress before, but somehow she looked different. Then it hit me – she looked happy.

She wasn't trying to cover up the latest bruise by constantly applying make-up or walking on eggshells frightened of saying the wrong thing. She was being herself – happy and getting drunk on a Christmas night out. She was being Julie, the woman I had fallen for before I went away.

I felt a physical pain strike up in my stomach, quickly rising towards my chest. My heart raced. I spun a beer mat on the bar to distract myself. The mat spun faster and faster. The music sank into the background, drowned out by the sound of water rushing through my head. The mat flipped onto the floor. I stared at it by my feet.

There was a commotion at the far end, Kail was yelling at the barmaid. At first, I thought he was ordering another round then I saw him thrust his pint into her hand.

'And I'm telling you it's off!' he bellowed.

The young woman busied herself pouring another and handed it to him.

'So is this!' he roared. The woman didn't know what to do.

'Fuck me, a pub that can't pour a pint,' he crowed at the top of his voice.

The manager appeared and tried to calm the situation. Kail was animated, stabbing his fat finger across the bar at the woman. The manager held his hands in a sign of surrender. It all calmed down. Next, I saw the manager hand over a tray loaded with shot glasses to Kail, while mouthing the words 'Sorry, sir.'

Kail forced himself away from the bar with a full pint in one hand and the tray in the other. He weaved his way to where Julie and the others were jigging around to the cacophony of noise blasting from the speakers.

'Oh yes!' Kail announced. 'What did I tell you? Who's the daddy!'

I chugged down half my pint trying to drown the pain in my chest. *The bastard had set that stunt up to get free drinks. What a wanker.*

'I told you. Now who's the daddy, who's the daddy?' Kail was rotating on the spot doling out the shots.

'You're the daddy, you're the daddy,' they chanted back, pointing at him.

He was accepting the adulation while strutting around doing some kind of gangster-rap walk. Julie was pointing and singing along with the others, downing the liquor.

She doesn't like shots either.

The knuckles on my left hand turned white as I gripped the rail running around the bar. I wanted to finish my drink but my other hand couldn't lift the glass. I was frozen. The pop-pop-pop of small arms fire went off in my head. My heart felt like it would rip itself from my chest at any moment.

The heat from the exploding IED roasted the back of my legs. I could taste sand in my mouth. I tore the glass from the bar and the rim clunked against my front teeth as I poured the remaining beer down my throat. I banged the pint pot back down making the woman next to me jump.

Bang-bang-bang, the exploding rounds were getting closer. I could hear them whistling through the air. Jono was screaming, but I couldn't find him. I scanned the faces of the people around me but none of them were Jono. Then there was a dull thud and the Snatch went airborne, the whole pub spun on its axis.

I couldn't breathe.

The side window shattered, spraying me with glass. Sand clogged my mouth, choking the back of my throat. I had to get out.

I looked around for my weapon. It wasn't there. *Where the fuck is it?*

I had to get out.

Crouching down I bumped my way through the crowd and shot one last look across at Julie. I saw Kail break away from the group.

'You're the daddy, you're the daddy.' They continued to chant.

He strutted away in triumph with his hands above his head. I tracked around the periphery of the room, watching him disappear through the door marked toilets.

I couldn't help myself.

Twenty seconds later I burst through the same door and followed him down the tiled corridor, past the Ladies, into the Gents. He was standing at the urinal with his hands on his hips, a couple of blokes were also in there finishing off. I made a beeline for one of the stalls and locked the door behind me.

Gunfire was all around. The wall behind me was peppered with bullets, showering me with shards of plaster. I peeped under the door to see two pairs of legs leave and the door banged shut behind them.

I unlocked the door and launched myself at Kail who had his head tilted back, still pissing like a race horse.

I slammed the heel of my hand into the back of his head and a loud crack echoed around the room as his forehead smashed into the wall. I grabbed a handful of hair and drove his face into the tiles. A plume of blood erupted across the white surface as his nose splatted flat against his cheek. I sunk my fist into his lower back, he gargled a cry of pain and slumped forwards.

I kicked his legs from under him and he went down hard, still pissing digested lager into the air. I slammed my boot into his neck and then his face. The flow of piss stopped. He went still.

'Incoming! Incoming!' cried Jono.

Where the fuck is he, I can hear him but I can't see him?

I ducked down and scurried to the door, crabbing my way back up the corridor. Mortar fire thundered all around me. I couldn't breathe. I burst into the main room, hurried through the knots of people and fell out onto the pavement.

One of the bouncers came over. 'You all right, mate?'

I held up my hand, bent over at the waist trying to suck air into my burning lungs. 'Asthma,' I croaked.

'Do you need an ambulance?'

Cold air hit the bottom of my lungs and I straightened up.

'No. No I'm fine thanks.'

I shoved my hands in my pockets and marched away. The freezing wind slapped me in the face and it felt good. For the first time in ages the dead space inside me had gone. It had been replaced by a feeling that I had not known in months.

The feeling of excitement.

The feeling of being alive.

Chapter 20

Kray made her way up the steps dressed in a white coverall, sporting overshoes and gloves. The hallway was a patchwork quilt of silver checker plates stretching down the hallway and into the lounge. She was met at the top by a tall man with spectacles dressed in much the same way.

'Morning,' he said with clipped tones. 'Jerry Atkins, crime scene supervisor.'

'Morning, Jerry, I'm DI Roz Kray. Who called it in?'

'The letting agent turned up with a young couple to view the property. They got more of a view than they bargained for.'

'That bad?'

'Well, let's say I don't think he'll be letting it to them.'

'The call said there was a body in the bath. Is it suicide?'

'Best you see for yourself. I've asked the forensics team to hold off until you arrived. Thought it would be good for you to take a look before we moved the body.' Two paper boiler suited figures were chatting in the hallway, ready with their boxes of tricks and high-resolution cameras.

They stepped to one side allowing Kray to pass.

'Phew, is that what I think it is?' she said wrinkling her nose. 'Smells like chicken tikka masala and bleach.'

'In here, Roz.' Atkins motioned with his arm at the room leading off to the left.

Kray edged open the door. Against the far wall was the bathtub with a shower cubical and toilet fitted to the adjacent wall. A large mirror hung above the sink.

The bath was brim full with crimson water. Puddles of it lay on the floor, visible between the silver plates. Kray moved closer.

The body of a man was lying face down, half submerged, with his arms secured behind his back and his lower legs standing proud of the water against the taps. Bleach fumes rasped at the back of Kray's throat.

She flicked on her torch and directed the beam at the surface of the water. The light penetrated the liquid to show the pale outline of two objects floating inches below the surface. She leaned over and peered at the illuminated shape.

It was the victim's severed hands.

'Shit.'

'Yes, that's what we thought,' said Atkins. 'We'll know more when we remove the body.'

'I guess that rules out suicide. What else have you got?'

'The killer didn't do his homework when selecting what bleach to use.'

'Oh, how come?'

'There are two types of bleach, one containing chlorine and the other containing oxygen. Oxygen bleach destroys bloodstains and DNA making them undetectable, chlorine-based products remove the stain to the human eye but the presence of haemoglobin can still be detected with an application of Luminol. Then it shows up under black light.'

'And what did our guy use?'

'He used a chlorine-based product. So, if he wanted to destroy any DNA evidence, he chose the wrong one. A simple Internet search would have told him that. Also, we found bleach-stained footprints in the carpet in the hallway, and it didn't come from the victim's shoes. We should be able to get a decent shoe print. He goes to all this trouble to cover his tracks then gets careless.'

'Thanks for that. I'll get out of your way.' Kray retreated back out into the hall and the two men in boiler suits swooped in. She checked the front door. The lock was intact with no sign of forced entry. Kray made her way to the lounge when she heard a familiar booming voice.

'How is Acting DCI Kray this morning?' It was Mitch Holbrook, Kray's favourite Coroner's Office doctor, coming up the stairs. He was approaching fifty with a bald head and straining waistline. He was old school and well respected. Very business like and abrupt to the point of being rude, just the way Kray liked it. He always wore the facial expression of somebody who had just stepped in dog shit, this morning was no exception.

'Hey, Mitch, how's tricks?'

'Pretty good, I hear this one is a bit different,' he said adjusting his overshoes.

'Yup you could say that.'

'When are they going to appoint a new DCI?'

'They already have.'

'Wow! Congrat—'

'It's not me, Mitch, they gave it to a guy from GMP.'

'Oh, I'm sorry.' Mitch paused realising he'd brought up a topic Kray would rather avoid.

The silence between them was broken by the swoosh of water as the body was exhumed from its watery grave.

'I think that's my cue to start work,' he said easing his way past her in the hall.

Kray wandered into the bedroom, opening and closing drawers and wardrobes. They were empty. It was the same with the smaller bedroom. She entered the lounge, the place was scrupulously clean with not a thing out of place. Apart from the Sky box laying in the middle of the rug. The morning sunshine streaked through the windows, ensuring the room was light and airy.

A small discolouration of the carpet at the base of the doorframe caught her eye. She crouched down and examined it. Despite the overall stink there was a strong scent of bleach coming from the floor. Kray went into the bathroom to find Mitch hunched over the body which was laying on a heavy plastic sheet on the floor.

'Do you have a black light?' she asked.

One of the men dressed in white handed Kray a torch from his bag. She went back to the lounge and shone the beam onto the base of the doorframe. Splashes of liquid fluoresced on the wooden frame and the carpet.

Why did you bleach the bottom of the doorframe? She thought. *What else did you bleach?*

She closed the curtains and continued to scan the room with the lamp. It yielded nothing until she directed the beam onto the armchair. The cushions glowed under the lamp, the other items of furniture were clear.

Did you sit here?

She ran the light across the fabric picking out the florescent particles on the arms of the chair.

Why did you sit here? Were you waiting?

'Roz!' It was Mitch calling from the bathroom. 'You might want to see this.'

She broke her train of thought and went to join him.

Mitch was kneeling by the side of the body. 'The vic sustained several blows to the side of the head but it is unlikely that's what killed him. More likely he bled to death.' He held up an evidence bag containing one of the severed hands. 'We will know more when they do the post-mortem.'

Kray stared down at the translucent face. 'My word, it's Billy Hicks.'

'You know him?'

'Most of the bloody force knows him. A one-man crime wave is our Billy. Did the killer cut off his hands when he was alive?'

'I think so,' said Atkins. 'The cut marks are ragged suggesting the victim was struggling when his hands were severed.'

'Do you have a time of death, Mitch?' Kray continued.

'Not with the body being immersed in cold water for so long. I need to do more tests.'

Kray turned to Atkins. 'I found bleach on the base of the doorframe leading into the lounge, there might be blood spatter. I will leave that to you guys.' She handed back the black light back to the SOCO. 'Also check out the armchair, it has some sort of residue on it. It doesn't appear on the other pieces of furniture, just the chair. It would be good to know what it is.'

Back in her car Kray stared into the distance, her mind churning over what she had seen in the flat. She could see the killer sitting in the armchair waiting for Hicks to arrive, she could see them fighting in the lounge and the killer emptying bottles of bleach into the bath.

You wanted to cover your tracks, then you leave dirty great footprints in the carpet.

Kray's head was buzzing.

That's not careless, it's like you only did half a job.

Chapter 21

I am now faced with a dilemma. It is fast becoming obvious how this is going to pan out. My target is swinging on the handrail running along the bar in the Cat and Mouse, screeching like a banshee. She's just been joined by three blokes who are pissing themselves laughing. One of them is scrawny like a recovering heroin addict, the second man is tall and gangly and the third is a pig ugly guy with a turn in his eye and a beer gut. It's a little after four in the afternoon and she is nine pints down, her friends are catching up fast.

'What's the matter, Biscuit, don't you know this one?' she yells across the bar, all four of them dissolve into gales of laughter. Biscuit ignores them and continues to sip his beer, staring into space. Sooner or later a song will come on and Biscuit will do his thing.

I have been coming here for two months, watching Biscuit do his thing is a sight to behold. He is probably early fifties and always wears the same battered parka coat and combat trousers. He carries a rucksack and sits on the same stool, feeding money into the jukebox mounted on the wall next to him.

Biscuit mimes to every song he puts on, but he doesn't simply nod his head in time with the music like the rest of us. No, when Biscuit mimes a song he goes all out. Facial expressions, arm movements and occasionally slipping from his stool to spin on the spot, are all moves within his repertoire. Along with pointing at the ceiling in a Saturday Night Fever pose when the choreography demands it.

'Don't you know the fucking words, Biscuit?' she yells at him again. Biscuit is somewhere else.

The truth is he doesn't know the words. Many weeks ago, after one particularly lively rendition of Mustang Sally, the landlord told me that twenty years ago Biscuit used to play lead guitar and sing in a band. They did the clubs and were pretty good by all accounts. Then he suffered a stroke while on stage and his path to stardom ended. Nowadays he knows every word to every song that comes from his era but anything produced later than that fateful day he fell into the audience, skips his memory.

I asked the landlord, 'why is he called Biscuit?'

'No idea. Don't think even he knows why.'

At last a song comes on that Biscuit knows and the show kicks off. It's Sandy Shaw singing Long Live Love, the song where Biscuit likes to spin on the spot while miming the chorus. From his seated position, his facial expressions and wind-milling arms go into overdrive.

'Hey, Biscuit, you fucking retard, what's in the bag?' pig ugly guy calls out.

'Oi! Biscuit, do you want to spin on this?' The gangly one holds up his middle finger. All four of them howl and slap each other on the back. 'I said what's in the fucking bag, Biscuit?'

Where is that judge now to see what he allowed to walk the streets when he was doling out his good deed for the day? I can feel the knot of anger in my belly. I glance across at the man working behind the bar. He is making himself busy cleaning glasses so he doesn't have to look at what's going on.

She pushes the lanky lad and he lurches across the pub like a stick insect, making a grab for the bag. But he is so pissed he keels over onto a table.

More howls of laughter.

'I'm gonna piss myself!' She screams clasping both hands to her crotch and scuttling off in the direction of the toilets.

I empty my glass and wave it at the barman. He raises his hand and pulls a fresh glass off the shelf. The lanky stick insect has managed to right himself and is leaning with his arm across the shoulder of the pig ugly one for balance.

Biscuit finishes with a flourish and plonks himself back onto his stool. The next song comes on and he doesn't know it.

She comes back. 'I did piss myself.' She thrusts her pelvis in the direction of the other three to show a dark stain on her jeans between her legs. 'I actually fucking pissed myself.' They fall about giggling.

Biscuit gets down from his stool, picks up his bag and shuffles off in the direction of the gents. This is the moment I've been dreading – I have to stay focused.

'What's in the bag, Biscuit?' She lunges at him as he passes but he manages to avoid her grasp. He disappears from the bar. She pulls the guys in close, whispering and chuckling, then the three men peel off and follow Biscuit through the door.

Fuck! Keep your eyes on the prize. Don't get diverted.

I spin my beer glass around on the bar.

Don't get diverted.

I can't do it, and go to the gents.

I push open the door. A stainless-steel trough runs along one wall with three stalls set against the opposite wall. Biscuit is cowering in the corner with the pig ugly one standing over him, the heroin addict is rooting through his bag.

'Fucking beat it,' pig ugly says as I walk in. The door bangs shut behind me. I stand my ground.

'You fucking deaf?' said the gangly one.

'Fuck off if you know what's good for you,' said the other.

'Yeah and that's the problem, I've never been great at knowing what's good for me,' I say, returning his stare.

'Are you trying to be funny?' said pig ugly guy, moving away from Biscuit.

I am buzzing. I can't stop myself smiling, I feel alive.

'What the hell are you grinning about?' pig ugly says.

'I don't know, I can't help myself,' I reply.

'There's fuck all in here,' said the heroin addict. He hurried over to Biscuit and thrust the bag in his face. 'Why the fuck do you carry around an empty bag?'

Biscuit reached out and tried to wrestle the bag off him. The pair of them have a playground game of tug of war over who was going to get the bag.

'He's gotta have money on him,' said the stick insect. 'Come on retard turn out your pockets.'

'I said fuck off.' The pig ugly one takes three steps towards me. He gets no further.

I slam the heel of my hand into his nose. He staggers backwards, clutching his face. The toe of my boot crunches into his bollocks and he crumples to a heap. The gangly one throws a clumsy haymaker as he runs for the door. I swing my arm and the inside of my forearm catches him full in the throat. His legs go from under him and he cracks his head on the floor as he lands on his back. I stamp twice on his face. The pig ugly guy is struggling to his feet, coughing and croaking. I march over and drive my elbow into his chin, snapping his head back into the wall.

The heroin addict still has hold of the bag but he's frozen to the spot, his eyes as wide as saucers. His sunken face says, 'No, please don't.' I drive a hammer blow into the side of his head and he goes down with a splat, and stays there not moving.

I put my finger up to my lips, crouching beside Biscuit. 'Shhh. Time to go back into the bar and pretend nothing happened. Do you understand?'

He nods.

He scrambles to his feet and is out the door.

I turn, kick the pig ugly bloke one more time in the head for good measure and stroll out.

I take my seat at the bar and sink my pint in one. Biscuit is sitting on his bar stool, sipping his drink and staring into space, despite the fact that I'm sure he knows this song.

I scour the room.

Fuck it, she's gone.

Chapter 22

The stick insect staggers out of the Gents at the same time that I step out onto the pavement. I can hear a commotion kicking off behind me. I'm mad with myself for having lost her. I stride up the high street, jerking my head from side to side, glancing up and down the side roads.

Where the hell are you?

The late afternoon air begins to clear my head following the effects of the beer. If this goes tits-up I have seriously screwed my schedule. A little further on I can hear raised voices, one of them is wailing like a banshee.

A bald-headed man dressed in an ill-fitting uniform is standing in the doorway of a shop with his arms outstretched barring the way in.

'You are not allowed in, madam and if you don't move away I will contact the police.' This must be one of her favourite shoplifting venues.

'Do what you want, you bald twat. I wouldn't be seen dead in your fucking shop anyway.' The banshee is slurring her words, she now seems oblivious to the piss stain on the crotch of her jeans. I breathe a sigh of relief.

Thank God for that.

I slow my pace to do a little window shopping.

'Stick your shop up your arse,' she says, giving the security guard the finger as she slopes away. She zig-zags up the road, shouting abuse at random strangers.

This is uncharted territory. Normally she would stay in the pub until either she keeled over or it was throwing out time.

Or in her case, throwing up time. It's five o'clock and all bets were off as to what was going to happen next.

She bumps into a group of people who are gathered on a street corner, all of them in much the same state as her. There is much backslapping and exaggerated hugs as she makes her presence felt. I can hear her voice above all the others.

'Then … then … I left them in the pub, what a bunch of muppets. They kept buying the beer so I legged it while they were chasing Biscuit in the toilets. I've only spent twenty quid all day and I'm fucking hanging. Oh, and I pissed myself laughing, look!' The damp crotch display seemed to bestow on her even more credibility within the group.

As I sober up, my rage intensifies.

She peels off the side of the group and waddles along, waving her goodbyes. Suddenly she slumps down on a seat at a bus stop. This is way out of the norm. While I'm trying to work out what the hell she has in mind, a bus shows up and she sticks out her hand to flag it down. The doors hiss open and she staggers on board. I turn my walk into a jog and follow suit.

'Where do you want to go, mate?' the bus driver asks as I stand on the front step.

'Oh, err.' I look at the route plastered onto the wall and it all falls into place. I give him my destination – figuring out she's on her way home. Perfect!

I sit and gaze at the houses passing by the window. My adrenaline pumping hard, my hands trembling. After twenty minutes I hear a 'ding' and the bus slows down for the next stop. She sways past me holding onto the seats to steady herself.

It's getting dark as we step down onto the pavement. She turns left and wobbles up the road. I wait a few seconds, pretending to look for something in my wallet, then follow her. It's a short walk to her home, a ground floor flat in a new development, all courtesy of the council. Two town houses have been knocked together to form six one-bedroom flats, all of them decked out with the latest mod-cons. She was given it after her partner, Leah Bramhall, had thrown her out. This followed a particularly violent episode when she had stabbed Bramhall twice, once in the leg and once in the shoulder. When the victim was admitted to hospital they found her body peppered with cigarette burns.

A judge decided that behaviour like that was okay and hence she's been walking around scot-free getting pissed every other Wednesday, after she's been to the job centre to bag more cash.

I spot the house coming into view and quicken my pace. I have to time this right.

She reaches the front door and opens it with her key, oblivious as I tailgate her through. She bumps her way up the corridor, bouncing off one wall then the other. Flat number two is on the right. She stops and fiddles with the key trying to get it into the lock. I pause about six feet away, leaning against the wall.

'Come on you little fucker.' She studies the key and turns it the right way up.

I hear the lock disengage and the door open up. I make one last check around me and rush forward, shoving her in the back with both hands. Her head slams into the door and she topples headlong into the hallway, landing heavily on the wooden floor. The door clatters against the wall as she skids into a heap against the far wall. In one leap I'm on her, punching her hard in the side of the head. She groans and goes limp below me.

I close the front door, grab her collar and drag her into the next room, heaving her onto a dining room chair. I take four cable ties from my pocket and secure her wrists to the arms of the chair and her ankles to the legs. I then head into the kitchen to find a couple of tea towels. I stuff one in her mouth and secure it in place with the other. Her head is slumped forward onto her chest, a purple bruise spreading across her cheekbone.

I return to the kitchen, it is certainly well kitted out. The item that interests me most is the knife block. I remove each one in turn and examine it, they have hardly been used and are razor sharp.

I can hear her coming around, groaning in the other room.

'You enjoy burning people and playing with knives,' I call out to her, removing the aerosol can and lighter from my pocket. She grunts and rocks back and forth, straining against the ties.

Eeny, meeny, miny, moe. I can't decide which one to choose.

I take the whole knife block with me into the lounge.

'I'll let you keep your clothes on, this isn't about sex.'

Chapter 23

Kray was a troubled woman. She had spent the rest of the day working with her team, progressing the leads on the Cadwell case while setting up new lines of inquiry for the untimely demise of Billy Hicks. Having arrived home late she was now slumped in a hot bath with a bottle of wine for company.

Millican had left a couple of voicemail messages but she was too preoccupied. She had called him back, made her excuses and promised to see him soon. She was alarmed at how easily she had transitioned from 'Sorry, I gotta dash' to 'promise to see you soon.' Normally that in itself would warrant a bath and a bottle of wine, but not tonight. She lay in the bath, her mind wrestling with the events of the day.

It's like you did half a job.

The bath and wine did nothing to quell her angst and she went to bed with the words still whirring around in her mind. After several hours of tossing and turning she got up and headed off to the station.

Tavener walked into the incident room to find Kray already there, surrounded by several half-drunk cups of coffee.

'Bloody hell, Roz, I thought I was early.' He looked at his watch, it read 7am. 'Has your house burned down?'

'Funny guy.' She flashed him a sideways look. 'I couldn't sleep so I came in.'

Tavener followed her gaze to the large whiteboard covered with photographs and printed notes.

'You've been busy,' he said taking a seat.

'I couldn't stop thinking about Cadwell and Hicks. Something was bugging me.'

'What?'

'Oh that doesn't matter.' Kray was not about to embark on a convoluted discussion about the significance of a job half done. She wasn't sure it made sense to her and, besides, Tavener thought she was crazy enough already.

'Before we get into this, did you apply for the role in CJU?' Tavener asked.

Kray looked down into her lap. 'I did.'

Tavener nodded his head, it was a real tumbleweed moment. 'Okay so why don't you tell me what's been keeping you awake?'

Kray smiled. 'We have—'

Dan Bagley burst into the office. 'Roz, can I have a word please?' While he phrased it as a question, it was certainly an order.

'I'm just in the middle of something.'

'Now, Roz, I need to speak with you now!'

Kray got up from her seat and followed Bagley out. He took her into the nearest available office and closed the door.

'I thought I made myself clear yesterday that I wanted the Stapletons front and centre of the investigation into the Cadwell death. Then I'm scrolling through my inbox to find you have de-prioritised them in an email you sent out at five this morning. What the hell are you doing?'

'Targeting our resources to those lines of inquiry which are most likely to bring a result.'

'I told you the Stapletons are our best chance of getting a result.'

'They're not.'

Bagley turned a shade of red which would be considered unhealthy for a man of his age.

'How can you be so sure?'

'Because of a man found yesterday floating face down in a bath of bleach with his hands cut off.'

'What the fuck has Hicks got to do with this?'

Kray punched down the handle on the door and stomped back into the incident room. Bagley followed gesticulating and wearing a 'What now!' look on his face.

Tavener was at his desk, keeping his head down.

Kray marched up to the whiteboard. 'The reason why I'm pretty sure it isn't the Stapletons is because here …' She pointed at the first mug shot. 'Is Jimmy Cadwell, small time drug dealer and all-round pain in the arse. He kills a four-year-old girl by running her over in his car while texting. He pleads guilty to a lesser charge, sings a sob story to the judge who hands down a driving ban along with an eight-month jail sentence suspended for two years. The judge in this case is Bernard Preston.'

'I know all this!' Bagley boomed. 'And that is why we need to—'

'This is William Hicks,' Kray ploughed on, pointing to the second mugshot. 'A twenty-three-year-old one-man crime wave. He gets arrested and brought to trial on eighteen counts of burglary. When in court he asks for five hundred and forty other offences to be taken into consideration – yes you heard me correctly, *five hundred and forty*! Just think about that number for a moment.' Tavener's eyebrows nearly hit the roof. 'He cites a relationship breakdown and a problem with drink and drugs as mitigation, along with having to look after his brother who has learning difficulties. The judge sentences him to a twenty-week jail sentence, suspended for one year. And guess who was the presiding judge? Bernard Preston. Now I don't believe in coincidences.'

Bagley was silent, listening to the story unfold.

Kray continued. 'Cadwell gets run over by a car, not once but three times. Coincidence? I think not. Hicks is a thief and dies by having his hands cut off. Coincidence? I think not. And both of them received suspended sentences handed down by Bernard Preston. Coincidence? I think not.'

Bagley looked like a landed carp. His mouth was moving but nothing came out.

'So, to answer your previous question, Dan, we are not looking at the Stapletons because I believe we should be looking for a vigilante.'

'It's a coincidence,' said ACC Quade having listened to what Kray had to say. Kray sat back in her chair and cast her eyes to the ceiling. 'Do you have any evidence to connect the two cases? Do you have any DNA?'

'No, ma'am.'

'Finger prints?'

'No, ma'am.'

'Boot prints?'

'We have a boot print—'

'That connects the two?'

'No, ma'am.'

'Similarities in MO?'

'No.'

'So, you have nothing solid, what you have is a plausible storyline that could connect both cases if you allow your imagination to run riot.' In the rarefied atmosphere that was ACC Mary Quade's office, this was not going well. 'What do you think, Dan?'

'I'm not sure, we have limited resources and can't be seen to chase ghosts.'

'What do you propose?' Quade asked.

'We should—'

Kray jumped in. 'We should run the investigations separately, with a small team looking at the 'coincidences'. The heavy lifting will still need to be done on both cases anyway. If the joint-work turns out to be a dead end then we've lost nothing.'

Bagley stared at Kray. 'Yes, that's what I think we should do.'

'We could get Brownlow to run the Hicks case allowing you to work the overlap, Dan,' said Quade.

Bagley gave Kray a sideways look.

'Ma'am, if we want to do a thorough job can I suggest Dan and I manage it between us? The Cadwell case has gone cold, we have nothing to go on. There is no DNA on the vehicle, other than Cadwell's, no CCTV and everyone who we've interviewed to date has alibis up to their neck. This might give us a new angle.'

'But why not use Brownlow?' Quade asked.

'He's pretty tied up at the moment …' Bagley pussy-footed around the issue.

'With all due respect, ma'am, we would make more progress if you gave the case to my cat.' Kray didn't do pussy-footing.

'DI Kray do I have to remind you I will not allow you to disparage a fellow colleague in my office.'

'Sorry, ma'am, I withdraw the comment. I want us to have the best chance of catching whoever is behind this.'

Quade paused. 'How would you propose tackling the overlap between the cases? I mean, who would have had access to the court findings and sentencing?'

'That's our first problem, ma'am.' Kray laid out a buff coloured file on the desk. 'The Cadwell and Hicks trial verdicts were in the public domain.' She removed two clippings from the local rag. 'They also made the local news at the time. Anyone could have seen them. We need to run through the evidence trail again and cross reference anything that could be common. The second action is to run a data trawl on all the trial cases that have resulted in a suspended sentence in the last three years. Especially those involving Bernard Preston. Then identify the ones that have the same characteristics as the Cadwell and Hicks cases.'

'Okay, but I want to be kept in the loop. If they are connected, I want us to be seen to have joined the dots up early,' said Quade.

Isn't that what I just did? Kray kept her lips sealed.

'Yes, ma'am,' they said in unison and rose from the table.

'Oh and one more thing,' Quade said as they headed to the door. 'I want you two to play nicely, is that understood?'

They both nodded.

Kray and Bagley walked two abreast down the stair well.

'You told her about our chat yesterday?' Kray said through clenched teeth.

'She asked how it was going.' Bagley had not expected his mate, the ACC, to drop him in it. 'I didn't know you had a cat?' he asked trying to keep it light.

'I don't.'

The rest of the walk was in silence. When they approached the incident room Kray turned to Bagley. 'I'll get the guys together and both of us can run through what we have.'

'Good idea, shall we say, thirty minutes?'

'Yes that's good. Oh and Dan the next time Quade asks you how it's going, you can tell her I've applied for the job in CJU.'

Chapter 24

The incident room was buzzing, not since the Palmer case had Kray seen so many eager faces waiting to be briefed. Bagley stood out front, explaining how the investigation was to be structured.

'I will be handling the Hicks case while DI Kray will be leading the Cadwell investigation.' Bagley was being very presidential. 'Now the reason we have you all together is there is a slim chance these cases are linked, so at this point I will hand over to Roz who will give you a heads up on her theory.'

Slim chance? You patronising twat.

'Thank you, Dan. I have provided each of you with a summary of the criminal records of Hicks and Cadwell. I think you will agree it makes toe-curling reading. I have also made note of the sentences that were handed down when they last appeared in court. I think you will agree that is equally toe-curling.' There was a general murmuring of agreement along with a few people uttering, 'Five hundred and forty!'

'In addition to working both cases, we will also be pursuing the theory that the killings are linked by them both receiving suspended sentences. Plus, in each case, the manner of their death could also be construed as a vengeance killing. Both cases were widely reported in the press and on the local news, so they would have been well known. We could be looking for a vigilante.' This word galvanised more chatter and knowing glances.

'I have to stress …' Bagley was on his feet. 'At this stage it is a working theory and nothing more. We investigate each case separately until such time as a positive connection is uncovered, or not. In other words, stick to your own case and don't be diverted.'

A small guy wearing a crumpled suit shot his hand up. His name was Mark. 'Roz, have you drawn up a list of other convicted criminals who have been given suspended sentences?'

'I have and they are pinned to the whiteboard. I went back three years and discarded the petty offences, which left us with ten possible candidates.'

'What criteria did you use to weed out the non-runners?' Mark asked.

'I'm not sure I would go so far as to call it a criteria, Mark. I asked myself the question: If I were the victim of this crime, on a scale of zero to ten, how pissed off would I be? The ones on the board all scored a nine or ten. We need to make contact with these people as a priority, to see if they've noticed anything strange in the past few weeks. So, if you do know any of them, let us know.'

A ripple of conversation ran around the room, Mark seemed satisfied with the answer.

'Are there any that score an eleven?' asked a woman scribbling on her notepad.

'One, I have no doubt you'll spot it a mile off,' said Kray.

Bagley was fidgeting on the spot, watching the team's reaction. 'Let me stress again, I want people to focus on the case they have been given. Roz and I will look for the crossover.'

The meeting broke up and everyone made a beeline for the board, Bagley was looking less than impressed. He sidled up to Kray.

'I don't want folk getting sidetracked looking for connections when they should be concentrating on what's in front of them.'

'Got it.'

'Have you lined up another crack at the Stapletons?'

'I have,' she lied, 'well worth another go, I reckon. What's your first move?'

'The letting agency. If the killer was lying in wait for Hicks he might have viewed the flat as part of his preparations.'

'Good thinking,' Kray said, knowing full well it was, because she had given him that idea an hour earlier. 'Nice one.'

The next fifteen minutes were spent answering questions and giving everyone their tasking for the day. Within twenty minutes the incident room was empty.

Kray was in her car, riding solo. She was travelling without her trusted sidekick, Tavener, because Bagley had nabbed him to work on his case. It felt good to be out from under Bagley's critical eye. She passed the turn-off for the Woodland View estate and headed out of town towards the zoo. It was easier to tell Bagley what he wanted to hear regarding the Stapletons rather than argue the toss that he was barking up the wrong tree. She passed the large bay fronted properties and turned into a less salubrious street, with semi-detached houses and rubbish in the front gardens.

When she parked up she hit two buttons on her phone. The inside of her car reverberated with the ring tone.

'Hey this is a nice surprise. Hang on one second …' It was Dr Ding-dong; the sound of footsteps and a door closing echoed through the speakers. 'That's better I can talk now. How are you?'

'Having a mare of a day but then, what's new? How about you?'

'Not having such a good day myself.'

'Why, have you lost a body?'

'No nothing so trivial. I text a woman asking if she would like to join me at my place tonight and I would cook dinner. She hasn't replied, what do you think of that?'

'She must be a right cow.' Kray smiled. 'If I were you I would steer well clear of that one.'

'I think you might be right.'

'About steering well clear?'

'No about her being a cow.'

They both laughed.

'I called, Dr Millican, to inform you I will not be paying you a visit regarding the body of William Hicks. For that, you will have the pleasure of DCI Dan Bagley. He may wish to attend or he may simply read your report.'

'Is that the newly appointed DCI?'

'The very same, see … you *were* listening.'

'Okay then I will expect his call.' Millican paused. 'Perhaps he might like to have his dinner cooked for him tonight?'

'I doubt it, he looks more of a takeaway man to me.'

'Shame, I guess I'll have a pig-out on a dinner for two.'

'I'll be there around seven-thirty.' She hung up smiling.

Kray looked up and down the street trying to locate the house. It wasn't difficult. It stood out from the rest with its fresh coat of paint and new windows. This was the abode of Catherine Stubbs. She had moved into the ground floor flat five months ago. The tenant manager had said she could normally be found at home in the daytime but not on alternate Wednesdays when she tended to be out all day.

Chapter 25

It was the day I carried my friend and made a vow.

We lifted the coffin high in the air and then down again. It felt like I was carrying the weight of the Brotherhood on my shoulder. All six of us adjusted our position to even out the balance. All of us were roughly the same height apart from Becket, who supported the casket on his upturned palm resting on his shoulder. We would take the piss out of him for that afterwards.

The vicar arranged the procession and gave a nod to the woman at the organ. She slipped effortlessly into *Jesu, Joy of Man's Desiring*, and the music drifted up to greet us as we walked into the church.

As we shuffled onto the red carpet I mused that friendship between men is an odd affair. It's a friendship where you can remember every joke your friend ever told, but not know that his wife left him a month ago. I had no idea Jono was religious.

The church was packed with members of the congregation, family, friends and soldiers from the unit. The vicar led the cortege, his bible in his hands, followed by Francine, Jono's wife, supported by his brother, Sam. He was the spitting image of Jono, which must have broken her heart every time she clapped eyes on him. Her arm was linked through his, as much for physical support as emotional.

A blood red carpet ran the length of the church to the altar. At the end I could see his children, sat with their heads bowed with an older woman, presumably the grandmother. They were ten and eight. It was a heart-rendering sight. Just when they had come to accept that Daddy had returned from war, and there was only half as much of him to love, they were now staring at the stone floor not wanting to see what was approaching from behind.

Jono had spent a lengthy period in hospital when he got back. There were times when it was touch and go, but he pulled through and was getting himself fitted with prosthetic legs.

'Look out, Robocop, cos here I come,' he would shout making the kids laugh.

I visited him a number of times, it was great to hear the old stories and remember those who hadn't been so lucky.

He once asked me, 'Did you really find my leg and put it in the chopper when we flew to Bastion?'

'Yeah, I did.'

'What the fuck did you expect them to do with it? Sew it back on?'

'I don't know. All I can recall is thinking it was the most important thing in the world. I had to find your leg.'

'Well it looks like they must have mislaid it along the way.' He waved his stump in my direction. 'It's a right bastard when someone mislays your leg.'

A short while after that he snagged his stump on a shard of metal protruding from his wheelchair and the wound got infected. As a precautionary measure he was admitted to hospital where they could administer industrial strength antibiotics. After a few days he contracted MRSA and deteriorated fast. An outbreak of clostridium difficile on the ward was too much for his weakened body to take. He died three weeks later. Even though he was in an isolation room the bug crept under the door and took him. I had received a call from his wife and arrived at his bedside ten minutes before his life drained away. Some precautionary measure that tuned out to be, admitting him to hospital.

We shuffled along between the rows of seated people and I could feel my cheek was weeping, the change in air temperature had set it off. I couldn't risk mopping it with a tissue so it had to run down my face. We lowered the coffin, slid it onto the trolley draped in red velvet and I took my seat next to Julie. She leaned into me, linking her arm through mine. The order of service was in the back of the seat in front of me, Jono's face beaming out of the front cover.

Every joke he ever told me flashed before me.

'I never knew you were religious,' I muttered.

'What's that?' Julie said.

'Oh nothing.' I turned my head and smiled a weak kind of smile at her.

The funeral was mercifully short. I constantly dabbed the weeping puss from my cheek while the vicar guided us through the order of service. Jono's brother gave a speech that had the whole place reaching for their hankies.

I could hear Jono's voice chirping in my ear. 'There, everyone's doing the handkerchief thing now. You don't look so much of a wanker mopping your cheek!' It's exactly what he would have said.

At the end we filed past the family. I found it hard to look at his two sons, standing to attention, being brave for their mum. I hugged Francine. Her face was damp.

'Thank you, Alex, I know Jono would have wanted you to be with him.'

'I'll always be with him, Francine.'

I squeezed her hands in mine and moved along the line. The eldest boy stuck out his hand, I shook it and placed my other hand on his brother's shoulder, leaning forward.

'Take care of your mum.'

'We will,' the elder lad said, his face was red.

I could take no more and bustled through the gaggle of people out into the courtyard, leaving Julie behind. I walked around with my hands thrust in my pockets trying to keep the tears at bay.

The hefty figure of Ben Pinner blocked my path. He had been our commanding officer during our last deployment, his broad shoulders and barrel-body made his head appear two sizes too small. He was a popular guy who looked after his men. I had always known him as Pinball. A nickname that ticked the boxes in so many ways.

'He will be missed.'

'Yes, sir, he will. He was a good friend,' I replied.

'When are you going to stop fucking about and come join me?' Pinball said, gripping my hand and pulling me in close. 'We are growing fast and need people like you.'

I smiled and squeezed his hand. 'Good to see you again, sir, shame the circumstances are shit.'

'How have you been?' He gestured to his cheek.

'It's on the mend.'

'Don't forget, when you want some of this?' He ran his hand down the lapel of his expensive suit. 'You only have to give me the nod.'

'It's not for me but thanks anyway.'

'Nonsense, of course it is, it's just a matter of time. Give me a call and you could be anywhere in the world in eighteen hours. Work for me, doing what you do best, and I promise it will set you up for life.' He smiled and handed me a card. 'When the time is right, call.'

Pinball slapped me on the shoulder, moving onto the next person. I drifted around waiting for Julie to appear.

I will deliver justice, Jono, I promise.

The phrase echoed in my head. At the time it seemed like the right thing to say, I had no idea what it meant.

Chapter 26

I slept like a baby again last night. My dreams were visited by Jono and Donk who both gave me the thumbs up as they floated by. I got to work early as usual but there was nothing of interest in the files. I keep looking even though I have a wall of suitable candidates at the Lakeland Hotel.

It's way past lunchtime but the office is still crammed with people. The sharply dressed woman standing at the front has her audience in the palm of her hand. She is surrounded by a garden of helium balloons and flowers, each one showering her with good luck messages and best wishes. There is a buffet lunch prepared, which to be honest looks a little beige.

'… So that's why I decided after twenty-eight years it was time to give someone else a chance. I'm not leaving immediately, they have asked me to stay on until a replacement has been appointed but I need to go before I become part of the furniture.' She pauses for the laugh.

'I thought you already were, Brenda,' replied a woman with red hair. The people gathered around laugh politely.

'My husband and I, oh, I sound like the queen now, don't I? What I meant to say is Tony and I plan to spend three months …'

I'm not really bothered how she and her husband plan to spend the next three months, I keep playing the events of last night over in my mind. The altercation in the pub was a bad idea, but I couldn't walk away from it. In reality it served as a tasty starter to the main course, and made the day all the more special.

Brenda is still in full flow. I've met her twice before and she seems a pleasant enough woman, well liked by her staff and good at her job. Now there's a rarity in this place.

They shouldn't let her retire, they should have her stuffed instead.

Despite the feeling of elation from last night, my cynicism is alive and well.

Brenda takes a hankie from inside her sleeve and dabs her eyes. 'I promised myself I wouldn't do this.' A warm ripple of 'Aww' goes around the large open plan office. I didn't catch her closing remarks, maybe because I wasn't listening. The room bursts into rapturous applause which has Brenda dabbing her eyes once more.

The party breaks up into clusters of people as they track back to their desks. Nodding heads and smiles all around. I go back to mine and sip at a plastic cup of lukewarm coffee. I flick the mouse and the screen bursts into life. Now where was I …

Ah yes, the complainant was given a three-month jail sentence for possession with intent to supply. My fingers tap away at the keyboard filling in the template. No appeal has been lodged, I check the box.

I'm aware of someone by the side of me.

'I'm Brenda Tillerson, we've met before I believe, Alex isn't it?' She has her hand outstretched. I take it, she shakes hands like a bloke.

'You have a good memory with all the people you get to meet.' I get up from my desk.

'I have a knack for it I suppose.'

'Good luck in your retirement. I enjoyed your speech.' I lied.

'Thank you. I'll let you into a little secret, you would not believe how much practice goes into making a speech appear off the cuff.'

'Well you made it sound so natural. The team appreciated it.'

'Thank you, Alex that's kind of you to say so.' I smile back in return, not wanting to overplay my hand by commenting further on a speech I hadn't listened to. 'I hear good things about you from Angela.'

Angela is my section lead, a university high-flyer with a brain the size of a planet and a level of self-esteem to match.

'She tells me you come in early every day to sort out the files, it has made a huge difference to the processing rate.'

'I'm an early riser and I like to set things up properly at the start of the day.'

'Well, thank you for doing that.' She shakes my hand again. 'You should submit a request to have it integrated into your job description, that way you would be formally recognised for the work.'

'That's a good idea, Brenda, I'll do that.'

'I wanted to come and shake your hand to say goodbye.'

'Thank you, Brenda.'

She turned and walked over to the next cluster of desks to repeat the same warm words.

I go back to my data entry.

Thanks for the advice, Brenda, but I won't be making any formal requests. Not sure how long I will be sticking around. Anyway, I have an appointment at the bank.

Kray pushed the buzzer to flat number two, there was no response. The control panel in front of her had six buttons each with a number beside it. She hit every button on the pad. Moments later there was a buzzing sound and the door unlocked.

She entered the building and flipped up the flap on the mailbox, bolted to the wall, marked with the number two. There were a couple of letters stuffed inside. She called the mobile number again, it went straight to voicemail. She rapped her knuckles hard against the front door and pressed the doorbell, the shrill warbling tones of the bell could be heard coming from inside.

Kray went back outside into the crisp cold of early afternoon and tried to peer through the net curtains at the front. The blurred interior of the bedroom gave nothing away, save for the unmade bed and a mound of clothes in the corner. She made her way across the front of the building and down the side to the back. She looked through the kitchen window to see a pile of dishes in the sink and cups lined up on the worktop. On one of the walls was a decorative mirror, with a built-in clock. She took a double take and strained her eyes, reflecting back from the other room was the arm, leg and shoulder of a seated person. The face obscured.

Kray banged her hand against the glass.

'Catherine! Catherine can you open the door please. My name is DI Kray, you are not in trouble. I just want a quick word with you.' The figure didn't move. Kray scrambled to another window to get a better view but it was no use.

'Catherine! Please open the door!'

Kray ran back to the car and returned with her retractable baton. She punched the handle through the window, reached inside and opened the door. A thick waft of stale cigarette smoke greeted her along with the acrid taste of burning. She snapped the baton open.

'Catherine, I am a police officer.' Kray edged her way down the length of the kitchen into the hallway. The lounge was on her left. The figure came into view, facing away from her.

Kray pushed the door until it connected with the wall behind. The figure of a woman was slumped forward in a chair with her hands and feet secured. The woman's back and shoulders were a patchwork of scorch marks where her clothing had been charred black. Around the chair, a circle of dark red stood out against the grey carpet.

Kray scanned the room and crept inside.

She stepped around the stain to face the seated woman. Her arms and legs were covered in the same circular scorch marks and an angry bruise protruded from her cheek. Kray removed a pen from her jacket pocket and picked at one of the black marks, the material of her clothing was melted into her flesh.

The woman's long blonde hair was singed at the ends and stained red from her blood-soaked chest. Kray put two fingers to the woman's neck, her flesh was cold to the touch. She lifted the woman's forehead and tilted her face towards hers. It was Catherine Stubbs, her eyes gazing out in a dead fish stare. Kray looked down to see the handles of six kitchen knives protruding from her chest.

He turned her into a human knife block.

'Fuck it!' she yelled at no one.

She stepped back, reaching for her phone. A control room operator picked up the call.

'This is DI Kray requesting immediate backup at number fifty-seven, Heathcliff Road, flat two. And tell DCI Bagley to get here ASAP, tell him I've found the body of Catherine Stubbs.' The voice on the other end protested. 'I don't care, get him here.' She hung up.

I want Bagley to see for himself what a 'slim chance' really looks like.

Chapter 27

I down my pint and order another. My hands are shaking and my mouth feels like its full of sand. The bar is full of early evening drinkers but I'm oblivious to them. The crack-crack-crack of small arms fire ricochets off the inside of my skull. I'm trying to hold it together but I swear insurgents are going to blast their way through the window at any moment.

I grip the brass rail that runs around the bar. The barman drops a bottle and it goes off like a firecracker when it bursts on the floor. I duck down and spin, facing the door. People turn and laugh but they don't understand what's coming.

A call of 'Hooray!' erupts around the pub and the bar man holds his arms aloft. I haul myself to my feet and look around.

I feel a hand on my arm and turn to face my assailant, fist clenched, ready to go.

'Whoa there, big guy. It's me.'

I stare at the man next to me, trying to unscramble his face. 'Sorry, I didn't mean to …'

'It's okay, do you want another beer?'

'Yeah.' I stand with my head bowed, both hands gripping the brass rail. 'Sorry, I don't feel so good.'

He orders two lagers. 'I know. Let's get a couple of seats away from the bar.' The drinks arrive, he picks them up and we find a quiet spot in the corner.

'Cheers.' He raises his glass and I do the same. He sips the bubbles off the top of his, while I down half of mine. 'I was surprised to get your message, it's been a while.'

'Yeah, I know, sorry about that. It's good of you to come along at such short notice. I'm trying to keep my head down and get on with things, but today got too much.'

'Okay well the first thing you have to do is stop apologising, and the second thing you need to do is sup the rest of that and think about what you want to tell me. I'll get us two more.'

I sat with my face in my pint, or would have done so had I not sunk the other half in one go.

He returns with two more and lines his up side by side on the table.

'What happened?' he asks.

'I told you Julie had moved out.'

'Yes you did.'

'We had a joint account and we decided to close it, you know, tidying up loose ends and all of that. I arranged to meet her at the bank to sign the necessary paperwork.'

'You could have done that separately, you didn't have to—'

'I know, I know. I thought it would be good to see her again and it seemed harmless enough.'

'And?'

'The bank woman took us through to a small office to complete the paperwork and share out the monies left in the account. It's been so long since I'd seen her, we got on well and she looked fucking amazing. When we finished we went outside and I couldn't see her car, so I offered her a lift. She said she didn't need one because she already had one. Then a car draws up alongside us with her boss in the driver's seat. You know the fat twat who she said she couldn't stand the sight of. She said her goodbyes and got in.'

'What happened next?'

'I saw fucking red. I wanted to drag his sorry arse out of the car and rip his head off - again.'

'Please tell me you didn't.'

'No, they left me standing there like a knob.'

'Thank God for that.'

'And then it all kicked off in my head. The explosions, the gun fire, the rampant paranoia, the full works. That's when I messaged you.'

'How do you feel now?'

'Better. I feel better now you're here.'

He picks up his beer and takes a slug. 'Good, and the noises?'

'Pretty much gone.'

'And the anxiety?'

'I'm coming down.'

He raises his glass and we chink. 'Cheers to that,' he says. 'And well done for not beating the shit out of him in front of Julie.' We chink glasses. 'Let me take a look.' He turns my face to the light and touches my cheek with his fingers. 'That's coming along a treat, are you still on medication?'

'No, not anymore. It occasionally itches like fuck but most of the time it's okay.'

'You've done well. That was tough to get through.'

We stay and chat for over an hour. He does the usual thing of trying to convince me that counselling is the answer. I tell him to piss off and go diagnose someone else. As we stand outside the pub we go through the same closing remarks we always do:

'Don't message me unless you're dying,' he says.

'The only time I message you is when I'm dying.'

He walks one way and I walk the other.

I probably won't see him again, until the next time I'm dying.

Kray stared down at her shoes, they were damp but minus the carpet of grass that normally clung to them.

They don't cut the grass in January.

She craned her neck to see cloaks of grey scudding across the night sky, blown along by the wind sweeping in off the Irish Sea. For once it wasn't raining. The moon cast a silvery glow across the grass, which was gradually turning white with frost.

She crested the brow of the hill and an expanse of beautiful gardens opened up in front of her. Even in the moonlight the flowers that carpeted the ground stood out against the solemn backdrop. Kray made her way along the manicured pathway, taking in the scene stretching out in front of her. It was peaceful and serene. She hated this place with a fucking passion.

Kray pulled her coat tight around her body in a vain attempt to keep warm, while stamping her feet like she was marching in time to a military band.

'Sorry I've not been for a while, things have been pretty hectic at work. And I thought, well, you're not going anywhere so anything I have to say can wait. I didn't get that job, you know, the one I went for, the DCI role. They gave it to Dan fucking Bagley, you remember, the prick from GMP who almost screwed up the Palmer case? Well anyway he got it. To be honest I don't think I stood an ice cream's chance in hell with Quade chairing the panel. But the worse part of it was, I convinced myself I did.' She pulled a cloth from her coat pocket and wiped the top of the marble stone.

'I don't know what it is about the guy but no matter what he says or does, he gets right on my tits.' She knelt down and began to clean the front, spitting on the material and paying particular attention to the lettering that made up the words Joseph Kray.

'So, I had a bit of a meltdown when I didn't get it and applied for a job in a solicitors. I know, don't laugh. Can you see me working in an office like that … no, me neither. I got an interview out of it though and absolutely nailed it, but I know that's not the right move for me. I've decided I need to get out of CID, so I've applied to head up the Criminal Justice Unit, which will be a welcome change for me. It will probably be a major fucking shock for them, but that's their problem.'

Kray picked the dead flowers from the vase and replaced them with a fresh a bunch of tulips, topping up the water from a bottle. She could see the brass pin sitting at the base of the headstone. The pin that saved her life.

'Don't know if I'll get an interview and with what's kicking off at the moment they might not let me go. Though I think Bagley would jump at the chance to see the back of me.'

Kray paused. Tears welled against her bottom eyelids.

'Oh yes and there was something else …' She coughed and wiped her eyes with the back of her hand. 'I had company the other night. He's a nice guy called Chris Millican, you'd like him. He reminds me of you, or at least his smile …' She stopped and choked back the tears. 'His smile reminds me of you. I'd had a shitty day and asked him to come over to have a chat and help me drown my sorrows. I think I did most of the chatting and most of the drinking, and one thing led to another … you know.'

Kray straightened up staring at the sky, mopping at the tears streaming down her cheeks. 'It's nothing serious, I think we share a liking for white wine and shit conversation. Anyway, I plan to see him again … I thought you'd want to know.' She scrunched the cloth into her pocket. 'So that's my news, do you have any?'

She trudged back and got into her car feeling drained and peered into the rear-view mirror, running her fingers through her hair trying to make herself presentable.

Who am I fucking kidding?

The engine kicked into life and she pulled out of the car park. A bottle of wine was waiting for her in a strange fridge. A bottle of wine that would be opened and poured by a Home Office pathologist with a liking for waistcoats and tight trousers.

Chapter 28

K ray rang the doorbell and stood in the cold, tapping both her feet on the ground and a bottle to her hip. She pressed the button again. The butterflies in her stomach were going berserk.

'Calm down, you silly cow,' she muttered to herself, 'it's just a meal.'

The door swung open.

'Hi, come in.' Millican stood before her dressed in jeans and a white T-shirt. Her heart did a little skip.

'Sorry I'm late ... work got in the way.'

'I knew it would. I decided not to start cooking until you arrived.'

'Wise move.' Kray stepped into the hallway, handed over the bottle and removed her coat. Millican took it from her shoulders and hung it up.

'You going to be sending me more bodies?'

'I'm afraid so, multiple stab wounds.'

'The last one had his hands cut off by some kind of powered jigsaw.' Kray looked at him and cocked her head to one side as if to say, 'Really? You want to discuss that now?' Millican took the hint. 'Welcome to my humble abode,' he said holding his arms outstretched.

'Not so humble, it's a beautiful place.' She had only seen the outside but judging by the neighbourhood this house cost three times what she paid for hers. She followed him into the spacious living room that was decorated in grey and silver, with a matching leather suite and a massive curved screen TV in the corner. 'You have taste, Dr Millican.'

'Yeah, something like that.' He went through into large open-plan kitchen, with a central island workspace and a dining table and six chairs at the far end. It was all chrome and glass. He picked up a wineglass. 'Do I need to ask?'

'Thank you.'

Kray looked around and thought how dull and dowdy her place must look in comparison.

'How long have you been here?'

'About two years.'

'It's stunning. Well, it's stunning compared to mine.'

'I like it, it's home.' He passed her a drink and they chinked glasses. 'Cheers, thanks for coming. I hope you're hungry, and I hope you like Thai food.'

'You cook Thai food?'

'No, I keep a Thai lady under the stairs for just such an occasion ... *yes* I can cook Thai food.'

'The closest I get to eating Thai is a ready meal and the microwave, and I tend to screw that up. Are you a good cook?'

'A bit of a frustrated chef, if I didn't spend my time cutting up dead bodies I reckon that's what I would do.'

'It doesn't sound so good when you put it like that.' She took a slug of wine and began to relax. This was nice, he was nice.

The wine flowed as did the conversation. Millican paraded around the kitchen like a Masterchef contestant cooking up a feast. He had not exaggerated his abilities, even to a picky eater like Kray. Memories of Joe burst into her mind, the rolling chopping action, the theatrical flourish when he added the spices and the way he flipped a tea towel over one shoulder. She tried hard to keep the memories locked away, determined to enjoy the present.

'I'm stuffed?' Kray said after the meal, as she collapsed onto the sofa.

'So, you don't want any more of this?' Millican waved the wine bottle in the air. She stuck out her glass.

'How long have you been single?' she asked.

'About eighteen months.'

'That's a long time.'

'Yeah it is,' he paused. 'I was in a long-term relationship and …'

'What happened, did you break up?'

'No, she died.'

Those three words stopped Kray in her tracks. She wanted the sofa to swallow her up. She was a detective for Christ's sake, why had she not done a little 'detecting' before opening her big mouth?

'I'm sorry.' Was all she could think to say.

'We hadn't long moved into this place when she was diagnosed with brain cancer. It was four months to the day from diagnosis to funeral, it all happened really fast. One minute she was here doing all this …' He waved his hand around the lounge. 'And the next she was gone.'

'I didn't know.'

'Why would you? I don't introduce myself by saying, 'Hi my name's Chris, my girlfriend died of cancer'.'

'I don't know what to say.'

'Say you'll have some more wine.' He filled her glass. 'Let's talk about something else.'

'Yeah, and while you're thinking what that could be I need to visit the little girl's room.'

'Upstairs, second door on your left.'

She left him staring at the table and headed up the stairs. Like every other room in the house the bathroom was huge, plus it had an oversized roll top bath and separate shower. She sat on the toilet and cursed herself for not having done her homework. While she was giving herself a good telling off she noticed a cluster of framed photographs on the wall opposite, each one depicting a group of men dressed in camouflage uniforms. She finished off, washed her hands and took a closer look.

The face of Dr Christopher Millican stared out of every one. He was either buried amongst a group of men corralled next to a Chinook helicopter or he was caught in a candid pose, checking his gear. The photographs had handwritten inscriptions in the corner, which read 'Afghan' followed by a date, or 'Iraq' followed by a date.

Kray went back down stairs.

'Not sure what you want to talk about but I want to know about those pictures in the bathroom.'

'Ah yes. I wanted to put them up in a prominent place but Alice wasn't keen. To compromise she said I could hang them in the bathroom, at least then I could look at them when I was on the toilet.'

'How long were you in the forces?'

'I graduated out of med school and worked in a hospital for a while, but it was dull, so I joined up to get a bit of excitement. I did four years in the Royal Army Medical Corps, then went back to the NHS and onto the Home Office.'

'Are you glad you did it?'

'It was the best thing ever. When I left I signed up as a reservist and saw a number of active tours … that's where the Afghan photographs come from.'

The conversation was back on track, with all the awkwardness regarding his late girlfriend forgotten. The evening drifted into a comfortable mix of conversation and wine.

Millican staggered into the lounge with a third bottle in his hand. 'More?' he said swaying slightly.

Kray looked at her watch, it was nearly midnight. 'Better not, it's late.'

He flopped onto the sofa with his legs outstretched. 'Yeah, you're probably right. We both got work in the morning. I've had a brilliant time.'

'Me too.'

'I'll call you a cab.'

'No don't bother.' Kray got up and went to find her coat, Millican could hear the rattle of keys.

'Whoa there, DI Rosalind Kray, you are going nowhere near your car.' He jumped up from the sofa.

'I am.'

'No you're not,' he said grabbing her by the hand.

Kray folded herself into his arms and kissed him on the mouth. She held it there long enough for him to run his hand across her back. She pulled away.

'I am, because in the car is my overnight bag.'

Chapter 29

Kray plugged her laptop into the widescreen TV mounted on the wall. Despite her night time activities she was feeling fresh and ready to go. She buzzed around the incident room arranging pens and pencils into regimented order and stacking papers into neat piles, all the while hoping no one would notice. The room was filling up with coppers carrying coffee and notepads for the 9.30am briefing. Bagley appeared next to her.

'You all set?'

'Yup.'

'How about if I give a bit of an introduction and then hand over to you?'

'How about if you don't?' Kray replied, struggling to locate the cable into the TV socket. 'This is the same group we spoke to yesterday, they already know what's going on. We need to give them new information and let them get to work.'

Bagley shuffled on the spot. 'Okay. Quade has asked me to join her this morning to brief the Chief, the trouble is I had already booked an appointment with the letting agent for that time.'

'That does sound like a problem.' She pushed the fitting home and the TV screen came to life.

'I wondered if you could fill in for me. I've already spoken to him once and he's compiling a list of people who have viewed the flat in the last three months. I'm sure you will be in and out pretty quickly.'

'I'll take a look at my diary and if I can fit it in, fine. If I can't you'll need to re-schedule.'

'Okay thanks.' Bagley beetled off to chat with the team.

Kray knew precisely what was in her diary for today but she wasn't going to tell him that. She checked her watch; five minutes to go.

'Roz, everyone is here,' Bagley piped up. 'We could start early.'

'Good idea.' Kray collated her papers and clicked the mouse, a picture of a woman's face filled the screen. 'Good morning, everyone. You will recall when we spoke yesterday I told you we were following a line of inquiry that the murders of Cadwell and Hicks were linked. The nature of how they died relates to the crimes they committed and they were both given suspended sentences. I put a list of names up on the board of other such convicted criminals who have received similar sentences. DCI Bagley was at pains to point out that this was only a theory and, until we had more evidence, we should plough on with the investigations in the normal way.

'This is Catherine Stubbs.' Kray pointed to the mugshot. 'I'm sure some of you will be all too aware of her. She is nasty piece of work. She has a history of assault and two counts of battery. She calmed down when she met this woman, Leah Bramhall.' The face of a young woman with short blond hair and glasses came up on the screen. 'Stubbs moved into Bramhall's home eighteen months ago where they cohabited as a couple. After a heavy drinking session, Stubbs assaulted her girlfriend twice and was convicted of ABH for which she was given a restraining order. She was later found guilty of harassment after she consistently broke the order. Bramhall took her back and in the weeks that followed Stubbs frequently kicked, punched and burned her with cigarettes. Things came to a head when Stubbs stabbed her twice with a kitchen knife.'

The door opened and ACC Quade marched in. 'I was told this was starting at half past.'

'Sorry, ma'am I was not aware you had been invited.' Kray gave Bagley the evil eye. 'If you take a seat I am more than happy to start again.'

'No carry on, I am being briefed later anyway.'

Kray continued. 'Stubbs was arrested and went to court where her barrister put forward the case that the defendant was only violent when she was in a relationship with Bramhall and under the influence of drink and drugs. She argued that as Stubbs was now on a drink and drugs rehabilitation plan, and had split up with Bramhall, the triggers for her violent outbreaks had been removed and Stubbs was no longer a threat. The judge agreed and concluded that she no longer posed a risk, she was given a ten months custodial sentence, suspended for eighteen months, plus a further restraining order.

'This is what I found when I broke into Stubbs' flat yesterday.' The image on the TV changed to show a woman strapped to a chair with the handles of six knives protruding from her upper body, her arms and legs covered in scorch marks. 'These are kitchen knives. The blades were plunged into her body in the same sequence as they occurred in the knife block. Initial forensic results indicate that the black circles are the result of the killer setting fire to an aerosol spray and using it to burn the victim - twenty-seven times. The heat from the flame melted her clothes into her skin. There was no sign of forced entry into the property so she could have known her killer.

'We have established a definite link between the murders and must work the three crime scenes together. We need to get to the other offenders on the list who have received suspended sentences, they could be next. That's all.'

The session broke up. Quade waddled over to Kray.

'Sorry about that, ma'am, I wasn't aware you would be attending.'

'Don't worry about that.' Quade walked to a quiet corner of the room and ushered for Kray to follow. 'I must say, Roz, how disappointed I am with your decision to apply for the CJU role.'

She had been expecting this. 'I need a challenge, ma'am and the role will give me that.'

'You could be challenged here in CID.'

'I need to feel I am progressing and if that cannot happen within CID I need to choose a different route. Dan will do a great job.'

135

Kray went back to her team to ensure they had their marching orders, she had no intention of prolonging the discussion with Quade. She left the station shortly afterwards in search of the letting agency.

Kray sat across the desk from a man the colour of corn flour.

'Are you okay, Mr Simmonds?'

'I don't think I should be in work,' he said wiping his face with his hands. Derek Simmonds was in his late-thirties with unruly hair and a stubbled chin. He was the letting agent who had shown the couple around their dream flat only to find a dead man in the bath with his hands cut off.

'We can do this at your home if you would prefer.'

'No this is fine, I'll go home when we're finished. I suspect it's delayed shock from yesterday.'

'That sometimes happens, I won't keep you long.'

Lockkeepers Letting Agency was on the high street. The company occupied the second floor of the building, the place smelled of fresh paint and new carpets.

'You spoke with my colleague DCI Bagley and he asked to see the letting diary. Do you have that?'

'Yes I do.' Simmonds handed over several sheets of paper containing names, dates and contact details. Kray scanned the information.

'A popular property, Mr Simmonds.'

'Yes we get plenty of interest, it's in a great location but I'm afraid we are struggling to find tenants.'

'We are working on the assumption that the person who murdered the victim had gained entry into the flat and was lying in wait for him. The killer might have visited the place posing as a prospective customer.'

'Oh, I didn't know that. When your colleague called he didn't divulge that information, he simply asked for the list of viewings.'

'Called?'

'Yes, he rang the office yesterday.'

'You've not been interviewed?'

'No.

I swear I'm going to swing for Bagley. Kray bit her lip.

'Okay, when you went into the property on that day you found the body did you notice anything out of the ordinary?'

'No nothing. Well, apart from the Sky box laying on the living room floor and the man ...' Simmonds tailed off into nothing.

'Sorry, what I mean is, did you notice if there was any evidence of forced entry, windows open, that type of thing.'

'No, the flat was as I had left it. You will see from the list I had done the previous viewing.'

'The killer and the victim must have got into the property somehow. Are you sure none of the doors or windows had been tampered with?'

'Nothing like that, all I can say is the flat was locked up tight.'

Kray looked at the list of viewers. 'You attended almost all of these appointments, Mr Simmonds.'

'That's right, we tend to operate on that basis where we can, it saves everyone in the office having to know the details about every property. We have hundreds on our books and it makes life easier.'

'Did you notice anything unusual about any of these people when you showed them around?'

'Like what?'

'Maybe someone who appeared nervous, or edgy, or disinterested. Was there anything that stood out as not being the norm.'

'Not really, but I remember I lost the key to the front door after doing a viewing. We looked everywhere for it and it never turned up.'

Kray almost fell off her chair.

Chapter 30

Kray was sat opposite Derek Simmonds who was no longer the colour of corn flower, he was more ashen grey. He was hanging onto a cup of police station coffee as though his life depended on it.

'I am not under arrest, right?'

'No, Mr Simmonds, we want you to help us with our inquiries,' Tavener said for the second time since they had taken their seats.

'I want you to step through what you told me earlier, Derek. Starting with when you realised the key was missing.' Kray took the lead.

'We have a system whereby we keep three duplicate keys for every property. That way if different agents are showing people around at different times on the same day we don't have the issue of handing over keys. On Saturday 13 January I remember showing a customer around the flat and noticing one of the keys was missing.'

'How can you be so sure of the day?' Tavener asked.

'We have a full staff briefing every Monday morning and I remember bringing it up in the meeting. It is recorded in the notes.' He handed over a copy of the minutes from the meeting. 'The key had not been booked out to anyone and I wanted to know who had taken it.'

'No one owned up?'

'That's right.'

'But the key was there on this date.' Kray jabbed her finger at a diary entry on 28 December printed on a sheet of paper. 'Because you had two agents showing the flat to different customers on the same day.'

'Yes, we did. The office was open between Christmas and New Year and I'm sure someone would have said if it was missing.'

'So, between that date and the Saturday when you noticed the key had gone.' Kray pointed again at the diary entry. 'You had six viewings.'

'We had four couples, a woman on her own looking for a place for her son and a man who was also on his own.'

'Okay, talk to me about the man.' Kray fingered the diary entry. 'Here, he gave his name as George Owens. Do you remember him?'

'Yes I do because I can remember thinking this guy isn't interested.'

'Why was that?'

'Because he didn't ask the usual questions.'

'Like what?'

'Normally, a serious customer will want to know about parking, how much council tax they can expect to pay, does the rental fee include bills, who would they contact if there was an urgent problem with the property ... that type of thing. But this guy didn't ask me anything, he simply walked about the flat.'

'Did you escort him the whole time?'

'No, that was the other odd thing. He kept wandering off. One minute I'd be talking to him and then I'd turn around and he'd be gone. I can remember thinking, 'this guy is a waste of time.' After you've done this job as long as I have you get a sense for these things.'

'I'm sure you do. Did you have your keys on you at all time?'

'I can't be sure, sorry.'

'Could you describe him?'

'Yes I think so, I'm pretty good with faces. He had a scar on his right cheek that he kept dabbing with a tissue.'

'If we sat you with one of our e-fit team would you be able to describe him?'

'Yes I would. Do you think he's the guy who murdered that man in the bath?'

139

'It's too early to draw any conclusions at this stage. We are exploring a number of lines of inquiry, and this is one of them. Now tell me again about the phone.'

'We have a process whereby we call customers on the day of the viewing to check they still intend to keep the appointment. You would not believe how often people don't show up. This …' Simmonds pointed at the diary sheet. 'This is the number he gave me.'

'And you called him on the day of the appointment?'

'I did and he confirmed he would be there.'

'You called this number and George Owens answered?'

'He did and we agreed to meet at the allocated time.'

Kray got up from the table. 'I will leave you with Detective Tavener. Thank you, Derek, you've been very helpful.' She left the interview room and headed down one floor, clutching a copy of the appointments diary and the minutes. She marched up to a geeky-looking guy wearing glasses and sporting a comedy comb-over. He was barricaded into his desk by a wall of four computer screens.

'Hi, are you Brian Taylor?' Kray said as the man looked up.

'Yeah, are you Roz Kray?'

Kray offered her hand. 'Yes, we spoke on the phone.'

Taylor shook her hand and Kray handed over the diary entries. 'That's the number I told you about. Can you work some magic?'

'I'll have a go.' He typed in the digits of the phone number and the screens lit up with information. 'This number is registered to a pay-as-you-go handset on the O2 network.'

'Could be a burner phone.'

'Yes it could be, have you called it?'

'No I didn't want to alert the person who owns it.'

'If it is a burner and the battery and sim card are removed I won't be able to track it.'

'It's worth a try, our man is prone to making mistakes.'

Taylor dialled in the numbers and switched the screens to a different view. 'If it connects we should be able to locate the position from the cell masts.' He hit the final digit and put his handset on speaker phone. It gave a single ring.

'The person you are calling is currently unavailable. Please try again later.' The metallic voice of the service provider buzzed through the phone.

'Nope, its dead.'

'Bollocks,' Kray said. 'I thought it was too good to be true, thanks for trying.'

'No problem.' Taylor went back to playing with code while Kray skulked back to her office.

She got there to find Quade and Bagley already seated around her desk, not the reception committee she wanted to see.

'Did we have a meeting?' Kray asked knowing damned well they didn't.

'No, we came to see you. Dan has been filling me in on the latest victim. With the link between the murders now established I will oversee the joint investigation teams and Dan will be SIO,' Quade announced.

'Ma'am with all due respect I have more experience of running investigations that involve multiple murders. Don't you think I should be SIO?' Kray fixed Bagley with a stare.

'Yes you do have the experience but not the seniority, and besides ...' Quade got up from her seat and hovered in the doorway. 'Dan hasn't applied for a job in CJU. I'll get out of your hair, you two have a lot to talk about.' She smiled at Kray and walked off.

Kray sat behind her desk and opened up her laptop. The silence between her and Bagley was deafening. She clicked on her crammed inbox and skipped through her e-mails, conscious she was pissing Bagley off big style. There was one that stood out from the pack.

Bloody hell, they don't hang about.

'How did you get on with the letting agent guy?' Bagley was not about to endure the silent treatment a moment longer.

'You didn't tell me you hadn't interviewed him.'

'I asked him for his appointments diary, that's all.'

'If you had asked some basic questions he would have told you that he probably met the killer and showed him around the flat. He could have also given you the mobile number he used to confirm the appointment. Oh, and explained how the killer gained entry into the premises. It was not just about the appointments diary, Dan.'

'Shit, what is he doing now?'

'He's with the e-fit team working up a composite picture.'

'Have we—'

'The phone is dead,' Kray said anticipating the question. 'It's a shame.'

'What is?'

'If you had asked the questions in the first place you could have given the ACC the good news that we have new leads to follow.' Kray could see the wheels in Bagley's head turning over.

'Yes maybe I'll—'

Bagley was cut short by Tavener sticking his head around the door.

'Sorry to interrupt,' he said.

'That's okay, I think Dan was just leaving.'

'Roz, it looks like we need to narrow our search.'

The temptation to impart good news had indeed proved too much for Bagley, who couldn't resist scuttling off to the top floor in search of Quade. Tavener and Kray sat in her office drinking coffee with the door closed.

'You okay?' he asked.

'This job never gets any easier. What is it you want? Oh, and thanks for the coffee.'

'While you've been otherwise engaged upsetting our new DCI, I've been busy.' Tavener showed Kray a photograph of a black, calf high, military boot, with eight lace holes running along the instep and up the sides. 'Behold the Spartan XTB.'

'I prefer a bit of a heel,' said Kray.

Tavener ignored the flippancy. 'Forensics have analysed the footprints found at the flat where Hicks was murdered and the prints have a distinctive tread. This is the most likely candidate, in size nine.'

'It looks like it could be service issue.'

'It is, they can be bought online or in specialist shops. My second piece of news is …' Tavener placed an electronic composite picture of a man's face onto the table. 'The woman from the e-fit team said Derek Simmonds was very particular and precise when relaying what George Owens looked like. In her opinion this is probably an accurate likeness.' The oval face of a man stared up at Kray from the desk. He had dark floppy hair above narrow eyes, with a square jaw, an angular nose and a blemish on his right cheek. Kray picked up the image.

'Should be a good likeness, you say? Only sometimes these things go horribly wrong.'

'That's what she said.'

'Okay … get it circulated. What did you tell me about having to narrow our search?'

'I've trawled the Internet and can find nothing on Catherine Stubbs. Not in the press and no coverage on the local news. That makes her different from the other two murders. The killer knew where she lived, the crimes she had committed and the outcome of the sentencing. I think we are looking for someone who works in the in the courts, CPS or—'

'Is a copper.'

Chapter 31

I sit with my back against the wall, my head torch dancing across the faces opposite. My civvy clothes are folded neatly away and I'm dressed in my combat gear, ready to go. Three of the pictures have red crosses drawn from corner to corner, a satisfying sight. I dig my spoon into the ration pack to extract the last of the pasta. To be honest, labelling it pasta should be against the trades description act. It could best be described as pasta-like, but it's a million miles from the real thing. The burn of copious amounts of Tabasco sauce just about makes it edible.

I go through the same ritual every time. My preparation takes place in the penthouse suite of the Lakeland. It reminds me of Afghan but without the heat, even the dust tastes the same. It helps me get into the zone. I can hear Jono clear as a bell.

Time to deliver justice boys, time to deliver justice.

Cold anger builds in my gut as I stare at her face. Her blonde locks tumble across her shoulder with her thin lips slightly parted in a cracked half-smile. The scar on my cheek begins to itch, I dab it with the paprika-red headscarf. I get to my feet and read the details beneath the photograph. I don't know why because I recite the punchline over and over before I go to sleep at night.

The woman was handed a six-month jail sentence, suspended for two years for sexually assaulting a child.

My kitbag is bursting at the seams, this one requires special attention to deliver suitable retribution. I close my eyes and think through what I am about to do, each action carefully planned and choreographed. I imagine the look on her face when I impale her with the baseball bat – a fitting end, I think.

I glance at the noose, dangling above the gap in the floor. The long shadow cast against the front wall is huge. It sits there motionless. Waiting.

Not tonight, I have things to do.

I pick up my bag and head back down the corridor to the stairwell. My boots echo against the confines of the hollow walls. I emerge into reception and squeeze through the gap in the brickwork. The night air greets me, pinching at my skin, my cheek goes crazy. The street lights bathe the surrounding area in an orange wash. I unlock my car and drive up the promenade. The place is deserted, save for the hardened dog walkers. I quickly turn off and head for the backstreets, avoiding the plethora of CCTV cameras.

My adrenaline is rocketing with every mile that passes.

Relax, it's just another op.

I repeat the thought over and over but I'm struggling to maintain focus. Thirty minutes later I swing the nose of the car over to the kerb, fifty yards away in Meadow Drive sits her house; a respectable mid-terraced property, in a respectable area with respectable neighbours. But the occupant of number one-four-four is anything but respectable. She is a convicted sex offender who abused a twelve-year-old boy and is free as a bird because our justice system is designed to protect the perpetrators of crime, not the victims.

I walk past her house noting that the lounge and hall lights are on. I hang a right and after ten yards there is an alleyway running along the backs of the houses. Darkness envelops me as I lose the glow of the streetlights. High brick walls flank me on either side, punctuated by wooden doors leading to the gardens on the other side. I negotiate my way around the rubbish bins to reach the back of her house and, with a final check on my surroundings, I jump up to peer over the top of the wall. All is clear.

I throw the bag over the wall and heave myself after it, dropping to a crouch on the other side. A dog in a nearby garden begins to bark. I wait, allowing it to pass. She has her kitchen light on,

I can see through the windows either side of the back door. The room is empty.

The dog finally falls silent.

I pick up the bag and crab my way to the back, keeping my eyes glued to the kitchen in case she puts in an appearance. All is quiet. I unzip the side pocket and remove a glass cutting tool. The diamond tip scores through the glass as I run it around the frame, the barking begins again.

Fucking dog!

I hear a door open a few houses along and a gruff voice cuts through night air. 'Shut up, Cyril and get in here.' After a few moments the door bangs shut.

Who the hell calls their dog Cyril?

I carry on scribing around the edge. After a while I replace the tool and stick a suction cup to the glass, one sharp strike and the pane will come away from the frame. The kitchen door opens and she walks in. I duck down, out of sight.

Shit, that was close. The fucking cup is stuck to the glass. Never mind if she comes out to investigate, it will save me having to break in.

I pull a telescopic mirror from the bag and ease it over the window ledge. She is putting the kettle on. I feel the adrenaline kick in again, the same tousled hair, the same thin smiling lips, my hands begin to tremble with anticipation.

It's time to deliver justice.

A uniformed police officer follows her into the kitchen and removes his hat.

Fuck!

Chapter 32

'I thought it would help to provide people with a forty-five-minute orientation session before we went into the formal interview stage. CJU has a wide remit that not everyone in the force understands. We think that giving candidates a heads-up on what we are all about will make for a better selection process,' said Brenda Tillerson, taking a seat at the conference table opposite Kray. The surprise email Kray had received while in the throes of pissing off Bagley had been from CJU inviting her along for a chat.

'I have to admit I know some of what goes on here but not everything. An orientation session would be helpful.' Kray sipped at her coffee while Tillerson powered up her laptop.

'Let's start with the people.' An organisation diagram popped up on the large screen. 'You can see we operate a tight ship, with spans of control which you guys at the sharp end might find surprising. I have five direct reports who cover the full gamut of the work we do.'

'There was a time when we would have raised an eyebrow at a structure like that, Brenda, but those days are over. Operating short staffed is common place for us so I'm used to managing people who are spread thinly.'

'Our staff have a primary role and a secondary role which they slip into when we need flexibility.'

I'm still rattled by that copper turning up at her house last night. I had expected that sooner or later Lancashire's brightest and best would join the dots up but it was still a jolt to the system when it happened. I had geared myself up to killing the bitch and now it's difficult to come down from such a high with no result.

She had made the officer a cup of tea and they stayed in the kitchen chatting for a good ten minutes. I have to admit to having a bit of a panic about the sucker attached to the pane of glass. Anyway, they failed to notice it and went back into the lounge where they must have had their drinks.

I suppose the copper wanted to know if she had noticed anything unusual in the last month or so, along with warning her to be extra vigilant. I craved putting a red X through the middle of her face, but it wasn't to be.

I'm finding it difficult to concentrate on my work. The new circumstances don't stop the mission, it simply moves it into the next phase. I didn't come in to work early today. I needed an extra hour in bed.

I need something to take my mind off all that's happened. I pull a file from my desk drawer, flip over the cover and scan the facing page.

Tillerson was breezing through her slide pack. 'Like the rest of the force, we are under increasing pressure to reduce costs while increasing productivity. To address this, we have a series of improvement projects that will deliver us a benefit of two hundred and thirty thousand pounds by the end of the financial year. They are a mix of cost saving, waste reduction and performance improvement initiatives that have been suggested by the staff.' Kray was impressed with Tillerson's grasp of her brief, but then by her own admission she had become part of the furniture.

'Do you have a headcount reduction target?' asked Kray.

'No as such, we have people who will retire this year and they won't be replaced. Do you have any more questions or can I move on to one of my favourite topics, our drive to digitise what we do?'

'No more questions, please move on.'

I forget all about last night and bury myself in the file. No matter how many times I read this it sets my adrenaline pumping. I clench my fist under the desk. This one is a charmer.

A twenty-eight-year-old woman with three counts of assault and two of causing an affray. She was cautioned for the offences and given a restraining order, which she persistently broke. She was arrested when she attacked a woman outside a nightclub, the assault was witnessed by an off-duty police officer who intervened to break up the fight. She smashed a bottle over his head, causing severe concussion and multiple lacerations to his face and neck. The officer spent several days in hospital recovering from the attack.

Jesus Christ!

'We are literally drowning in paperwork, Roz,' said Tillerson. 'There is a major push by the CPS and the Courts to scan critical documents and where possible create them electronically to speed up the paper chase.'

'That sounds like common sense.'

'You would think so, but it is an initiative which has been going on for years with little progress. I'm afraid it is a massive lip-service project with precious little appetite to embrace such a change. Whoever takes on the role will be knee deep in treacle trying to play their part.'

'We have our fair share of treacle at the sharp end, I'm used to that as well.'

'Do you have any more questions, Roz?'

'No, that was very informative, thank you.'

'How about if we take a walk and meet a few people?'

'That would be good.'

My blood is boiling.

She stood trial and gave the court a sob story about being two months pregnant. It's the same fucking idiot judge who sat in the big chair on the Hick's case. Every choked back tear, every watery-eyed apology - he lapped it up.

I remove my phone from my pocket and tap the details into a search engine. The third article down shows a photograph of her and a friend emerging from court. They are puffing away on cigarettes, both of them pointing at the camera and laughing their heads off. No wonder she is happy - Judge Fuckwit handed down a fourteen-months custodial sentence suspended for eighteen months, plus four hundred pounds costs. Which of course was on a payment plan.

Tillerson shepherded Kray about the office, a huge floor space with offices dotted around the perimeter, the whole floor housed a couple of hundred people. She pointed out the different teams and explained what they did. She made a beeline for a desk located in the corner.

'This is one of the people I spoke to you about earlier, Roz, he has implemented a new working practice which has reduced our file processing time. It's a piece of work he introduced completely off his own bat and the results have been amazing. Roz, I'd like you to meet Alex Jarrod.'

Chapter 33

Jarrod was lost in his own little world, a world consumed with the need to deliver retribution. So engrossed was he in the file that it took a moment for him to register the two women standing at his desk.

He recognised Tillerson. 'Hi, Brenda, sorry I was miles away.'

'I was telling Roz about the good work you do here.'

Jarrod got up from his seat and offered his hand. Kray was struggling to maintain her composure.

'Hi Alex, my name is Roz Kray.' She shook his hand. Their palms touched and the scar running across her back exploded with the pin-pricks of a hundred needles.

'Looks like my ears should have been burning.' Jarrod's hand went limp to end the shake but she held on, not allowing it to fall away.

Their eyes locked and Kray's scars burned beneath her clothing.

Jarrod pulled away and wiped his palm on the leg of his trousers.

'Roz is here to have a brief tour looking at what we do in CJU,' Tillerson continued. 'I thought that as I had been singing your praises, Alex, I would bring her over to say hi.'

'Brenda has been very complementary about the work you've been doing,' said Kray boring her eyes into him. 'She tells me you come in early to sort through the intake of files from the CPS and the Courts in order to ensure they reach the right people.'

'Yes, they come from all over, I've been doing it for a while now and it seems to be working.'

Kray clasped her hands behind her back to prevent them from fidgeting. Jarrod looked away to avoid Kray's stare, occasionally flicking a glance in her direction. He removed a tissue from his pocket and dabbed his cheek.

'Shall we continue, Roz?' Tillerson waved her hand to show the way.

'Good to meet you, Alex,' Kray said, her whole body on fire.

Jarrod held his hand up in a 'thank you' gesture and returned to his seat. He watched Kray move between the clusters of desks with Tillerson at her side.

'So, Roz …' said Tillerson.

'Excuse me, Brenda, I need to take this.' Kray fished her phone from her jacket pocket, holding it to the side of her head. 'Okay I'll be there in five.'

'Problem?'

'Yeah, sorry I have to cut the tour short, we've got an incident that has blown up and requires my attention.'

'No rest for the wicked. I hope you have found this useful and I look forward to seeing you at the interview stage.'

They shook hands and Kray walked to the front of the office and through the doors, every muscle in her body telling her not to look back. She stood on the landing and pushed two buttons on her phone.

Jarrod watched Kray leave, every muscle in *his* body telling him to run. The taste of sand in his mouth.

Tavener answered the phone. 'Roz.'

'Go to the incident room and pick up the e-fit picture of the suspect then get your arse over to the third floor of CJU. Hurry.'

'What is—'

'Do it now!'

Kray stole a glance through the glass panel in the door, she could see Jarrod at his desk. He looked up and pretended to carry on working. Her heart was bursting from her chest. Jarrod had his eyes glued to the door.

The minutes ticked by. Jarrod got up from his desk to look out the window. People milled around outside, none of them were Roz Kray.

Kray could hear the sound of size eleven boots pounding up the stairs two at a time.

'What is it?' Tavener puffed and panted. Kray snatched the paper from his hand.

'Fuck, that's him.'

'That's who?'

'The guy in the picture. His name is Alex Jarrod and he works in CJU.'

'Shit. Where is he now?'

'At his desk in the far corner of the office. I met him and I think he rumbled me.' Kray opened the door and marched inside, closely followed by Tavener.

Jarrod was gone.

They weaved around the office, scanning the faces. Kray pointed to the back corner, Tavener nodded.

'Roz, are you back so soon?' It was Tillerson, still out and about chatting with her team. Kray ignored her.

Fuck, where is he?

They reached his desk. The computer screen was still on and the usual clutter lay untouched on the desk. His jacket was draped across the back of the chair.

'Check the toilets, I will take the side offices,' said Kray.

'Roz, is there a problem. Can I help?' It was Tillerson again.

'Have you seen Alex Jarrod?'

'Yes he was … oh, he's not there. He was here a second ago.' Kray dashed off to the nearest office and burst inside. 'Roz, what is this about?'

The place was empty. Kray checked under the desk and behind the door. Nothing. She moved on to the next office and did the same.

Tavener appeared. 'The Gents and the Ladies are clear.'

'Check with facilities and find out if Jarrod has a car registered on site. He might be in the car park.'

Tillerson took hold of Kray by the arm. 'Roz you need to tell me what this is about.'

Kray looked around the office at the collection of faces staring at her.

'We believe Jarrod may be involved in a murder investigation. I recognised his face from the e-fit, do you have any idea where he might have gone?'

'Fuck me,' Tillerson said, her professional veneer cracking wide open. She turned to face the room. 'Did anyone see where Alex went?' Her voice boomed around the office.

There was a general murmuring and shaking of heads.

'Is there another way out of here?'

'There is a fire escape at the back, but it's been—'

'Where, where is it?'

'Through here.'

Kray followed Tillerson along the back wall to an area filled with banks of metal shelving, holding hundreds of dusty files. 'It's been out of commission ever since I took over. The metal work had deteriorated beyond repair.'

Behind one of the shelving units was a wooden door, the glass fire bolt lay on the floor in pieces.

'Shit!' Kray yanked it open and stared down at the rusted metal staircase, running down the exterior of the building. She seized the handrail and darted down the steps.

'Roz they are unsafe,' Tillerson yelled, but it was too late, she had already reached the first landing below.

Kray could feel the metal contraption sway and creak as she paced down it. She had a good view of the rear staff car park. Several people were walking to their vehicles while others were on their way into work. None of them looked like Jarrod.

She reached solid ground and gave a big sigh of relief. There was a horrible groaning of metal above her and for one awful moment she thought the whole structure was going to come crashing down. Tavener stood next to her.

'Jarrod has a black Vauxhall, here's the reg number.' He handed Kray a slip of paper and they ran in between the cars, looking for the one matching the description. After several minutes Tavener called out, 'Roz, over here.'

Kray ran across to find him standing next to the car.

'He has to be here somewhere,' she said. 'Tell facilities to pull up all the CCTV they have for the last half an hour. I will alert Bagley to get Jarrod's mugshot circulated … and post a couple of uniform at the gate.'

Tavener and Kray both reached for their phones.

'Fuck it!' Kray yelled at the top of her voice just as Bagley picked up her call.

Chapter 34

My hands are stuffed deep into my pockets as I force-march along a side road. It is bloody freezing and the wind cuts right through my shirt. It's no big deal. Cold is good.

I pull my phone from my pocket and drop it onto the ground. I look around me to see if anyone is watching and smash my heel repeatedly into the touch screen. The glass shatters while I continue to stamp the life out of it. I pick the remnants off the pavement and toss them over a wall.

I trudge for almost an hour, trying to control the explosions going off in my head. The physical exertion helps me focus. I keep my head down and trudge on.

Back at the office, when Kray had disappeared from view, I had brought up the internal phone directory. The letters DI in front of her name made me realise it was time to hit the eject button. I have to say I wasn't looking forward to climbing down the disused fire escape but it was my chosen escape route if ever events took a turn for the worse. And meeting DI Roz Kray certainly gave things a turn for the worse. The way she looked at me, I knew my time was up.

I march on and hit a fork in the road, choosing the street leading south, running parallel to the Promenade. I've managed to avoid the major routes with their CCTV cameras and passing traffic, but the constant criss-crossing around the city has made the journey far longer than I had imagined. My legs are burning with the cold.

The corrugated fencing looms in the distance. I reach the corner, look around and pull the sheeting free, slipping inside.

After crossing the rubble and mud I do the same with the security shuttering on the back wall, the familiar smell of plasterboard and dust welcomes me inside.

I dash up the service staircase to the top and feel my way through the dark corridors, arriving at the penthouse. I tug my combat jacket off the nail and put it on. My limbs are shaking and my teeth chattering. Bars of horizontal light stretch across the walls as the sun cuts through the gaps in the shutters. I pick up a bottle of vodka and crack the top off. The fiery liquid burns on the way down and gets to work straightaway, easing the tension in my body. I don't like the stuff but buying spirits was a matter of space and volume. While I would much prefer to sink a beer, it would have been far too onerous to manhandle crates of lager into the penthouse. I took the decision that if I needed alcohol it would have to be hard liquor. Four bottles line up against the wall. Alongside the booze are bags of dried food and bottles of water, plus a camping stove and gas canisters. It has taken several months to kit the place out but then I have been planning this for a long time. I think I've thought of everything even down to buying spare batteries for my head torch and a supply of basic medicines, plus a couple of cheap pay-as-you-go phones and a smart phone. I'm conscious I need to conserve the battery life so I have yet to switch them on.

Today has been a panic, that's for sure. But this is an inevitable phase of the operation. Sooner or later I was always going to end up here, needing a bolt hole to run to. The supplies would enable me to remain hidden. The police could have the car, it contained nothing of interest and they could ransack the flat all they liked - they would find nothing there either.

The plan was simple, when the situation became too hot to handle I would disappear. I sit on the floor, position a mirror between my feet and begin hacking away at my hair with a pair of scissors. Soon my scalp is peppered with dark tufts which I scrape away with a disposable razor. In a few days my goatee beard will complete my new look. While it is a change in appearance that wouldn't stand up to close scrutiny, it was good enough to deflect a casual glance.

The tension eases from my shoulders and the banging and screams in my head have subsided. I reach for the bottle and take another swig.

Fuck, that was close.

'Jarrod got away on foot by using the old fire escape at the back of the admin building.' Kray was in the imaging suite scrolling through CCTV footage under the watchful eye of Bagley and ACC Quade. Grainy images of cars and people scurried about the screen. 'This is Jarrod caught on the camera at the back and here he is again walking off site and turning down King's Street.'

'Why didn't you arrest him when you clocked him in CJU?' asked Bagley, fidgeting with his pen.

'I needed to be sure, plus I needed back up. For all I knew he could have been armed in an office full of people, I couldn't take the chance,' Kray replied.

'You could have—'

'Yeah I could have but I didn't. Maybe if you had asked the right questions when talking to the letting agent we would have had the e-fit a day earlier.'

'Okay, okay.' Quade held up her hands, getting fed up with the sniping comments. 'Pack it in. He was too quick for us and we have to work with what we've got. What do we know about Jarrod?'

Kray consulted her notes. 'He's thirty-eight years of age, joined the police after a spell in the army where he saw active duty in Afghanistan. He was discharged on medical grounds and came to work for us a little over a year ago. When I spoke to Tillerson and his line manager they both said Jarrod was a bit of a loner, a pleasant enough guy but he didn't mix with the others in the office. The intervening period between leaving the army and appearing on our radar is a bit of a blank I'm afraid. We have a request in with the MOD to see his records but as we know that can be a little hit and miss on times.'

'What's his domestic circumstances?' asked Quade.

'Don't know a great deal as yet, we are working up a media profile to identify his social network and it looks like his phone is dead. We also have a couple of uniform posted at his flat, just in case we get lucky. We got there pretty fast and don't believe he returned home after he left here, I will be going there after we have finished. One of his neighbours told an officer that he used to live with a woman but she hasn't been seen there in months. We are doing some digging to find out who she is. His vehicle is still in the car park and the details held at the DVLA all check out, we will be handing it over to a forensics team as soon as we can get organised. And we've put a watch on his bank accounts. We also have the local bus and train stations on alert as well as the airports.'

'Does he have a criminal record?'

'No, he's clean.'

'Do we know anything about this guy that tells us why he's doing this?'

'No clear motive as yet. Other than what we surmised before, that he is performing a kind of vigilante role against people who have received suspended sentences.'

'Anything else?'

'The footprint found at the flat where Hicks was murdered came from a military boot. So that fits given his background.'

'We have to assume he has gone to ground somewhere, maybe he's laying low at a friend's place,' said Quade.

'But that doesn't fit with his loner profile,' replied Kray.

'I think we need to go public.' Bagley finally made a contribution. 'Make a television appeal and see what falls out. That might spook him into making a mistake and could also put the brakes on him travelling if he believes he could be recognised.'

'I can sort that out,' said Quade. 'What do we intend doing with the other people on the list who could be potential victims?'

'Jarrod has now had a major spanner thrown into his works,' Bagley said leaning forward. 'I think he will be concentrating on getting away. His mind won't be on murdering more people.'

Kray stared down into her lap spinning her wedding ring.

'What do you think, Roz?' asked Quade.

'I think he's on a mission. Jarrod isn't going anywhere until its complete.'

Chapter 35

Kray sat on the edge of the settee, taking in her surroundings. This was her last task of the day before returning home to put her feet up and sink a bottle of wine. Julie Clarke came in holding two cups of coffee.

'Here you go,' she said handing one over. 'You said you wanted to talk to me about Alex. Is he in trouble?'

'When was the last time you saw him?' Kray avoided the question.

'I saw him the other day when we were at the bank. We had a joint account which required us both to sign before it could be closed. And I know that could be done separately but for some reason I wanted to see him.'

'How was he?'

'He was fine, we chatted about all sorts and he seemed happy enough. He said work was going well and he was still living at the flat. Alex doesn't say a lot ... you kind of have to read between the lines.'

'Do you meet up often?'

'No, not at all. That was the first time in almost a year. We ceased contact when I moved out.'

'How long were you with him?'

'Six years.'

'Why did you split up?'

'Alex came back from his last tour of Afghanistan a different person. He was medically discharged after he contracted leishmaniasis.'

'What the hell is that?'

'It's caused by being bitten by a sand fly which injects a parasite into your skin that causes your flesh to erupt into huge sores.

He was bitten on the cheek and was in a terrible state. It took ages to heal.'

'Is that what changed him?'

'It didn't help matters, but that's not what did it. On his last tour he and his team were out on patrol when they were attacked. Most of the team were killed but Alex survived. It was awful and he developed PTSD.'

'What type?'

'Every type you could think of. He had panic attacks, voices in his head, night terrors, day terrors, the works. It started off small and quickly took over his life.'

'Is that when you left?'

'I couldn't take it anymore. When he was suffering one of his attacks he would lash out and sometimes hit me. He wouldn't mean to, he was fighting off an invisible attacker and occasionally I got too close. It was scary and he flatly refused to get help, so I packed my things and went. Sooner or later I was going to get seriously hurt, we both knew that.'

'Where did you go?'

'I moved in with my mum, but that only lasted a week.'

'Why was that?'

'If you knew my mum you wouldn't ask. That's when Kail said I could crash here until I got on my feet.'

'Kail is …?'

'Kail is my boss at work, he gave me his spare room and one thing led to another. You know … and now we live together. We've been a couple about five months.'

'Where is Kail now?'

'He goes to the squash club once a week; I'm not sure they play a lot of squash but he enjoys it.'

'Does Alex know about Kail?'

'I don't think so.'

'Does Alex have any friends? Does he use social media?'

'He had loads of friends before Afghan but when he came back he pushed them away. He kept in touch with his team leader, a guy named Jono, who returned with horrific injuries and subsequently died. So, you see when you ask about his friends, I don't think he has any, and his idea of social media is sending the occasional text.'

Kray nodded and scribbled in her notebook.

'You didn't answer my question, is Alex in trouble?' Clarke asked again.

'We believe Alex was involved in the murders of three people.'

'Jesus!' The coffee slopped out of Clarke's cup onto the back of her hand. She placed the cup on the hearth. 'Murders? But how?'

'We are conducting our investigations, so it is too early to confirm any details. We will, however, be going live with a public appeal asking for anyone who sees Alex to get in touch.'

'Shit. You mean he's disappeared.'

'We need to find him, a press conference has been scheduled and it will be aired on the TV tonight. I did not want you to see the appeal without being notified first.'

'I don't believe it.' Clarke was on her feet, pacing around the lounge.

'I don't want you to panic, Julie, but I do want you to get in touch if Alex makes contact.' Kray fished around in her coat pocket and handed over a card. 'Anytime, day or night, you can reach me on that number.' Kray drained the last of her coffee and stood up to leave. Clarke was still on her walkabout around the living room.

'I'll let myself out.' Kray made her way back down the driveway to her car. Through the bay window she could see Clarke stood in the centre of the room trying to comprehend what she had just been told.

Kray's phone buzzed on the dashboard. It was a text from Dr Ding-dong. It said one word: *Food?* She called and his voice came over the speakers.

'That was quick, are you hungry?' Millican said.

'Nope, but I'm thirsty.'

'Fancy having an impromptu wine tasting at my place?'

'No; but how about you come over to mine and I'll fix dinner.'

'You don't cook.'

'I know, see you at half-eight.' She hung up; what a lovely end to a shit day.

At eight thirty on the dot there was a rap on the door. Kray raced downstairs dressed in jeans and a top. 'I'm coming, I'm coming,' she said having only just got home and taken a quick shower.

She opened the door to find Millican holding a bottle of wine.

'Hey, I heard there was a thirsty woman on the premises. Sounded like an emergency.'

'Come in.' He stepped across the threshold but she didn't move back to allow him inside. Instead his body pressed into hers and she kissed him on the mouth. 'Definitely an emergency.' She took the bottle from his hand and walked through into the lounge where a large wine was already sitting on the coffee table next to an empty glass.

He threw off his coat and joined her on the sofa.

'It was looking like I was going to drink the first bottle on my own,' she said.

'That would constitute as an emergency. I can see the headlines now; 'Lone woman drinks whole bottle of wine on her own.' That's hardly breaking news for this house, now is it?'

She poured him a drink and they chinked glasses. 'Cheeky sod.'

'Bad day then?'

'Yeah, one of the worst. We had that guy who's been murdering people and lost him.'

'That is bad.'

'Actually, to be more precise … I had that guy who's been murdering people and lost him.'

'Ouch! That's worse.'

'If only I had leaned over the desk and punched his lights out, we would be down the pub celebrating now.'

'So, now I'm the booby prize. Very nice.'

'No, I didn't mean that.' Kray swung her feet up onto the sofa and leaned into him. 'I wanted you to come over, but that doesn't change the fact that I fucked up today.'

'You'll get him.' Millican kissed the side of her neck. There was a comfortable minute when neither of them said a word. They sipped their wine and melted into each other.

'I can't smell cooking,' he said breaking the moment.

There was a rap on the front door.

'I said I would fix dinner.' Kray put her wine on the table and walked into the hallway clutching her purse. 'I didn't say anything about cooking.'

Minutes later she returned with two flat, square boxes. 'I assume you like pizza.' She slid them on the table and flipped open the lids.

'Bloody hell, Roz, you shouldn't have gone to this much trouble.'

'I know. I had to call them twice because the first time they were engaged. Fucking exhausting.'

Kray stuffed a wedge of pizza in her mouth. There was one positive thing to come from her association with Dr Ding-dong; at least now she ate real food with her wine rather than chocolate … or simply more wine.

'You are a great cook,' he said helping himself to another slice of garlic bread.

'I know.'

Two hours later they were still curled up on the sofa. The food was gone as was the wine.

'I can't believe you only brought one bottle,' she said.

'I can't believe you only had half a bottle left in the fridge.'

'I couldn't help it, when I got home and I was thirsty.'

'Do you have an off-licence around here? I will pop out for some more.'

'Wait, what's the time?'

'It's just gone ten-thirty.'

'I need to put the news on, you don't mind, do you?'

'No what is it?'

The TV came on and Kray flicked between the channels. The anchor woman said, '… our correspondent was at the news conference.'

The segment cut away to ACC Quade, flanked by DCI Bagley, with a cluster of microphones sprouting up at them from the table. The force badge and logo served as a backdrop.

'We are investigating the murders of …'

'Mrs Blobby said she would organise a news conference today and I've been so busy I've not seen it,' said Kray. 'Look at Bagley, he looks scared shitless.'

'… we want to trace this man. His name is Alex Jarrod …' Quade read from her pre-prepared script. The face of Jarrod filled the screen. 'We want any member of the general public seeing Alex Jarrod to contact us on the number at the bottom of your screen. I will read it out: It's …'

'That's the guy I had today and he got away,' Kray purred. Millican stared at the screen, blinking his eyes. The news article finished and Kray switched off the TV. 'Fingers crossed someone spots him.' She half-turned into Millican and kissed him on the lips. 'Let's both go to the off-licence, I don't trust you.'

Millican said nothing.

'Are you all right?' Kray asked.

'No, no I'm not feeling so good.'

'Oh no, was it the pizza?'

'I don't know.' Millican pushed Kray to one side and stood up. 'I need to go.'

'Go! What do you mean *go*?'

'I need to leave.' He pulled on his shoes, retrieved his coat from the hallway and grabbed his keys.

'Hang on, Chris, where are you going? You can't drive.'

'I'll be fine I've only had a few glasses.'

'Chris you've drunk far too much.'

'I need to get home.'

'Chris, you can't …' And with that, the front door slammed shut.

Chapter 36

I put the fork into my mouth, my taste buds wonder what the hell they've done to upset me. I scan the ingredients off the packet. The title at the top reads 'chilli con carne.'

I doubt that very much.

The food is hot and that is about all you could say for it. I reach for the Tabasco sauce. The dead eyes of Alice Fox, the child rapist stare down at me. I imagine myself drawing a big fat X across her face – all in good time.

I put down the food, unpack the phone from its box and assemble the components. There is one good thing about being located on the Promenade; there is excellent 4G coverage and in no time I am downloading the Facebook app. I tap it with my fingertip, input the necessary details and my false identity comes up on the screen. To anyone searching my history they would see a boring man who has never posted a single message or photograph. Which is true. I do, however, belong to a closed group; an exclusive group with three members, one of whom had his legs blown off and is dead, and the other helped me come through the darkest time when recovering from my Bagdad Boil.

When we came back home from Afghan we decided to keep in touch and Jono came up with the closed group idea. 'Let's keep things between us three', he said. Not sure why. The phone emits a shrill *ping* and an alert comes up. It reads: We need to talk, urgent. The message was sent an hour ago.

I tap out a response and immediately get a reply.

I pull on more layers of clothing and make my way down the dark corridor to the stairs, my head torch blasting a white cone of light at the red-pink walls. The wind is picking up as I stroll along the prom, the clear black sky confirming that we will have a covering of frost and ice by morning. The moon is big and bright, casting a wedge of silver across the sea. I descend the steps onto the sand and head past the tower to the central pier. The cast iron structure juts out at right angles into the sea, a wooden boardwalk held aloft by what looks like old man's fingers. The skyline is dominated by a Ferris wheel, one hundred and eight feet tall, stretching into the night sky.

It is low tide and I walk towards the surf. I am soon under the pier surrounded by the thick legs supporting the massive structure. I stop and lean against the iron skeleton, surveying the beach. I can hear the waves behind me lapping on the sand, it is a comforting sound.

Out of the darkness I see the silhouette of a figure coming towards me. I give a low whistle, he flicks his head in my direction. A minute more and he is stood beside me.

'Hey, I got your message, what's so urgent?' I ask.

'What the fuck are you doing?' He is out of breath.

'Standing under the central pier talking to you.'

'Don't be funny. What the fuck is going on?'

'I love this place, don't you? I really identify with it. I know people prefer the tower or the Winter Gardens or the Pleasure Beach, but this is my favourite. Did you know it was engulfed in flames twice; two fires nine years apart, both of them threatened to destroy it, and yet here it is. Standing tall. It's a survivor, just like me.'

'I saw your picture on the television. They said you were wanted in connection with three murders.'

'Oh, yeah … that.'

'Alex what the hell have you done?'

'Was it the police putting out a public appeal?'

'Yes, it was, why the fuck do they want to speak to you?'

'Because I killed those people.'

'What! Why the fuck …?'

'They needed to die, that's why.'

The man walks in small circles with his head looking up. 'What happened? Did they do something to you, is this about revenge?'

'No this is about retribution. These are people who have got away with the most heinous crimes and they need to pay.'

'You cannot go around killing people.'

'Yes, I can.'

'No you can't. You went to war to protect people, you can't come back and start killing them.'

'That's where you're wrong. We like to think we were in Afghan fighting to protect our way of life but we weren't.'

'You're talking bollocks.'

'You don't understand.'

'That's the most sensible thing you've said so far ... no I don't understand. What the hell is going on inside that screwed up head of yours?'

'I look at it like this: We all live in a fucking big house, in the middle of nowhere in a strange land—'

'What is this? Jackanory time?'

'Bear with me, I'm trying to explain in simple terms. It's like we all live in a big house, in the middle of nowhere in a strange land. Other people live there too, in their own big houses. In our place we have a set of rules that makes us happy, but the others have a different set of rules. Their rules are not like our rules. In their house it is okay to kill people, to sexually abuse children, to beat those who are weak or to steal from your neighbour, and we live in fear that they want to impose their rules on us. So, we send our people to fight those with different rules and its dangerous outside, and people die. And after you've taken your turn fighting you are allowed back into the house. It is then that you discover that what you've been fighting for doesn't count for anything.'

'Where is this going?'

'It is then you find out the rules you were fighting to protect don't exist. It's wrong to kill a kid – no it isn't. It's wrong to sexually abuse children – no it isn't. It's wrong to threaten people and hurt them – no it isn't. It's wrong to steal – no it isn't. You find the rules you've been defending no longer apply. What was the fucking point? We may as well have let the other people in, to impose their will, and saved the ones who died.'

'That's bollocks!'

'Wake up! People are killing kids and getting away with it, sexually abusing kids and getting away with it; assaulting people, threatening people and stealing from people and getting away with it. We didn't fight for that.' I grab hold of his shoulders. 'I fought for my country but I never fought for this.'

'For fuck sake, Alex, you have to hand yourself over to the police. You're ill, the PTSD has skewed your perspective. You have to stop.'

'I can't, the mission isn't over.'

'Mission? What mission? We are not in Helmand Province now! This is not Sangin or the Northern Valleys. This is England, the place we fought to preserve.'

'Then why the hell aren't *they* fighting to preserve it as well?' I shove him and he stumbles backwards. 'You're part of the Brotherhood, you cared for me in Bastion and you helped me when I got back. I thought you of all people would understand.'

The tide is coming in and water is lapping around the soles of our boots.

He comes back at me hard, ramming his fists into my chest, pinning me against one of the stanchions. 'I looked after you because that was my job and now you need to allow others to do their job. This is not your fight. The police, the CPS, the judges all have their part to play and sometimes they get it wrong, but it's not your job to put it right.'

I press my face into his. 'Yes, it is. For the sake of Donk, Jono, Bootleg, Ryan, Pat and all the others who have either not returned, or come back with limbs blown off, I owe it to them to put things right.'

I hook my foot around the back of his leg and slam him into the sand. He lands hard on his back in the water. My knee knocks the wind out of him as it thuds into his chest, the point of my knife digs into the skin of his cheek. I can see his wide eyes, glinting in the half-light.

His legs kick at the sand and he throws a punch, I block it and seize his wrist.

'Don't.' He struggles below me, his hair sticking flat to his head with sea water. 'Don't.'

'You have to stop. You can't go on killing people.' He chokes out the words through gritted teeth.

'The reason this blade is not sticking out of your eye socket right now is because you are part of the Brotherhood. You helped me and we're friends. This is me being your friend. You need to stay out of my way. Do you understand?'

He stares up at me and struggles to free himself. I force my knee into his sternum and press the blade across his throat, my face inches from his.

He freezes.

'I said, do you understand?' He nods and blinks his eyes. 'Because if you don't, Brotherhood or no Brotherhood, I *will* kill you, Chris.'

Chapter 37

I can see the silhouette of a copper sitting in his car outside the house. What a thankless task that is. The pavement is glistening with the onset of a heavy frost. I skirt around the corner using the hedge for cover and lose myself in the darkness of the alleyway.

To avoid the officer playing sentry, I'm approaching the house from the other side so I have to judge when I'm level with the property. A couple of times I heave myself up to peer over the wall – twice I get it wrong. At the third attempt I'm in the right place.

My elaborate plan has had to go out of the window. For a meticulous planner like me this is tantamount to winging it. I've had to leave the kit bag filled with toys back at the penthouse, a man walking around at 2am is bound to raise suspicion, one carrying a large holdall is even worse. I'm packing light tonight.

The back gate is locked so I leap up onto the top of the wall and drop down the other side. The grass is crisp underfoot. Cyril the guard dog must be sound asleep because all is quiet. I crab across the lawn and crouch below the kitchen window. The house is silent. I attach the suction cup to the glass and give it a light push, the pane breaks away from the frame. I tilt it and draw it back through, placing it at my feet. My arm snakes through the gap and I unlock the catch. The door creaks opens inwards.

I creep inside and close the door behind me. I tune in. All I can hear is the hum of the refrigerator. I make my way into the hallway, the stairs are off to my right. I keep my feet tight to the wall as I ease my way step by step to the next floor, blinking my eyes to adjust to the changing light conditions. I see four doors leading off the landing. Two are shut and two are ajar. I sneak a peek into the first, it's the bathroom. I move to the door opposite and push it open with the tip of my finger. I see a wardrobe in one corner and the foot of a double bed. The bedspread is rolled down to the bottom. I hold my breath. The sound of deep breathing drifts towards me from an unseen person.

This has to be the one.

I edge the door open a little more and slip inside. The room is dark, the thick lining of the curtains blocking out the street lighting outside. The figure is barely visible, just the side of a head and an arm poking out from under the heavy duvet.

I move to the side of the bed, watching the covers rise and fall in time with her breathing. The hunting knife slides free from its sheath attached to the back of my belt. The blade shines silver-grey against the darkness. The figure roles over, her right arm tugging at the quilt cover.

That is my cue.

I jam my left hand across her mouth and bring the blade up to her face. Her eyes burst open and she lets out a muffled scream. I make sure she can see the blade.

'Shhh. Don't make this worse.'

She hits me on the back of the head with her hand. I flatten myself against her, shoving her body into the mattress. She continues to scream behind my hand and kicks her legs in an attempt to throw me off. She catches sight of the blade and her body goes rigid.

'Shhh,' I whisper into her ear. The struggling stops.

I land a heavy blow to the side of her head with the butt of the knife.

She is out cold.

I'm ready to deliver justice, Jono.

Chapter 38

K ray was at her desk staring at the shift rota pinned to the back wall of her office, the second cup of coffee of the day going cold in her hand. The place was empty and the sun had not yet got out of bed. The events of the previous evening churned over in her head, which was exactly what they had been doing since 3am.

She twisted them one way, then the other, but no matter how many different ways she posed the question, she reached the same uncomfortable conclusion. Her phone buzzed. Kray read the text and got up. The desk phone warbled into life but she ignored it.

The lift doors opened and she entered the reception area, raising her hand to the officer behind the desk. She scribbled in a book and opened up a small side office, taking the seat facing the door.

'I went to your house, and when I found you weren't in, I came here,' said Millican, adjusting the visitor's badge dangling from his lapel. He looked like he hadn't slept for a week.

'How long have you known him?' asked Kray.

'Three years.'

'Did you meet when you were in Afghan?'

'Yes, I was posted to Bastion and his patrol team were wiped out by a Taliban attack. All bar two of them were killed and miraculously Alex survived, even though he'd been shot in the head and blown up by an IED. Then he contracted leishmaniasis and because I was in the reservists I was part of his rehabilitation team when he was discharged. How did you know?'

'It wasn't that difficult. One minute we are playing the happy couple curled up on the sofa and the next you are running out the door like I'd bought a do-it-yourself vasectomy kit. You seem to forget, it's my job to put two and two together.'

'Yeah, sorry.'

'What did you do when you left my place?'

'That's why I'm here. I met Alex and I tried to persuade him to give himself up.'

'You fucking did what?'

'I know, I know.'

'You had better start from the beginning.'

Millican stared down at the desk, plucking up the courage to betray a Brother. 'I contacted him using a closed Facebook group, there is only me and him in it since the other guy died. I told him we needed to talk.'

'Where did you meet him and what did he say?'

'We met under the Central Pier. He was very agitated and said he was on a mission to right the wrongs in the justice system. He is fixated by people getting off with crimes they should be sent to prison for. He said he was on a mission.'

'Did he use the word mission?'

'Yes he did. He told me there was more to come, the mission wasn't over. I pushed him hard to hand himself over.'

'Is that when he attacked you?'

'How do you …' he asked.

Kray ran her thumb across her throat describing the red line visible on Millican's neck. He nodded, running a finger along it.

'Did he give any indication who was next on his list?'

'No, he talked about people getting away with killing others, getting away with sexually abusing kids, threatening and stealing. He was banging on about how we all live in a house where the rules were different, he wasn't making much sense.'

'Was he on foot or did he have transport?'

'I don't know, he walked away and left me under the pier. It was dark and I didn't see where he went.'

'What was he wearing?'

'Combat gear.'

'How did you leave it?'

Millican put his hand up to his forehead. 'He said if I got in his way again, he'd kill me.'

'Wait, what did you say about sexually abusing kids?'

'That's what he told me. He said people were sexually abusing kids and getting away with it.'

'Shit,' Kray spat the word into the air. 'You wait here, we will need to do a thorough debrief.'

'Where are you going?'

Kray didn't answer, she simply bolted for the door.

'Her name is Alice Fox, she is the only one on the list who is a convicted sex offender. It has to be her, we have an officer posted outside her house.'

'On my way,' said Bagley, still in bed squinting at the illuminated digits on the clock.

Kray sped out of the station car park.

'Can you patch me through to the officer outside one-four-four Meadow Drive. It's urgent,' she said to the operator, the line went dead as he made the connections. By the sound of it, the call woke up PC Reynolds.

'PC Reynolds.'

'This is DI Kray, do you have eyes on the Fox house?'

'Yes, ma'am, the place is still in darkness, she said she wouldn't be getting up until around 7.30am.'

'Are you looking at the front?'

'Yes.'

'Have you checked the back?'

'No, ma'am, I can check it now. Is there a problem?'

'Bang on the front door and wake her up.'

'Okay, is there a problem?'

'I'm not sure, call me back.' Kray gunned the engine and tore through town. Moments later PC Reynolds was on the phone.

'No response, ma'am, I will go around the back.'

'I'm on my way.'

The line went dead.

Kray skidded to a halt, double parking next to the police car. She leapt out and ran to the front door, hammering on the wooden frame. She hammered again. Reynolds opened the door, every ounce of colour drained from his face. Kray shoved past him and ran up the stairs. The bedroom door was open. She burst inside.

Alice Fox was lying face down, spread-eagled on the bed with her limbs pointing to each of the four corners. Her naked body shone translucent white against the gloom. The pillows, quilt and under sheet lay in a heap against the far wall.

Kray flicked on the light and clasped her hand to her mouth. The bottom half of the bed was awash with blood, pooling into the recesses of the mattress and onto the floor. The handle of a hunting knife protruded from between her legs.

Chapter 39

'You're in a fucking what?' Bagley was leaning over with his hands on the desk. He was so close Kray could feel specks of saliva landing on her face.

'You heard me.' She pulled away.

'A relationship? You're in a relationship with Doctor Christopher Millican?'

'That's right, we've seen each other a couple of times.'

'I don't believe this. Quade is upstairs with the Chief talking reputational damage, and you're telling me your boyfriend has a hotline to a fucking serial killer.'

'It's not like that.'

'Which part? The bit about him being your boyfriend or the one about him having our murder suspect on bloody speed dial? Which part is it?'

'It came as just as much of a shock to me.'

'Have you arrested Millican?'

'On what charge? Being a dick? Christ if we did that half the people in the station would be in custody. He saw the appeal, asked Jarrod outright and came to us with the response, he is under no obligation to do anything else.'

'Maybe not, but he is a Home Office Pathologist who has been up close and personal with Jarrod's victims. So excuse me but I would have expected him to act differently to Jo Public.'

'He did what he thought was right.'

'And how does he contact Jarrod? Through some bloody Facebook group? What do they call themselves, 'Serial Killers R Us'?'

'Now who's being a dick? They had set up the group as a way for them to keep in contact. Jarrod's team leader, a guy named

Jono, was the instigator, he's dead now so it's just Millican and Jarrod.'

Bagley sat down and bunched both fists under his chin. 'Did you know?'

'Of course I didn't know.' It was Kray's turn to explode onto her feet. 'He was at my house, saw the news item and left. Then he turned up here early this morning and told me everything. Until he saw Jarrod's mug on the TV, he had no idea. And I believe him. Don't you insinuate that I have been colluding with him on this.'

'It's not me saying that, but it will be every bugger else. We will have a hard enough time explaining how a woman under police protection gets murdered in her bed, let alone that the DI working the case happens to have a boyfriend who is best mates with the man who did it. Fucking hell, the way this is shaping up, we're all gonna wind up on Jeremy Kyle. When the IPCC and Internal Investigations Team get hold of this our collective bollocks will be well and truly in the vice.'

Kray was about to correct his anatomical error but thought better of it

'How is he?' asked Bagley.

'Who?'

'Millican, how is Millican?'

'Not good, as you can imagine. He blames himself for the death of Alice Fox.'

'That's understandable but he didn't kill her, Jarrod did. What have you got there?'

'It's the forensics report on the dust found at the flat where Hicks was murdered, you remember, I found residue on the arm chair?'

'Yes, what of it?'

'It turns out it was all over the driver's seat in Jarrod's car as well. The analysis says it's a composite of plaster board dust and powdered concrete. They also found it in the footwell of his car along with traces in the carpet at the flat.'

'So is our guy hiding out at a building site? He hasn't returned home, we have his car and he has no friends. Well apart from Millican, are you sure he's—'

'Jarrod is not staying with Millican. I had the same thought about Jarrod laying low in a building which is undergoing renovation, so I set Tavener to work on it.' Kray flipped over the page. 'Looks like there are over five hundred businesses for sale in the Blackpool area. Of those, two thirds of them are being sold as going concerns which leaves one hundred and sixty as unoccupied premises. There are plenty of examples of developers scooping up failed hotels with the intention of turning them into flats. But they start the work only to find the council planners won't grant them a change of use certificate, so the work grinds to a halt. You only have to take a walk along the Prom to find huge hotels closed down in various states of repair. Plaster board dust and concrete says to me he's in a place where construction work has been carried out but it's now vacant, allowing him to stay there.'

'He could have worked on a site?'

'No, sir! He worked across the car park in CJU, that's where the fucker worked. I think it unlikely he was doing cash in hand jobs, shovelling rubble.'

'Point taken. What do you propose?'

'Millican thinks Jarrod was on foot when he met him last night. We make a list of all the unoccupied premises within a five miles radius of town, then look at which ones have had work done on them and target the most likely candidates.'

'We could do that. Alternatively we could use the Facebook group chat to lure Jarrod out into the open.'

'That comes with a hell of a risk. Jarrod was clear that if Millican gets in the way again he's a dead man. Any message we post will put him directly in the firing line.'

'What if we don't involve Millican?'

'How would that work?'

Bagley spent the next ten minutes setting out his plan. The more he spoke, the more enthusiastic he became. When he finished he looked at Kray and said, 'Well?'

'That's a stupid idea!' Kray replied.

'That's a brilliant idea,' Quade said to both Kray and Bagley as they stood in front of her desk. 'I like it. I like it a lot.'

'What do you think, Roz, you've spoken to her?' said Bagley.

'You know what I think. I hate to be the one to pour cold water on such a brilliant plan but there is too much risk.'

'Roz, we are up to our necks in shit here and we need a result.' Quade was pacing. 'This gives us our best opportunity to flush Jarrod out into the open. I understand the new forensics narrows down where he might be hiding out but there are too many properties to search. It could take weeks.'

Quade's PA came in with coffees on a tray.

How the other half live, Kray helped herself.

'Of course we would need to have their full co-operation,' Quade said spooning sugar into her cup.

'That goes without saying,' replied Bagley waiting his turn. 'I'm sure they will be on board with our proposal.'

'This is not right. You want to use Millican's Facebook account to send Jarrod a picture of his ex-girlfriend, Julie Clarke, with a message from her telling him to hand himself in. Is that really what is on offer here? This man is a ruthless killer and you want to put both Clarke and Millican in harm's way?'

'We have a direct line to Jarrod and we can use Julie as leverage, he won't listen to Millican but he might listen to her,' said Bagley.

'And what if Jarrod feels betrayed by the two people he trusts most in this world and comes after them?' Kray said.

'We will protect them,' replied Bagley.

'Like we protected Alice Fox?' Kray was getting nowhere.

'That's enough, Roz, I take your concerns on board but we have to look at all the angles here and Dan has an innovative plan.'

It's a fucking dangerous plan, that's what it is.

'Jarrod must have picked up the message from Millican on a new phone, he wouldn't risk going to an Internet café.' Kray couldn't let it drop. 'Jarrod can't be sure how Millican will react, so he will err on the side of caution, and consider that channel of communication to be compromised. In my opinion that phone will be in a bin somewhere. If you send him a message, he won't receive it.'

'Maybe he will, maybe he won't. It has to be worth a shot. It's better than trawling our resource around every disused property in Blackpool that happens to have some building work going on.' Bagley refused to let go of his good idea.

Quade and Bagley began to flesh out how to trap Jarrod. Kray picked up a sheaf of paper containing the transcripts of the Facebook posts. It ran to five pages. In the early days there was a lot of chatter about how Jono was recovering and how Jarrod was having to change his medication. Millican had played a key role in keeping both men on an even keel, seeing Jarrod regularly to check his progress. When Jarrod started to go downhill with PTSD Millican tried hard to get him to seek help. But Jarrod would have none of it.

Kray scanned the messages.

I'm missing something, what the hell is it?

Her eyes raked the densely packed print, scouring the pages.

What the hell was it, there was something I've missed?

That little voice inside her head that told her something wasn't right was now yelling at the top of its lungs.

'So, what do you think, Roz?' said Bagley.

Kray was zoned out and continued to read.

'Roz, I realise you are not enthusiastic about Dan's plan but you are part of this team and I will—'

Kray raised her hand to interrupt Quade.

'I know where Jarrod is hiding out.'

Chapter 40

Kray was standing in front of her biggest audience of the week. Thirty expectant faces stared back at her; uniformed officers, CID, members of the armed response unit and the woman who headed up the dog unit.

'We have information to suggest that Alex Jarrod, who is wanted for four murders, may be hiding out in a vacant property that has recently undergone building work. You all have a background briefing note regarding Jarrod, please read it and see me afterwards if you have any questions. He used a Facebook account to communicate with two people, Ellis Johnston and Christopher Millican, and in the messages they talk about their experiences of coming home having served in Afghanistan.'

Kray tapped the touch pad on her laptop and the Facebook comments came up on the TV screen. 'On two occasions Jarrod referred to how good it felt to come home to the place he loves the most - the Central Pier. He talks about how he sits on the Promenade watching the sun setting behind the Ferris wheel.

'He met with Millican last night and chose the pier as their rendezvous point, and in his discussion Jarrod said that he could relate to the place. He said the pier was a survivor, just like him. This place obviously has resonance.

'I believe Jarrod is holed up in a building near to the pier, maybe in a position where he can see the structure. This is a map of the area identifying all the vacant sites in that location.' A map came up on the screen with the premises outlined in red. 'Jarrod has probably been planning this for a long time so we can exclude those that have recently become empty.' The map changed to show fewer buildings coloured red. 'And if we also exclude those that have not had any building work done to them we have this.' The final map came up.

'We need to search these locations. This will not be a high-profile raid and we will be led by Inspector Yates. Do you have everything you need, Donna?'

'Yes, Roz, we have several items of clothing from Jarrod's flat. If he's in there we will find him.'

'Good. I cannot stress enough how dangerous Jarrod is. He has a military background and we have to assume he is armed. I want the dog in first, then the armed response unit, then anyone else. Is that clear?'

'Yes, ma'am,' was the murmured reply.

'I do not want us blazing in with blues and twos. We lost him once and I don't want to scare him into running. Uniform, you will be posted out on the street in case he does make a break for it. We've contacted the landlords and property developers and asked them to open up for us but if they are not there, we go in anyway. Does anyone have any questions?'

There was a general shaking of heads as people rose to their feet.

An hour later everything was set. The first target was a huge three-storey hotel on the front, the car park was now home to three yellow skips containing discarded beer cans, bottles and domestic rubbish. The landlord turned the key and the heavy padlock clicked open.

Inspector Yates went in first with an enormous Czech Shepherd dog called Cracker. She gave the command and the dog went into tracking mode. He sniffed at the floor and shot off, followed by two armed officers and Yates. Kray and Tavener brought up the rear.

The place was completely gutted, only the walls and stairwells remained. The overwhelming stench of wet clothes and mould hung in the air. Torch beams flashed around the interior as Cracker sniffed his way up the stairs and along the corridor. Rows of empty rooms with no doors stretched along the length of the building. Cracker bundled along, checking out every room, but nothing of interest turned up. It was the same on the next floor.

They came to the last room and scurried down the service stairs, through the ground floor and back out into the breathable air.

Yates made a fuss of Cracker for a job well done. Kray blew her nose when she emerged outside.

'The next one is one street back, we've not heard from the landlord.'

The team made their way along the front and took a left, then a right. This hotel was on four floors and much smaller. The bolt cutters made short work of the lock. They went inside following the same routine, the place had been stripped bare, with naked block walls and concrete floors. In minutes Cracker had decided this was worse than the first and they were all outside on the pavement again.

'Back to the Prom,' Kray said pointing the way. 'We'll need the bolt cutters for this one as well.' They turned the corner and the massive hotel opened up in front of them. Kray gazed up at the sun-baked orange front. The big bay-fronted windows standing proud on the top floor made her shudder. She could see the Central Pier in all its glory, the Ferris wheel standing out against the clouded sky.

Tavener cut through the lock and shoved open the door. Yates removed the clothes from the sealed plastic bag and once again allowed Cracker to bury his snout in the material.

He shot off.

This one was different to the other two. Woodwork and pallets were strewn across the floor and the upended reception desk lay on its side. The damp stench they had experienced in the other buildings was replaced by the smell of plasterboard.

She put her hand on Tavener's arm.

'Be careful.'

Cracker made a beeline straight for the service stairs, sniffing at the floor and walls as he went. Up and up they climbed, until they reached the top. He hurried down a windowless corridor then he froze, standing absolutely rigid and silent.

Yates caught up with him and signalled to the others. 'He's found something.' Pointing further on.

The armed officers skirted around Yates and the dog with their weapons raised and crept along the last few yards of the passage way. The entrance opened up into a big space with horizontal bars of light cascaded onto the pink walls. One of them peered down the big round hole at the end. He gave the 'All Clear.'

Kray slipped on a pair of overshoes and stepped inside, casting her eyes around the room. Sachets of packet food were lined up in regimental order in one corner, along with bottles of water and a gas stove. Three bottles of vodka stood in a line against the wall next to three mobile phone boxes. Against the other wall lay batteries, medicines, spare laces, cutlery and two bottles of Tabasco sauce all lined up in order. A black holdall and a neatly folded set of clothes sat beside them.

'And I thought I had OCD,' Kray muttered under her breath.

Then she noticed the faces of two women and two men staring at her from across the room. Four pictures were stuck to the wall, each one with a fat red X through it. Tavener joined her, staring at the photographs.

'Shit,' he said.

Kray went up to the faces, examining each one carefully. 'There's one missing.'

'How can you tell?'

'These are blu-tacked to the wall. Look at this.' Kray pointed to the space next to the mug-shot of Billy Hicks. She clicked on her torch and directed the beam at the plasterboard. Four round blue marks stained the surface. 'There was a fifth picture, he's taken it with him.' Kray took out her phone, enabled the flash and started clicking away.

'Who do you think it is?' asked Tavener.

'I don't know.'

'This is great, now all we need to do is wait for him to come back and nab him.'

Kray looked around the room. 'I'm not so sure.'

'Why?'

'Where's the bedding? He has this place kitted really well, but where does he sleep?'

'After all the preparation, you wouldn't leave this lot.' Tavener waved his hand at the supplies.

'You would if you had some place else to go.'

'Hey.' Tavener nudged Kray's arm and nodded in the direction of the hole in the floor and the rope suspended from above. 'Looks like Jarrod is on a suicide mission.'

'That's what I'm afraid of.' The flash went off and the hangman's noose was preserved for prosperity.

Chapter 41

The woman wearing Ugg boots drops a pound coin into my Costa cup. I'm sitting cross-legged on the pavement and can only see up to her knees because my head is bowed. I grunt a 'thank you' as she walks off feeling better about herself.

I'm in a place that catches the sun but I can still feel the cold of the concrete chilling the bones of my arse through my sleeping bag. I've pulled it around my legs for extra warmth but, in reality, I am hiding my boots and combat trousers. They still don't look right.

Whenever I went to the Lakeland I always changed into this gear to give it a worn lived-in look. I didn't wash the clothes I'm stood up in for six weeks and made a point of ensuring they got grubby. But while they are soiled, they are not street soiled – there is a big difference.

It is an amazing feeling. Scientists don't have to waste their time inventing an invisibility cloak, all you have to do is sit on the ground in a busy shopping centre and abracadabra! - no one can see you. Which is good because the next part of my mission requires me to hide in plain sight.

In my peripheral vision I see a police officer and a PCSO ambling up the pedestrianised thoroughfare. An old lady stops them to have a chat. It seems they know one another. She is smiling, throwing her head back and cackling while waving her arms about. The coppers are smiling back and nodding. Eventually she goes on her way and the officers resume their preamble up the street.

I watch them stop and the PCSO flicks her head in my direction. They are ten yards away and the police officer is looking straight at me. My pulse rate spikes.

Stay calm, stay calm.

They change direction and head towards me. I keep my head down and control my breathing.

'Are you all right, sir?' The polished boots of the PCSO enters my field of vision. I look up shielding my eyes from the sun. She looks about fifteen years old.

'Yeah, I'm fine, officer.' I lower my gaze back to the floor and the second pair of bright shiny boots come into view.

'Do you have somewhere to stay?'

I raise my head again, peeking through my fingers. This lad looks about twelve.

'Oh, erm, I have a bed at the B&B on Clevedon Road.' I lied.

'I know it, up by the Hilton?'

'Yeah, that's the one.'

'I'm afraid, sir, you have to move on,' said the man.

Shit what do I do now? How would a proper homeless person reply? Would they argue or simply go away?

'I'm not bothering anyone, officer,' I said.

'I know but you have to move on.'

'Okay.' I step out of my sleeping bag and pick up the cup containing the money. 'Sorry if I've ...'

'That's okay, sir, but we do have to ask you to move on.'

All right, you've told me three times, I get the picture.

I shuffle to my feet, maintaining a slight stoop when gathering up my things. Then I hold my hand up as a sign of goodbye and slope away.

'Excuse me, sir.' It's the PCSO calling after me. I keep my head down and pretend not to hear her. 'Sir, excuse me.'

I carry on going. Then I feel a tug on my sleeve.

Every sinew is poised to take the knife from my boot and slice her head off. Instead, I stop and turn slowly.

'You dropped this.' In her hand is a pound coin. She gives it to me and I grunt a 'thank you.'

If only she knew how close she came, if only she knew.

Chapter 42

The sun had long since given up the last of its glow as it disappeared below the Irish sea. Kray and Tavener were in a car watching the back of the Lakeland Hotel. The rest of the team were dotted around doing the same while the armed response officers were cooped up in the back of a van. The digital clock on the dashboard read 20:50.

The sky was grey with clouds and fine rain cast an opaque veil over the windscreen. The streets were empty save for the occasional passer-by.

'I hate stakeouts,' Tavener said offering Kray a mint. 'They start off with a buzz of high expectation, and dissolve into a pool of boredom.'

'Bloody hell, that's a bit poetic for you. How many have you done?'

'Including this one ... two.'

'You're hardly a seasoned veteran.' She shook her head and popped the sweet in her mouth.

'You only have to stub your toe once to know how much it hurts. It's not necessary—'

'Thanks for that stunning piece of insight. You are making this so much more fun ... after all, it could be shit.'

'Yeah, well it looks like it's about to get worse.' Tavener nodded out of his side window at the figure scampering towards them with his jacket pulled over his head. The back door flew open and Bagley piled into the back.

'Evening,' Kray said staring into the rear-view mirror as Bagley shook water all over her back seats.

'Evening. Nothing has moved at our end,' Bagley said.

'Same here,' muttered Kray. 'The most exciting thing we've seen is a man picking shit up off the pavement.'

'Bloody hell, was he taken short?'

'He had a dog with him at the time.'

'Oh … anyway, I came over to tell you I've arranged for us to be relieved at nine o'clock. So I suggest when they arrive, you get off home. I will handle the handover. We have also doubled up on the uniform officers babysitting the other convicted people on the list. The Chief and the ACC are still in damage limitation mode and we can't afford another slip-up.'

'That sounds a sensible move. You could have told us that over the phone, you didn't need to get soaked.'

'I suppose but I wanted to check in on you.'

The headlights of two cars came into view, cruising to a stop on the other side of the road. Kray switched on the windscreen wipers.

'That will be them,' Bagley said opening his door. 'You two go home and get some rest, we will resume at seven in the morning. I will leave instructions that if anything happens during the night they will contact both of us, Roz.'

'That sounds fine. Good night, Dan,' Kray replied.

'Goodnight, sir,' said Tavener.

Bagley bundled out into the rain and trotted across the tarmac to the first car.

Why the hell can't you behave like this all the time? Instead of being a complete wanker. Kray started the engine and pulled away.

She stared at the road ahead and said nothing.

'Do you think Jarrod will return? He has that place well prepared. If it were me I'd be loathed to leave it,' asked Tavener.

'My gut feeling says he won't be back. We have to go through the process of watching the hotel because that is the right course of action but I think he's done a runner again.'

'Are you making that judgement because the sleeping bag and the picture are missing?'

'Yeah, but more than that the place didn't feel right. The food supplies were so well organised it looked like he had stored them away with a rule and a spirit level. Everything was lined up with precision but there was something out of place, and I can't for the life of me put my finger on it.'

They rode the rest of the journey in silence. After five hours of sitting together in the car there was not much left to say. Kray dropped Tavener off at the station and headed home. Feelings of anxiety raged in her belly.

Kray slid the key into her front door and stepped into the hallway, stooping down to pick up the mail off the floor. She placed the letters on the side table along with her keys. Her phone buzzed, it was Millican calling for the fifth time today.

'Hey, that's good timing I've just walked in,' she said. The voice on the other end was erratic. 'Yes I'm sorry, I couldn't take your calls earlier we were tied up.' Kray hung her coat on the hook and kicked off her shoes.

Millican babbled on while Kray walked into the kitchen, retrieved a bottle of wine from the fridge, a glass off the draining board and sauntered upstairs.

'You are not going to feel good about any of this, Chris, so that's to be expected.' She held the phone in the crook of her neck and turned on the taps, pouring a hefty glug of bubble bath into the swirling water. The bottle and the glass sat patiently on the wooden bridge that spanned across the bath, waiting for the full-frontal assault to ensue. She undressed, leaving her clothes in a pile on the floor.

'If you don't mind, Chris, I'm going to say no. I'm dead on my feet, having only had three hours sleep, and I need to take a bath and go to bed. I've got an early start and if you come over that won't happen.'

The line went dead.

'I don't have the time nor the inclination for that shit.' She muttered under her breath, unscrewing the cap and filling the glass. She watched the bubbles grow into a thick white carpet on the surface of the water. The first chug of wine felt cold in her mouth.

She eased herself into the bath, shutting off the taps. The hot water burned her skin, making her shudder. The image of Catherine Stubbs flashed into her mind with her clothing melted into her flesh under the heat of the flaming aerosol. Kray sunk beneath water until only her head was visible, her anxiety running riot.

The second gulp of wine was followed by a third and in no time the glass was empty. She topped it up.

Should have brought another bottle with me.

Kray ran her fingers across the puckered skin of the scar sliced across her belly. It tingled to the touch. The wine began to do its job and Kray's eyelids slowly closed.

She was drifting down the promenade on a warm bed of fat, white bubbles, past the tower with the Central Pier in the distance. The sun bathed the Ferris wheel with an orange glow against the horizon. Then she was in a kitchen, Joe was preparing a meal. He had that rolling chopping action going on and was laughing, drinking beer. Chris Millican was standing beside him, slicing vegetables with the same chopping action. When Joe drank, so did Chris, they were mirror images of one another. Their mouths were moving but she couldn't catch what they were saying. They flung their heads back and laughed.

Then the scene cut away to the inside of the penthouse at the Lakeland. The blushing pink walls were frosted up with the cold. Four floating faces stared at her, their faces scared with a red X. A blank sheet of paper was pinned to the wall. The hangman's noose dangled above the hole in the floor, next to it Kray could see Jarrod looking out of the shutters at the pier.

Jarrod's supplies were lined up with regimental precision. Everything in perfect alignment.

Kray awoke and sat bolt upright, knocking her glass into the tepid water, the suds were gone. She hauled herself from the bath, wrapped a towel around her body and grabbed her phone, flicking through the photographs she had taken at the Lakeland.

'Where is it? Where is it?' she growled at herself. Then she found it. 'Fuck!'

Kray hit the buttons and called a number. A sleepy Bagley picked up at the other end.

'Roz? What is it?'

'I know who Jarod's next victim is going to be.'

Chapter 43

The woman sitting on the floor to the right of me is called Primrose – quite an odd name for someone who smells of shit. Next to her is Bulldog and the guy on the end is Ken. I guess he's the one with no imagination.

The three of them are in their late-twenties to early forties but look like they have a combined age of two hundred. During the day others have come and gone. It is a transient arrangement where nods and glances are exchanged for the ones who choose not to say anything. One guy turned up, sat on the floor, only to get up and walk off two hours later, and I swear no one registered he was there.

Bulldog rummages in a plastic bag and pulls out an aerosol can. He snaps off the top and puts the spray nozzle into his mouth. He bites it off and spits it onto the floor, revealing the plastic spigot at the end. He grips it between his rotting front teeth and forces the can towards him. His cheeks inflate as the gas fills his mouth and throat. His eyes roll back and he hands the can over to me.

I pretend to have a go.

'Thanks man,' I say in a woozy voice.

The others are so high they don't notice I'm faking it. A metal bucket is ablaze in the centre of the room, the naked flames give the place a demonic feel and fat clouds of smoke cling to what is left of the ceiling. It's like a bizarre campfire scene from a low-budget horror film. I half expect people in robes to burst and sacrifice a goat.

The heat radiates out in a tight circle. The other three would be cold but for the solvent. It keeps them numb. I don't mind the chill seeping through the walls but I miss my view.

Bulldog keels over sideways and wraps himself in his piss-stained sleeping bag, bunching a roll of cardboard under his head to serve as a pillow. He turns his back and lets out a long, low fart. No one stirs.

Primrose takes another blast of solvent gas and follows suit. She struggles to pull her sleeping bag around her and ends up laying half-in, half-out. I lean over and tug it around her, she doesn't even feel it.

Ken and I stare into the flames. He is the youngest of the group but the ravages of sleeping rough and getting high or pissed every day has left its mark on him. He has the haunted look of a man counting down time; his eyes are sunk deep into dark sockets and his cheekbones are sharp. He counts a fist-full of coins into a sock for the fifth time tonight, maybe he can't remember how much money he's made today, or maybe it simply gives him something to do. He wraps the sock into a ball and stuffs it into his pocket.

'Where did you say you were from?' he asks.

'Kind of all over,' I say pretending to sway.

'Cos I'm sure I've seen you around. Have you been to the shopping precinct?'

'Once or twice, I guess. I really appreciate you guys letting me join you. I will pay my way, you know?' I change the subject.

'Yeah man, like every fucker else pays their way. I went to the job centre today.'

'How did you get on?' I say, amazed at the spectacular change of topic.

'Like fucking always, it's a simple equation - no address plus no bank account equals no money. Anyway I only went in for a warm cos it was fucking Baltic.'

'Yeah it was cold all right.'

I am conscious that I don't look or smell right and I'm sure Ken is wary of me. The one thing I'm struggling to hide is my three hundred quid sleeping bag. It was the most expensive one in the shop when I bought it. Still, so far I have managed to keep it under wraps and it is gradually getting soiled from sleeping on floors. I flip my pound coin in the air and catch it. The look on Ken's face says, 'I've had a better day than you.' I'm conscious of the five hundred pounds I have concealed in each of my boots.

Maybe not, Ken.

The fire is dying down to embers, casting a red and orange glow around the brick and breeze block walls. Ken stares into the bucket, drifting off to a better place. I stare at the bucket thinking this is exactly where I want to be; daydreaming about the woman who bottled that off-duty police officer. Two months pregnant my arse. The last time I saw her there was no hint of any pregnancy.

'I've had enough,' I say shuffling to my feet and staggering over to the wall where my belongings are lying on a sheet cardboard.

'See you in the morning,' Ken says, continuing to zone out.

I climb into my sleeping bag and pull it around my shoulders. I don't zip it up in case I have to make a fast exit in the night. Turning my back to the fire I face the wall and unfold the picture stuffed into my shirt, her face stares at me out of the gloom. In my mind's eye I see something different - she is on the steps of the courthouse with her friend, both of them puffing away on cigarettes and laughing. I reach down with my hand and wrap my fingers around the cool glass of the vodka bottle stashed away in my sleeping bag.

A gift for her, when next we meet.

Chapter 44

'Have you checked?' Kray asked attaching a cable to her phone.

'Yes I've checked,' Bagley replied.

'With both of them?'

'Yes, with both of them. I spoke to both officers myself and each one confirmed that she is safe at home.'

'Roz, what the hell is this all about? You weren't making a lot of sense when you called at one this morning. Step through it again.'

Tavener scurried into the incident room, looking bleary eyed. 'I got your text, Roz. I thought we were meeting at the hotel at seven.'

'We were but I need you to see this.' She plugged the other end into her laptop to access her photographs. The large flat screen TV behind her blinked into life. 'There was something bugging me about where Jarrod was hiding.' A picture of the penthouse came up on the screen. 'What do you see when you look at this picture?'

'The result of somebody carefully stocking up on supplies.' Bagley jumped in.

'What else?'

'I see someone who was intending to stay for a few weeks, judging by the quantity that's stashed away,' said Tavener. 'Oh, and Jarrod was contemplating suicide.'

'Don't look at the supplies, focus on the way they have been stored. What does that tell you?'

'He's a tidy freak?'

'Tidy! This guy makes *me* look messy. Everything is put away with precision, this is a guy who likes symmetry and clean lines. Look at the pictures on the wall.' The image changed to show the mugshots. 'If we went down there now I reckon we would find those sheets of paper are dead level, perfectly aligned and exactly the same distance apart. This is a man who obsesses with things looking right. Now look at this ...' The screen changed to another shot. This one showed the sachets of food, the water bottles, the vodka and the camping stove, plus a few kitchen utensils - all of them lined up perfectly. 'What do you see?'

'Nothing new,' said Bagley.

'Look at the gap,' Kray said, pointing at the screen. 'We have a bottle of vodka which has been opened and partly drunk, followed by a gap and then two more bottles. My guess is that gap is the width of a vodka bottle. Looking at the rest of the room I don't believe somebody with that level of OCD could sit there and ignore that anomaly. He's gone and he's taken a bottle with him.'

Tavener was up close to the screen. 'I see what you mean, it's out of kilter with the rest of the room.'

'That's what I think. Now consider his potential next victims.' Kray walked over to the white board and removed a sheet of paper. 'This one was convicted of breaking a bottle over the head of an off-duty police officer. That's who the vodka is for. He's going after Casey Lang.'

I wake with my nose inches from the brickwork, the place is dark and still. I check my watch and the luminous dial tells me it's time to get up. It's de-camp day.

I chomp on a flapjack while stuffing my sleeping bag into the cover. I'm going to need all the energy I can get today. In minutes I am ready to go. I peel three ten-pound notes from the money stashed away in my boot and drop one each beside the sleeping heads of my house mates. They don't stir.

Outside the dank air wraps around me and the pale orange glow of the streetlights washes across the puddles in the road. I set off, heading east across town. This one was always going to prove a challenge but it will be worth it in the end.

I trudge along the side roads, occasionally the local bus service stops to pick up people on their way to work. I envy them sat in their heated environment, nodding gently with the motion of the bus. I munch on another energy bar, the temptation to buy a ticket and save myself a heap of trouble weighs heavily on me. But that would be stupid. What is the point of avoiding the CCTV on the streets only to jump up onto the platform of a bus in full view of the on-board camera? No - as painful as this is - I have to stick to my plan.

After a two hours forced march I emerge through a group of houses onto a disused trading estate. The perimeter fence has long since been dismantled and the security hut lays in ruins. There must have been something worth guarding at some point but that time has long since passed. A huge concrete and metal clad warehouse stands tall in the centre of the plot, its saw-toothed roofline cutting a bleak silhouette against the morning sky. I walk across the yard, the crumbling tarmac and rubble crunching beneath my feet.

I put my full weight behind the door and it grinds open on rusted hinges. The cavernous echo reverberates off the walls as I slip inside. The huge space opens up in front of me; black metal stanchions stand in regimented lines holding up the roof, reminding me of the underneath of the central pier. Maybe that's why I chose this place.

The racking has gone but the tyre marks of forklifts are still visible on the floor. I weave my way through the support structure to the back and through a door into what used to be the changing room. There are no signs of tramps or homeless people living here because the building is too far out of town, making the daily ritual of begging for money almost impossible.

I flick on my torch and the outlines of low benches come into view along with banks of lockers lined up against the walls. I walk over to a pile of wood stacked in the corner, reach down and pull out a screwdriver. I push the flat edge into the lock of the nearest locker, slam the heel of my hand into the handle and twist.

The metallic bang reverberates around the room. I do the same with the locker door next to it. There is a screeching noise and the door opens. I shine the torch inside the two lockers to see food packets, water and a camping stove along with a box of essentials such as cutlery, cable ties, rope and a couple of cheap mobile phones. I check off the supplies in my head, it's not as extensive a larder as I had in the Lakeland but it will do for what I have in mind. This is my bolthole location. I was hoping not to use it but it's better than bedding down in a solvent sniffing hovel.

I dump my sleeping bag inside, lock the doors and make my way back through the warehouse and out onto the yard. It's a relatively short walk from here.

Forty minutes later I am stood in a bus shelter at the mouth of Craven Avenue, looking up the road. The drizzling rain patters onto the Perspex canopy above my head. I can see the police car, a uniformed officer wearing a high-vis jacket stands on the pavement outside one of the houses. He's looking up and down the road as if he is expecting someone.

A bus turns the corner. I shake my head and wave my hand, but it stops anyway and a woman carrying a toddler gets off. The doors hiss shut and it pulls away. I look up the street to see the copper has been joined by a man and a woman, both wearing suits. I strain my eyes – that's the woman who recognised me in CJU, DI Kray I think her name is. All three of them are chatting. Another vehicle pulls up behind them and a man jumps out.

I watch as the new guy walks towards the others. Kray breaks off to meet him.

Fucking hell, now that's a turn up.

The new guy is waving his arms in the air and his head is moving in short jerky movements. They look like they are having an argument. Kray turns her back on him to join the others and all three of them troop into the house. The man returns to his car, sliding himself into the driver's seat.

I expect the car to pull away, but it just sits there.

My head is reeling.

What the hell is he doing there? I have a plan but this is a game-changer.

I pull the hood forward on my coat and stride out, keeping my head down. My breathing is heavy and my heart thuds in my chest. Thirty feet, twenty feet, ten feet – I count down the distance. When I am level with the back-passenger door I yank it open and pile into the back seat.

I pull the knife from my boot and stick the blade into the side of the man's neck.

'Don't turn around, Chris, just fucking drive.'

Chapter 45

Millican jumps in his seat as my knife bites into his neck. 'What the f—'

'Shut up and drive.' I press the blade into his flesh. He swivels a quarter turn and the knife scores a red line about an inch in length to the left side of his Adam's apple.

'Ah!' he yelps and pulls away, bringing his hand up to the wound.

I grab hold of his shoulder with my free hand. 'Drive or I will open you up right now.'

'Okay, okay.'

Millican starts the car and pulls away from the kerb, shifting quickly through the gears. His eyes are fixed on the rear-view mirror.

'Keep your eyes on the road, we don't want any accidents.'

'What the fuck are you doing, Alex?'

'Where's your phone?'

'What?'

'I said where's your phone?'

'In the pocket of my jeans.'

'Keep your right hand on the wheel, lift it out between your thumb and finger of your left hand and give it to me.'

'What the hell?'

'Do it or so help me I will slice you up.' The blade draws more blood as I dig it into his skin.

Millican reaches down to his hip and fiddles with the pocket, shuffling around in his seat. He draws out the mobile and holds it up, I snatch it from his grasp.

'Where are we going?' he says turning his head.

'Take a left at the end.' I push the button in the armrest and the window lowers to half-way, I toss the phone onto the road.

'Alex, this is not what you think.'

'Oh and what am I thinking?'

'I am not helping the police, I was—'

'Shut it, Chris, I'm not interested. Take the next right.'

'Honest, I wasn't. Me and the detective woman are seeing each other.'

'Do you usually date her in the street surrounded by a bunch of coppers?'

'No we had a fight and she wouldn't talk to me, so I showed up at her place of work and saw her driving off. I followed her. That's all. I swear to you, I'm not helping them.'

'Fucking hell, Chis, that is a cracking cover story. Go straight over the traffic lights then turn left.'

'I'm telling you the truth.'

'The Brotherhood, Chris, do you remember the Brotherhood?'

'Of course I do.'

'You don't break the Brotherhood.'

'I didn't, I mean I haven't. Me and Roz are seeing each other, that's it. You got to believe me.'

'No, Chris, I don't.'

We drive along a dual carriage way and turn right off a roundabout into a housing estate. After weaving through a tight labyrinth of streets, we eventually emerge onto a narrow road and pull through a set of gates onto the yard of the disused warehouse.

'Around the side.' We skirt the front of the building and into a large covered lean-to which was once used to wash the lorries. The car is not fully concealed but it will have to do. 'Kill the engine.'

Millican turns the key and sits with his hands in his lap, blood soaking into his shirt collar. I yank at the door handle and jump from the vehicle, brandishing the knife. He had anticipated my move.

Millican launches himself across the driver's seat and flings open the passenger door. I am on the opposite side of the vehicle, forced to watch as he claws himself across the passenger seat. His feet hit the ground and he's away.

'You little shit.'

Millican darts across the yard and disappears through a side door into the building. He has ten metres start on me, but I figure cutting up dead people for a living isn't conducive to honing your fitness. I slam my hand down onto the bonnet and give chase.

The sound of his trainers slapping against the concrete floor echoes around the cavernous space. I am gaining on him as he dodges between the metal stanchions towards the back of the building. I am nearly on him but he switches direction, doubling back on himself. I can see the exertion etched into his face, his arms and legs pumping at the air.

He has his eyes fixed on the door at the front. If he makes it he will be across the yard and onto the estate. I power forward, gaining on him with every stride. His head is tilted back as he gulps air into his burning lungs like a sprinter going for the tape.

He's tiring - I'm not.

I shove him sideways. He spirals off and collides with one of the girders holding up the roof. There is a sickening splat as his face leaves a bloody smear on the black metal surface. His body corkscrews in the air and he lands in a twisted heap on the floor. I stand over him with my hands on my knees, still clutching my knife.

He doesn't move.

'Fucking hell, how many more of you are there?' Casey Lang was standing in the centre of the room with her hands on her hips, ash dropping from her cigarette onto the carpet. She was dressed in jeans and a baggy top, her blonde hair drawn back in a top knot so tight it made her look permanently surprised. A PC was stood in the doorway to the kitchen clutching a cup of tea, her expression read *please get me out of here*.

Kray, Bagley and the uniformed officer walked single file into the lounge.

'Yeah, come in why don't you, every bugger else does,' Lang continued, slumping down onto the sofa, puffing a plume of smoke into the air.

'Casey we need to talk to you,' said Bagley taking a seat in the armchair to the side. Kray remained standing, happy for her boss to take the lead.

'Is that all you lot do? Talk? I thought there was some guy out there wanting to kill me and all you people want to do is chat. Shouldn't you be out there catching the fucker?'

'We are, Casey,' said Bagley.

'Really? I have Policeman Plod sat outside in his toy car all day, while Mrs Plod here sits on my sofa drinking bloody tea. Now you two show up and I suppose it's party time?'

'Casey we think it might be best if we move you to a safe house until we have the suspect in custody.'

'A safe house! Does that mean I will have more of this to deal with? Does that mean I can't see my friends? Because if it does, then I don't think so. I knew you lot were up to something.'

'We cannot force you to go but we think it would be wise in the short term.'

'Well you can think again, Tonto, cos I'm not going anywhere. This is you lot trying to make life difficult for me.'

There was a knock at the front door. Lang stubbed her fag out on a saucer, glared at Bagley and walked into the hallway.

'Oh hi, babe, I got your text,' said a woman's voice.

'I'm fucking swamped with them now.' Casey came back into the room to resume her position on the sofa, the new woman waddled in sporting the same top-knot facelift.

'Who the fuck are all these?' said the new woman flopping down beside Lang and pulling a packet of cigarettes from her pocket. She offered one to her friend. 'I can see why you needed backup.'

'I am DCI Bagley and this is DI Kray.'

Kray stared at the new woman, her face looked familiar.

'Can I ask who you are?' said Bagley.

'You can fucking ask.' She exaggerated every word and bobbled her head from side to side. Both women laughed.

'She's my mate, 'nuff said.'

'Casey, can we continue this discussion in private?' asked Bagley.

'Anything you say to me, you can say in front of her.' Lang turned to her friend, offering a light. 'Do you know they want me to go into a safe house?'

'You what? I thought you were under police protection already,' she said drawing hard on her cigarette and puffing smoke against the yellow ceiling.

'It will be easier for us to control the environment,' said Bagley.

'Control the environment? What are you David Attenborough now?' Lang slapped her friend on the leg and they both rolled back their heads with laughter. 'Look DCI whatever-your-name-is I am staying here and you need to give me more protection if you want to 'control the environment'.' She did the same bobbly head thing, over pronouncing the last three words.

'You're Jenny Wilks,' Kray said staring at the heavily pregnant woman.

'Are you fucking psychic or something?' Wilks replied, slapping her hand on her thigh. 'How'd you know that?'

'I saw a photograph of you taken outside the courtroom on the day of the trial,' Kray replied, the jigsaw falling into place.

'Oh yeah, remember that, Jen,' said Lang. 'That was a belting day that was, we got proper leathered.'

Kray continued to stare at Wilks.

'What are you looking at?' Wilks said. 'Is it because I'm pregnant and smoking?' Kray shook her head. 'I smoke because I want a smaller baby to make the birth easier. My brother was nearly ten pounds and it tore my mum to shreds and I don't want none of that. And he ended up in intensive care with complications. So, before you give me any of your judgemental looks just remember I am doing this for my baby, all right?' Wilks raised her cigarette in the air in a salute.

'No I wasn't thinking that,' replied Kray.

'Well it looked like it to me.'

'I was thinking you two are very close.'

'Yeah we are, like sisters.'

'You must have been delighted when you discovered you were both pregnant at the same time.'

The women looked at each other with a double take. You could smell the wood burning as both women worked out the implications of what had just been said.

'Yeah well sometimes things don't work out.' Lang finally remembered her lines.

Kray decided to leave Bagley to it. She wandered out of the house and stood on the front step, looking up and down the street for Millican's car. She pulled her phone from her pocket and dialled his number. It went straight to voicemail.

Why do blokes always give it the little-boy-sulk routine when things don't go their way?

Chapter 46

I drag Millican across the warehouse floor into the changing room and loop his arms through the inlet pipework of a radiator, securing them behind his back. He flops onto his side. An ugly blue ridge has developed down the side of his face and his left eye has blown up to the size of an egg. His nose is bent over to one side with blood running down the side of his mouth. He doesn't look good.

I take an energy bar from a box and munch on it, my head spinning with permutations. The opportunity to snatch Millican and use his car is an unexpected twist, neither of which I had factored into my plan, but then a good soldier will always adapt to suit the circumstances. With the police buzzing around Lang like flies around shit I need to rethink.

I break another one from the box and chomp on it as if my life depended on it.

Think man, think. Keep the mission goals in mind and think.

Millican's breathing is shallow and a circle of blood has grown around his head on the concrete floor. His face is the colour of uncooked pastry.

My head is fuzzy, I'm not thinking clearly.

Then Jono's words thunder into my brain, 'It's time to deliver justice, boys.'

I leave Millican, walk out of the changing room and scout around the vast warehouse. Ten minutes later I find what I'm looking for - a heavy metal bar. There is a set of double doors at the back of the building and the bar makes short work of the padlock, I swing one of them open and run to the car, then drive into the warehouse.

With the keys in my pocket I close up the door and head out into the yard. I have no idea which direction to go. I stride off in search of a shop, a pharmacy and a phone box.

I return an hour later to find Millican lying on his side with his eyes shut. My immediate reaction is that he's faking, but the closer I get the more it becomes apparent he's still out cold. He hasn't moved since I left.

'Come on, Chris, wake up.' I dump the bag, kneel beside him and tap his shoulder. I try again – nothing.

I walk to the car and pull one of the newly acquired tea towels from the pack, then proceed to wipe both of the number plates clean. I fish around in the bag to pull out a small bottle, the top twists off and I remove the tiny brush, scraping off the excess. The smell fills my senses and I'm transported back to the squat where you had solvent for breakfast.

Sitting cross-legged on the floor, I steady my hand and draw a black line across the white surface of the number plate. After several more strokes I have transformed the letter F into a convincing E. I repeat the process on the rear number plate. That is the easy one. I do the same trick and the number 0 becomes an 8.

I stand back to admire my handiwork. The amended plates would not stand up to close scrutiny but to a NPR camera they will do fine.

Millican looks like death. I place my fingers to his neck, his pulse is strong. I unbox both the phones and insert the battery into one of them, the screen comes to life and I page through the basic set-up. The flash illuminates the locker room and I spend the next ten minutes working out the menu settings.

How can it be easier to steal a car than work a bloody phone?

Eventually I have everything I need. I pocket the SIM card and walk back to the car. The plates must have dried by now and I drive out onto the yard closing the door behind me.

My new strategy fizzes in my head.

This is not what I planned … it's better.

Chapter 47

'You've reached the voicemail of Chris Millican, please leave a message.' The recorded voice played once more in Kray's ear. She disconnected the call. It was her third attempt and she had an uneasy feeling in the pit of her stomach that would not go away.

His phone must be dead.

Since returning to the station time had passed by in a blur. Leads were being generated on an almost hourly basis as the intelligence gathering gained momentum. The public appeal had produced a deluge of Jarrod sightings, each one leading to nothing. Every scrap of information needed to be assessed, prioritised and inputted into the huge logistical nightmare that was the investigation plan. Bagley trudged into her office and slumped himself in a chair.

'Sometimes I wonder if we protect the right people.' He flung his head back with his arms in the air, arching his back.

'I didn't think you would get anywhere with the lovely Ms Lang so I came back to get some work done.'

'You'd think I was the one trying to kill her.'

'She didn't like you.'

'She didn't like any of us. The PC took me to one side and asked to be reassigned.'

'What did you say?'

'I said I would see what I could do.'

'How did you leave it?'

'The short answer to that is – badly. The more I tried to persuade her that moving to a safe house was in her best interest, the more abusive she became. We had tears and tantrums and she ended telling us to leave. And we are the ones trying to help!'

'Just remember, she bottled the last copper that tried to help so, I would say, you got off lightly.'

'We will maintain the protection unit but I'm not sure how long Quade will allow us to drive a horse and cart through the overtime budget. I got an email from her saying she wanted an update this afternoon, which is ACPO speak for 'Come and see my spreadsheet'.'

'Let me know if you need anything.'

'Yes I will. By the way, we can't have your boyfriend turning up whenever he feels like it.'

'I know, I'm sorry about that. I've been cooling things off and he followed me to Lang's place. It won't happen again.'

Bagley nodded his approval. 'Something's been bugging me.'

'I know, I saw her.'

'No not that. We have a heavy presence at Lang's place and Jarrod is bound to see that. It's unlikely he will have a crack at taking her out. But what about the other convicted people on the list?'

'He killed Alice Fox when we had an officer parked outside so he's not averse to taking risks.'

'We believe his sights are set firmly on Lang but it would be worthwhile running through the outstanding people just to me sure.'

'I'll take another look.'

'Good, well I've got to prepare for a meeting with an ACC and her spreadsheet.' He got up from the chair and left. Kray watched him go and shook her head.

One minute you are a delight to work with and the next you are jumping on the dick-head button for all you're worth.

Kray pursed her lips, annoyed at Bagley's inconsistency. Taking a fresh look at the list was a good idea. Jarrod might well change tack and have a person in reserve. She picked up the phone and spoke to Tavener to set the wheels in motion. He had wanted to meet with her straightaway but Kray stalled him, she had her own bug that needed sorting out first.

Kray pulled up a chair next to the geeky-looking guy wearing glasses and sporting a comedy comb-over. She wasn't going to spend her time looking over the top of the wall of computer screens on his desk. Brian Taylor tilted his glasses onto the end of his nose and looked up.

'Oh hi, how are you?'

'Fine thanks, I wonder if you could take a quick look at a phone number for me?'

'I'm just in the middle of something—'

'It will only take a minute. I have a bad feeling and I need to check it out.'

'Give me a second.' Taylor's hand whizzed around the mouse-mat closing down screens and minimising windows. Kray sat patiently, playing with her wedding ring

Her heart was pounding from having ran up the stairs, she had just arrived back at the station having visited Millican's place. The house was empty and his car was gone. She had called the hospital and they advised her he had not shown up for work today. The sinking feeling in the pit of her stomach would not go away.

Kray pulled her mobile from her pocket and retrieved a number from the address book.

'This is it.' She handed Taylor the phone. 'I've called it several times and it goes straight through to voicemail.'

'What do you want me to do?'

'Can you locate it?'

'I can try.' The screens lit up showing maps of the area and the locations of the cell phone masts. 'It is not currently responding which would indicate the handset has been immobilised in some way.'

Kray sat back in her chair, running her fingers through her hair. 'Can you give me its last known location?'

'I should be able to.' The screens changed again and he jabbed a finger at the map. 'Borland Way was when it stopped transmitting, around here, opposite the garage. You can see for yourself.'

Taylor wheeled his chair to the side and Kray slid into his place. She traced the map with her finger.

Two roads, situated close together, made her stomach fall through the floor – Borland Way and Craven Avenue.

Fuck.

Chapter 48

Kray flagged down the first police car that swung into the station.

'You on a shout?' she asked the uniformed woman behind the wheel.

'No, ma'am, I have some paperwork to complete.'

'Good.' Kray slid into the passenger seat. 'Drive to the south end of Borland Way and put your lights on - we're in a hurry.'

'Okay, do we need back up?'

'No, but we need to get there fast.'

The woman radioed into the control room to report her change of movements as she sped out of the gates. The vehicles up ahead parted like the Red Sea as the flashing blue lights filled their rear-view mirrors.

'What are we doing, ma'am?'

'We need to find something. What's your name?'

'Sergeant Angela Hucknall. You're DI Roz Kray, aren't you?'

'Yes, just Roz will do.' They hurtled along leaving lines of stranded cars in their wake.

'Borland Way is a dual carriageway. When we get there I want you to straddle both lanes and slow down. About half way up there's a garage on the left, I want you to stop.'

'I know where it is.' Hucknall pulled the car onto the roundabout, turning left, straddling the white line separating the lanes. A procession of cars crawled along behind.

'Okay, stop here. You get out and make sure the people behind are behaving themselves, I need to go find a phone.'

They both jumped from the car. Hucknall went to the back with her arms out stretched while Kray walked up the carriageway towards the garage. The road surface glistened with the earlier rain and puddles hugged the gutters. Kray scanned along the ground, her head twisting from side to side. Step by step she combed the surface in front of her, there were food cartons, cans and plastic bottles but nothing that looked like a phone.

Then she saw it. Tucked against the kerb was a silver-grey casing. Kray pulled a glove from her pocket, slipped it on and picked up the remnants of the phone. The innards were smashed and the battery missing. She dropped it into a plastic bag and scoured the area for more fragments. After a couple of minutes, she gave up and walked back to the car, the roundabout behind them was in gridlock.

'Okay, let's go,' Kray called out, getting into the passenger seat.

'Got what you came for?'

'Got some of it.'

'Back to the station.'

'No, my house.'

'That's very kind, Roz but I don't have time for tea.'

'Neither do I.'

Kray was sitting behind her desk, nursing a coffee and staring into space. She had been back at the station for an hour and in that time had managed to upset the forensics guys and piss off ACC Quade by refusing to engage in a discussion about overtime projections. She would have to buy biscuits to say sorry to the one and chop her arm off to appease the other.

Bagley stuck his head around the door.

'Hey,' he said.

'How did it go with Quade?'

'She is covering her back for when the month-end reckoning comes around. We are spending a shit load of money on this case and she needs to be able to justify it. She'll be fine, much better than the head of forensics.'

'Oh, how come?'

'Did you tell one of his supervisors that unless he dropped everything and dusted a wine bottle for prints, you were going to shove it up his arse?'

'I might have said something along those lines. The guy was being difficult.'

'He's not a happy bunny.'

'Okay I'll make it a whole tin of sorry biscuits. I'm waiting for them to call me with the results.'

'They called me instead. I'm sorry, Roz but the prints they pulled off the phone casing match the ones on the wine bottle from your house. That phone belongs to Chris Millican.'

'Oh shit.' Kray put her head in her hands.

'There could be a whole host of reasonable explanations why his mobile ended up on the road.'

'Is there any CCTV in the area?'

'No, I checked. I asked the garage if their forecourt surveillance covered the road and it doesn't. It's late. Why don't you call it a day and go home? We can pick this stuff up in the morning. I know what you're thinking, but Millican is probably pissed in a pub somewhere wondering where the fuck his phone's gone.'

'I got a bad feeling about this, Dan. I reckon Jarrod has him. He said he would kill him if he got in the way again. Chris is not at home and hasn't showed up for work.'

'You're involved, you're bound to think the worst. Go home and get some rest.'

'Yeah, maybe you're right.'

Kray gathered her things together and waved Bagley goodnight. The drive home was a damned sight calmer than her blues and twos ride with Hucknall. She opened up her front door, walked into the hallway and dumped her stuff on the floor. It was eight thirty and the only thing she wanted was a hot bath and cold wine.

Armed with a bottle and a glass, she ran the bath, emptying the last of the foam into the water. The first glugs of wine felt good. She tried to relax but the nagging sensation would not leave her alone.

Where the fuck was he?

She dipped her toe into the water and heard the letterbox snap shut downstairs, followed by a clunk as something landed on the mat.

What the hell was that?

She wrapped a towel around herself and headed downstairs, clutching her wine. A small, oblong object lay on the floor by the front door. She picked it up, turning it over and over in her hand – it was a mobile phone.

What the ...

Kray went to her front room window and looked up and down the road, all was clear. She pressed the on button, the screen shone blue and the menu came up. Kray stared at the handset trying to fathom why someone would drop it through her letterbox. The phone dinged and a message logo appeared.

She scrolled down and hit open.

The picture of Chis Millican filled the screen. He was lying on his side with his hands behind his back, an angry bruise ran along the left-hand side of his face and his eyes were closed. The floor beneath his head was stained red. At the top of the picture was written: *Lose the security around the Lang house or lose your boyfriend. Tell no one.*

Chapter 49

The office was empty, which was no surprise as the clock on the wall read 2.20am. Kray and Bagley were perched at a desk surrounded by a fortress of monitors, drinking coffee and waiting.

'How long did he say?' asked Bagley.

'He had to drive in from Preston so he said he'd be here around half past.'

Kray was struggling to keep her emotions in check. When the picture of Millican flashed up on the phone she almost dropped it. For the next hour she wandered about her house torturing herself with what she should do next. Eventually her copper's brain kicked in and she called Bagley.

The double doors swung open and Taylor paced in.

'I got here as soon as I could, it sounded like an emergency.'

'Thank you, it is. Brian, this is DCI Bagley, we need you to tell us everything you can about this phone.' She handed over the device in a plastic bag.

'Can I take it out?'

'Yes, it's already dusted negative for fingerprints. It dropped through my letter box and when I switched it on I received a text message.'

Taylor pushed a couple of buttons and the picture of Millican popped up.

'Oh shit. I see what you mean,' said Taylor screwing up his face. 'Okay let's see what we have.' He pushed more buttons on the handset and input the information into the system. 'This won't go any faster with you looking over my shoulder,' he said. 'Go get yourselves a coffee and bring one for me while you're at it.'

'Of course.' Kray walked over to the vending machine, followed by Bagley.

'You were right,' he said.

'I had a feeling something was wrong.' The machine whirred away brewing brown liquid, masquerading as a satisfying beverage.

'We'll need to run the plan past Quade in the morning, but I'm sure she'll go for it.'

'It's the obvious play, I'm not sure we have other options.'

'You don't have to do this, you know? No one would blame you if you took a step back.'

'And do what? Sit on my sofa eating chocolate and getting drunk? No thanks, I'm better off here. Anyway, you would soon get fed up with me calling you every five minutes.'

'You're developing a bit of a track record for calling in the middle of the night.' Bagley paused to remove a drink from the dispenser. 'Did you consider keeping it to yourself?'

'Yes, but that would have been a stupid thing to do.'

'It's tough. We'll get him back.' He placed his hand on her shoulder.

'I was able to contact most people and they will be in for six. Tavener is coming in at five.'

'He's a good lad.'

'Okay, I've got something,' Taylor called out, the two of them trooped back to his desk and handed him a coffee. 'We are dealing with two mobiles. This one …' He held up the one Kray had given him. 'Is brand new and has never been used. The second phone, which was used to take the photograph and send the text, has also never been used. They have no call or messaging history other than the text.'

'Where is the second phone now?' asked Bagley.

'Hold your horses, I'm coming to that. The photo was taken a little after 3pm yesterday afternoon but the phone was not active at that time.'

'How do you mean?' asked Kray.

'This phone is pretty basic, it makes calls, sends texts, takes pictures and that's about it. My assumption is that the second phone is the same type. Whoever took the picture installed the battery but left out the SIM card. The only way to track the device is when it pings against the cell masts using the phone network.'

'So, there is no GPS?' asked Bagley.

'Not on a cheap device like this.'

'There is no way to identify the location where the picture was taken.'

'Not from the phone.'

'Bollocks,' rapped Bagley.

'So, we could contact Jarrod on the second phone?'

'Have you tried the number?' asked Taylor.

'No, not yet,' said Kray.

'Do you want to try it now?'

'Yes, do it.'

Taylor dialled the phone number into the system. There was an agonising few seconds of silence, all three of them held their breath – then the network's message service clicked in.

'The handset is not responding.'

'When did they become active?' Kray asked.

'That's the interesting part. Both phones became active within a minute of each other at around nine o'clock last night. The person must have assembled them in the same location because they were both picked up by the same three masts. He installed the batteries and the SIM cards and sent the text.'

'Where was that?'

'It was here.' Taylor brought a map up on the screen with a blue dot pulsating on one of the roads.

'That's my street,' said Kray, 'that's where I fucking live!'

Chapter 50

'Are we all clear on what needs to happen?' Kray was on her feet in the incident room, briefing the team. 'We need to do this quickly and with a minimum amount of fuss. Jarrod could be watching. He is going to expect a certain amount of movement but we cannot over play our hand. Brian, you have the second phone, contact us the moment Jarrod's mobile becomes active.' Taylor raised his hand and nodded.

Kray checked her phone. 'Has anyone heard from DCI Bagley?' A mumbled 'No' reverberated around the room. 'Okay, let's go.'

They piled into cars and vans and drove out of the station. Tavener was riding with Kray.

'You okay?' he asked.

'As okay as I could be given the circumstances.'

'How do you think Jarrod knew where you lived?'

'I don't know, it could be as simple as he followed me to my house. It seems too much of a coincidence that fifteen minutes after I get home he's dropping the mobile onto my doormat. It's the easiest explanation. It also means he has use of a car and we have to work on the assumption that it belongs to Chris Millican.'

'We've put out a description of the vehicle, everyone is aware. How is Baggers behaving?'

'You mean DCI Bagley?'

'Yes I mean him.'

'One day you are going to slip up and he'll have your bollocks in a sling.'

'Point taken.'

'He's being bloody marvellous, if you must know, which is pissing me off no end.'

'Maybe he's settling in?'

'Yeah, maybe.'

The early morning start was catching up with both of them and they travelled the rest of the journey in silence. They pulled up in a side street and walked to the back of Lang's house. Kray opened the gate and the reason for Bagley not having called earlier became clear.

If Jarrod is within half a mile of this we're fucked.

Kray could see through the kitchen window that events had taken a turn for the worse. She and Tavener opened the back door, stepping into the mad house.

'I'm telling you, I'm not fucking going.' Lang was toe-to-toe with Bagley, screaming in his face.

'I have explained to you, Casey, that you are required to vacate the premises as part of our ongoing investigations. Failure to do so—'

'Fucking hell here's another two!' Lang waved her arm in Kray's direction. 'It's Mystic Meg and the one out of Game of Thrones.'

Bagley continued, 'I have told you—'

'And I've told you to fuck off.' Casey stormed off into the other room.

'Everything okay?' Kray asked.

Bagley shook his head and traipsed after Lang into the lounge. Tavener went to follow but Kray took his arm.

'Probably best not,' she said wrinkling up her nose.

'Game of Thrones?'

'I think she means the tall one.'

'That would make you ...'

'Don't ask.'

The row continued unabated; the more Bagley tried to persuade the more abusive she became. In the end Bagley snapped. 'Casey Lang, I am arresting you for obstructing a police officer ...'

Ten minutes later the house was quiet.

'The custody sergeant is going to love you,' Kray said to Bagley.

'Yeah, plus the two PCs who had to get her into the car and down to the station. I am not going to be a popular boy.'

A woman dressed in jeans and a baggy top, with her hair drawn back into a top knot came into the room. She wasn't a dead ringer for Lang but could pass at a distance.

'Have you familiarised yourself with the house?' Kray asked.

'Yes, I have, ma'am.'

'There will be no overt police presence anywhere near here. An officer will be with you in the house, keeping out of sight, at all times. Your job is to watch TV, make tea and do normal things, it's important for Jarrod to see you. We will be a stone's throw away. You have your radio and we will alert you of any movement. When we see Jarrod it will be a call to all units.'

'I understand,' she said.

Bagley and Kray walked out the back door and returned to their car. She gazed out of the window with a one-thousand-yard stare.

'Let's hope he makes a move,' he said.

'Yeah and let's hope he switches on that bloody phone.'

Chapter 51

'Come on, Chris, time to wake up.' I shake his shoulder and he stirs. He's been moaning and groaning for the last half an hour, so I figure he is floating just below the surface. 'Come on, up you get.' I kneel down and sit him upright, his head slumps forward and he coughs blood and saliva onto his chest.

'What …' He falls way short of completing the sentence.

'You ran into a pillar and knocked yourself out.'

'Shit, what is this?' He tries to move his arms but the ties bind them in place.

'You took quite a bang to the head, it must hurt like a bastard.'

'Where the hell am I?' He manages to lift his head up. It looks like someone has inflated the left side of his face with a bicycle pump, pushing his nose over to one side, his eye completely closed.

'You're safe, for now.'

'You attacked me!'

'We went for a ride in your car and you ran into a metal stanchion. So, technically—'

'You held a knife to my throat.'

'Oh yeah, I forgot about that.'

He strikes out with his legs and kicks me in the thigh.

'Remember your hostage training, Chris. The first priority is to work out how to stay alive, and kicking me isn't going to help.'

'You're not going to kill me. If you were you would have done it by now.'

'Maybe the time isn't right.' I jump up, forcing my knee into his chest and drawing my knife. I hold the blade inches from his good eye. He gasps for air and stares at the tip of the blade. 'Here, eat this.' I step off him to unwrap a flapjack and hold it near his mouth. 'If you bite my fingers I will remove your teeth one at a time.'

He leans forward and takes a chunk out of the bar. I hold up a water bottle.

'You need to drink.'

He slurps at the water. 'It tastes funny.' He pulls his mouth away.

'With the shot you took to the head everything is going to taste weird, now drink.'

He gulps down the fluid and motions for more to eat.

'How long have I been here?'

'Long enough.'

'What are you going to do?' He pulls away again splashing water down his chin.

'Complete the mission, Chris.'

'There is no mission, Alex. I told you before.'

I force more liquid into his mouth and he chokes. 'I told you before, there is.'

'What's up with my eye?'

'It's swollen, like the rest of your face. Good job I don't have a mirror for you to see for yourself.'

'Don't go through with it, Alex.' He looks up at me, squinting through his distended eyelids.

'Too late for that. As the man says, 'I've started so I'll finish'.'

'That's a fucking quiz show, this is real life.'

'Yes, it is real life and that makes it all the more important to finish the job. Now that's enough talking.'

'What are you going to do with me?'

'I said that's enough!' I hold the blade against his throat. 'One more word and I will finish this now.'

For the next half an hour we sit in silence. I occasionally walk from the changing room to look outside but there is no one about. Gradually his good eye closes and his head lolls over to the side. I lay him down onto the floor.

The dosage on the side of the box read *one to two tablets for a restful night's sleep*. I gave him six crushed up in the water so he should be out for a while.

I check my watch and pick up the keys. I can't spend all day chatting. I've got things to do.

I glide the car over to the side and park up. I check the mirrors and step out onto the pavement, jangling a handful of change in my pocket. *Do you know how difficult it is to find a working public telephone these days?*

I open the door and push at the filthy buttons. A woman answers and I feed a pound coin into the slot.

I state my business and the line goes dead and, after what feels like a lifetime, a man picks up. Two minutes of blunt conversation later and I'm back in the car heading out of town towards the zoo.

I stick to the side roads as much as possible which makes the journey long and tiresome, but I arrive without incident. The clock on the dashboard reads 2:40. The house up ahead is quiet. There is no visible police presence but I cannot take anything for granted. I sit and wait with my latest purchase lying in the boot.

You would swear I was trying to buy an assault rifle, there were so many questions.

'Who is it for, sir?'

Never you mind.

'Have you considered other models?'

No, I want this one because I can take it away now.

'Paying cash, sir, that's unusual.'

It's fucking legal tender, you idiot.

'How about if I throw in this blanket, free of charge.'

Oh all right then.

My wilting smile and a slight nod of the head was my answer to every question. I handed over the money and walked out. If everything goes to plan I'm going to need this. The problem is, I'm not sure when.

I'm mulling over the uncertainty of what lays ahead when the front door opens. My pulse rate spikes.

I might get to use my new purchase sooner than I thought.

Chapter 52

Kray had reached the conclusion that Tavener's assessment of stakeouts was very perceptive – she was going off her tits with boredom. But then eight hours spent waiting for something to happen will do that to a person.

The passenger door swung open and Bagley jumped in carrying a couple of pizza boxes and two cans of coke.

'They were shutting up shop for the night, I got the last two. I hope you like hot and spicy?'

'What's the alternative?' He handed her the coke and one of the boxes. 'I guess it's hot and spicy then.'

'Do you think Jarrod will put in an appearance?' Bagley said cramming half a slice into his mouth.

'Jarrod is a night owl, it might still be too early.'

'That wasn't what I meant.'

Kray shook her head and nibbled at the doughy mess. 'The longer we sit here the more I'm unsure. I'm not saying this is the wrong response but it feels too contrived, too obvious.'

'I'm confident he'll show up and when he does we'll find Millican.'

Kray had shoved any thoughts of Chris Millican to the back of her mind. She was not going to function well if her anxieties got the better of her. The pizza tasted as bad as it looked, stealing away her appetite. She ran her finger along the scar on her cheek. It had been itching for the past two hours.

'When this case is done they will resume the recruitment process to head up CJU,' Bagley said.

'Oh, how do you know that?'

'You're in the prime spot for that role you know?'

'And … how do you know that?'

Bagley munched on his pizza and tapped the side of his nose. 'I just do.'

Kray put the box and can onto the dashboard and turned square on to Bagley. 'No, come on, how do you know that?'

'I had a chat with Mary and told her you would be perfect in the role.'

'You had a chat with Mary Quade?'

'Yes, I told her your man-management skills are excellent, your attention to detail is off the scale and you know what good policing is all about. You'd be great.'

'Do you and *Mary* chat often?'

'Yes, we go back a long way. We were on the same course at Hendon, she was head and shoulders above anyone else and we've kept in touch ever since. We did our last posting together in Manchester, then when she came here I thought, well …'

'Why did you do that?'

'Do what?'

'Feel the need to speak to the person running the selection board on my behalf?'

'I think it's the best thing all round.'

'You want me out of CID?'

'Oh come on, Roz, don't be so dramatic. You applied for the role so I figured a helping hand could do no harm. She listens to me, you'll be fine.'

Kray straightened in her seat and glared out of the windscreen. 'Is that what the last few days have been about?'

'What, I don't follow?'

'Normally, Dan, you are a complete arse, yet lately you've been acting like we're best mates.'

'Christ, Roz, steady on. I was giving you a friendly leg-up, nothing more. Don't throw it back in my face.'

Kray balled her fists in her lap.

'I don't need a fucking leg-up and I sure as hell don't need one from you! You came into the department and made it clear from day one that we were on a collision course. You saw me as a threat and attacked me at every opportunity. Then you start playing nicey-nicey. I get it now.'

'Get what?'

'The change in your behaviour.'

'You are way out of order, Roz. I'm prepared to overlook it because you are under stress but this had better stop.'

'Or what? You'll go back to being DCI Nasty Twat. You've only been acting like a normal person because you think I'm on my way out the door. You take the fucking biscuit, Dan, just when I was beginning to like you, you come out all guns blazing acting like a dick.'

'Roz, that's enough!'

'Yeah, you're fucking right about that.' Roz picked the pizza off the dashboard and got out of the car, slamming the door behind her. She marched up the street, turned right at the end and launched herself into the passenger seat of another parked car.

'I need a change of scenery. Have some pizza.'

'Cheers, Roz,' said Tavener. 'It's all quiet here, how about you?'

Chapter 53

I watch as a satellite scuds across the black emptiness of the night sky. It is freezing cold and the first signs of frost are forming on the ground. My breath condenses in the air, I check my watch and move back inside the warehouse. I've waited long enough ... it's time to go.

I sever the ties binding Millican's wrists and pull his arms free of the pipework. He is heavy as I drag him through the changing room into the warehouse. The car door is open and I dump him onto the back seat, covering him with the blanket. My heart is racing, I can feel the blood surging through my temples. I get in and drive out into the yard, pulling onto the main road passing through the estate.

Keep the speed down.

I am less concerned about CCTV cameras, so choose the major routes through town. The streets are almost empty. My mind is oblivious to the journey, all I can see is the destination and the outcome. In what seems like no time, I swing a left turn onto Chapel Street and pull into the car park on the right. I get out of the car and remove the wheelchair from the boot, snapping it open and clicking the foot rests into place. I open the back and pull the limp figure into a sitting position, then heave him into the chair. I tuck the blanket tight around his legs and chest to hold him in place, pick the holdall from the boot and close the lid, then toss the keys onto the front seat and slam the door shut.

Time to say goodbye, Chris.

The gravel on the ground snatches at the wheels as I walk out of the car park and turn right towards the promenade. I have to grab his collar every now and again to prevent him toppling forward. I sing a suitable tune: *'Rock-a-bye baby, on the treetop.'*

We cross the main road and the entrance to the Central Pier stands in front of us in all its past glory. The yellow and red lettering look grey against the white corrugated flashing and the promise of 'Family fun above the sea!' seems a little overstated.

It is out of season so the pier is closed to visitors, but is open to the tradesmen who maintain and renovate the structure and the rides. I walk around the side to the compound where they store their gear, manoeuvring the wheelchair through the bollards to the fencing at the back. I unzip the bag and pull out the metal bar from the warehouse. There is a wire mesh gate in the fence, the chain gives way as I lever it open and push the wheelchair through the gap.

Inside is a wooden boardwalk which runs for about twenty-five yards either side of a parade of kiosks and gaming huts. This part of the pier bridges across the sand from the road to the structure itself. I used to love running under it as a child pretending it was a big American flyover. The clatter of the footfall from the tourists up above was the rumble of cars and lorries travelling overhead.

'Rock-a-bye baby, on the treetop. When the wind blows, the cradle will rock.'

The wheels clatter against the gaps in the planks. I reach midway and roll the chair up to the barrier at the side, rummaging around in my bag for the rope.

I tie one end to the rail and slip the noose over his head. The slip knot is beautifully crafted with thirteen turns of the rope just like the one in the Lakeland Hotel - the one I never got to use. I fish out the marker pen and tilt his head back so his face is illuminated by the moon. I write on his forehead.

The knot slides comfortably to the side of his neck and I heave him onto his feet. The rail is chest high and it's a struggle to lift him up. I put my shoulder under his arse and drive with my legs, he folds at the waist, hanging over the side.

'When the bough breaks, the cradle will fall.'

I take the mobile from my pocket and flip the back off. The battery snaps into place as does the SIM card. I replace the back, push the on button and tap a message onto the screen.

I slide the phone into the pocket of his jeans along with a folded piece of paper and grasp his feet. My chest fills with the pride of a job well done, a job that would have made Jono and the boys proud. Bringing justice to those who deserve it – that's what we did.

'And down will come baby, cradle and all.'

I flip his legs over the top. There is a moment of silence then a jolt as the handrail takes the full weight. I can hear the strands of the rope squeezing together as the knots tighten.

I take one last look at the towering Ferris wheel and bid it farewell. I never thought there was anything that could make this place more beautiful. I was wrong.

The wood and iron structure fades into the night as I make my way down the promenade, the silhouette of the body hanging below the walkway no longer visible against the sea.

Chapter 54

Kray was drumming her fingers against armrest.

'I know you don't want to talk, Roz, but can you stop doing that?' Tavener was finding his boss's anxiety infectious.

'This doesn't feel right,' Kray said.

'Of course it doesn't. Two people sat in a car at half one in the morning isn't natural.'

'It's too contrived. Jarrod isn't going to think we've *really* pulled the security from Lang's house. I think he's getting us to look in the wrong direction.'

'It can't be to target the others on the convicted list. You've contacted their support officers twice in the last hour and they're all fine.'

'Ah! I can't stand this.' Kray slapped her hands onto the dashboard.

Her phone rang, it was Taylor. She listened to the voice talking fast on the other end, then her phone beeped. She pulled the mobile away to read a copy of a text message.

'Fuck!' Kray yelled at the top of her lungs.

'What is it?'

She disconnected the call. 'Jarrod's mobile went active three minutes ago at the Central Pier. Taylor received a text on the second phone.' Tears welled up in her eyes, she held up her phone so Tavener could read the screen. It read: Come and get your boy.

'Shit, that's a good thirty minutes from here.'

'I fucking knew it.' Kray slapped the dashboard again. 'Get going we can brief Bagley on the way.'

Tavener gunned the engine and screeched away from the kerb. Kray called into the control room to mobilise any officers located in the vicinity of the pier then called Bagley. She called the coppers who were baby minding the other offenders – this could be another diversion.

The blue lights reflected off the shop front windows as they hurtled towards town. Bagley took on the role of co-ordinating a ground team to lock down the area, leaving Kray to manage whatever was at the pier.

The same words bounced around in her head.

Please don't let him be dead, please don't let him be dead.

She tried to force it to the back of her mind but it refused to give way. It kept repeating, over and over again.

Please don't let him be dead ...

Kray called Taylor who confirmed that the phone hadn't moved. She then took a call from Bagley.

'Roz, I have a police officer at the scene and he says there is a body hanging from the pier.'

'Oh my God.' She clasped her hand to her face. 'Who is it?'

'He can't tell. It's twenty feet in the air, there's no way we can get to it, he's called in the fire brigade to assist.'

'Is it male?'

'He thinks so.'

Kray let the phone rest in her lap, the tinny voice of Bagley still buzzed on the line, urging attention. She gazed out front at the urban scenery speeding past, tears running down her face.

'Roz, what is it?' Tavener asked. 'Roz!'

'They found a body hanging from the pier, looks like it's male. I think it's Chris.'

'It might not be, Roz get a grip.'

'It's Chris, I know it is. Jarrod made us look the other way and killed him. He said he would kill him if he interfered and now he's dead.'

The car skidded to a stop and they both jumped out. Kray ran along the promenade and down the concrete steps onto the sand. Tavener got a search lamp from the boot and chased after her.

Kray was sobbing as she ran, she could see the black silhouette of the man dangling at the end of the rope. The lone copper was stood beneath it, looking up.

Fucking hell, Chis, what have I done?

Kray reached the pier first, straining her neck back to look up at the figure twisting in the sea breeze. She ran one way then the other trying to get a better look.

What have I done?

Tavener arrived and the torch beam flooded the underneath of the boardwalk. Kray yanked it from his grasp and aimed it at the man hanging from the handrail. The powerful light hit him full in the face.

Who the fuck is that?

Chapter 55

Three weeks later

Kray tapped at the door and entered Bagley's office. He was elbow deep in paperwork and looking stressed. It was early afternoon, and despite the hour, she had her bag in one hand and coat in the other.

'I have news.'

'Can it wait, Roz? Quade and I are in front of the cameras again in an hour doing another public appeal.'

'Bloody hell, they are going to give you two your own slot on daytime TV.'

'Yeah, very funny. Plus, she's breathing down my neck about the overtime.'

'I may be able to help with both of those.'

'I doubt it.' He bent his head over his laptop and bashed away at the keyboard.

'I'll tell you anyway - we can stop looking for Alex Jarrod.'

Bagley's head snapped up.

'Have we found him?'

'Kind of. Do you remember I took the precaution of informing the security services about Jarrod, just in case he popped up on their radar?'

'Yes.'

'They've been in touch and it would appear he didn't so much show up on their radar as show up on a mortuary slab in Jalalabad.'

'Shit.'

'Turns out he was working for a private security firm in Afghanistan and was killed in a car bomb attack. The details are pretty sketchy.'

'Are they sure it's him?'

'It's him all right. He left instructions that in the event of his death any money in his account was to be transferred to his ex-girlfriend, Julie Clarke. She's confirmed the cash is in her bank.'

'Have we spoken to the security firm?'

'I have and they insist they enlisted Jarrod when he was already in Afghanistan. I put it to them that they played a role of getting him out of the country and they simply told us to prove it. One of their head guys used to be Jarrod's commanding officer. I'm sure if we look hard enough the evidence will point us in their direction but we will never make it stick.'

'Good news - we found him, bad news - he's dead. Christ, I've been living and breathing this damned case for so long it will take a bit of getting used to not having it hanging around my neck.'

'You getting used to it? I think you'll find we've *all* lived and breathed it. Still, you can tell Quade the resources are freed up which will help with the figures.' Kray turned to walk away having delivered her update.

'You going somewhere?' he asked.

'Yeah, you signed off on me having an early finish.'

'Wait a moment. I've been meaning to talk to you. The internal investigation team are wrapping up their inquiry into what went on in CJU and they have reopened the recruitment process to appoint a new head.'

'Yes I received an email to that effect yesterday.'

'Let me know when you need to take time away from the job.'

'That won't be necessary, Dan, I've withdrawn my application.'

'Whoa! Hang on, what do you mean?'

'I've pulled out.'

'We need to talk about this.'

'No, Dan, we don't.'

'I think we do. And where are you going?'

'That's none of your business.'

'Are you applying for other roles?'

'Nope, I'm staying on in CID.'

'What? You should have told me.'

'I'm telling you now.'

'But … but … how—'

'I guess me being around just one more thing you'll have to get used to.' She walked out.

'Kray get back here.'

'No, Dan, right now there's somewhere I need to be.'

Chapter 56

Kray gazed out over the Irish sea from her position on the hillside, shielding her eyes against the low February sun. She could see the array of wind turbines in the distance, the day was clear and bright.

'Chris didn't die, how about that? Fuck knows how. He had a fractured cheekbone, a fractured eye socket and a bleed on the brain. Not to mention a busted nose. I should carry a government health warning saying: Caution, getting close to this woman may result in death or severe injury. And before you say anything I know he made a catastrophic error in judgement. If he had involved us when he met with Jarrod under the pier we would be two bodies less and he wouldn't have been wired up to fuck knows what in a hospital bed. But as you and me both know we are all prone to errors in judgement. I mean I can't talk – my error got you killed, so I can hardly judge him too harshly. A police officer found him wandering along the Prom after he woke up and made a run for it from the car. Well, when I say run, it was more of a stagger.'

Kray bent down and wiped away the grime from the top of the stone, the black marble glistened in the sun.

'The guy hanging from the bridge was Judge Bernard Preston. He had enough sleeping pills inside him to put an elephant to sleep. In his pocket was a note saying: *Sometimes you have to lose a battle to win the war*. A reference to Jarrod not killing Casey Lang. Preston also had a note written on his forehead which said: *Prevention is better than cure*. You got to hand it to Jarrod, he played us like a penny-whistle. He made us look one way while he took care of business.

'We never caught him. He disappeared into thin air only to show up dead in Afghanistan. He managed to get himself blown up in a car bomb explosion. I briefed Bagley this afternoon and I think he was pleased, though it was difficult to tell. Oh, and I told him I wasn't going for the CJU job. He was not happy and looked like I'd kicked him in the balls, which I suppose I did in a way. It felt good. Speaking of the delightful Casey Lang, she submitted a formal complaint against Bagley and was suing the force for wrongful arrest, but that's all gone quiet after we found a stash of drugs at her home along with a ton of cash. No wonder she wasn't keen on giving us the house. Oh, I do have something that will make you chuckle. You remember I went for that job as office manager at a solicitors, well ... the fuckers said no! Can you believe that? I aced that interview. I don't know what Amanda from HR was doing, she obviously didn't have a clue.'

Kray took a letter from her pocket. 'Listen to this, 'we do not feel you have the experience we are looking for'. No shit, they only had to read my CV to know that. And what about this, 'please feel free to apply for any of the other exciting opportunities Willis and Broughton have to offer'. Cheeky bastards. They can stuff their job up their arse.'

Kray took a deep breath and turned her face to the sky. Her bluster and bravado melted away and tears began rolling down her cheeks.

'There is something else I need to tell you.' She wiped them away with her sleeve. 'It's about Chris, well, erm, I like him and I think he likes me, and it's difficult for me to let go. When I'm with him, half of me is with you, half of me is here talking to a lump of marble and I can't do that anymore.' Kray sunk to her knees, placing her hands on top of the gravestone. 'I love you and will always love you, but you're dead and I'm not.' Her tears dripped from her face into her lap. 'I know you would want me to be happy, and I think I can be with Chris, but not if half of me is on this hillside with you.'

Kray rummaged in her bag and drew out a chef's knife. 'The last time I brought this here I wanted to slice my wrists open and you said no. You gave me the strength to put the knife down and now I want you to give me the strength to move on.'

She dug the blade into the grass and began to hack at the soil. Using both hands she carved away a square of earth.

Kray dropped the knife and licked the third finger on her left hand, easing the wedding ring over her knuckle.

'Every time I see this I think of you, every time I feel it, I think of you. If I keep it in a drawer at home one day I will find it and I will be right back here again. I can't do that, I can't risk that.' Kray held the ring to her lips, then placed it into the hole, covering it with the square of grass and pressing it flat.

'I'll still come to see you, but I can't go on living my life with one foot in the land of the living and the other in the land of the dead. I know you'll understand.'

Kray put the knife back in her bag, stood up and wiped her face, emotional exhaustion washing over her.

She meandered back to her car, wondering what the traffic would be like between here and Chis Millican's place. Reaching into her bag she pulled out a white plastic object, it was four inches long with a small window in the side. She turned it over and over in her hand.

Across the window were two blue lines. She tossed it into the glove compartment. There had been enough revelations for one day. That one could keep.

Acknowledgements

I want to thank all those who have made this book possible – My family, Karen, Gemma, Holly and Maureen for their encouragement and endless patience. Plus, my magnificent BetaReaders, Nicki, Jackie and Simon, who didn't hold back with their comments and feedback. I'm a lucky boy to have them in my corner.

I would also like to thank my wider circle of family and friends for their fantastic support and endless supply of helpful suggestions. The majority of which are not suitable to repeat here.